What Goes Around

Comes Around

By

O.C Shaw

Maggie - so sorry
for the delay. Thanks
for your support
him
x .

Chapter 1

Do you ever have conversations with people where they remark how they seem to have blinked and an hour has flown by, or a week, or a year? This morning I have been having one of those moments, except that I find myself standing in front of my mirror at home, looking at my reflection and realising that somehow eighteen years have gone by. And I can't for the life of me really tell you much about it – what I was doing, what I achieved, what the hell happened. What I'm most afraid of is that the next time I wake up, another eighteen years will have gone, and I'll find myself fifty-five years old and feeling like somehow I missed virtually my whole life. So today, this morning, as I stand there looking at myself, I take stock: I decide that I, Lily Lambert, am unremarkable, and not in a good way, at least not in a way I am happy with. As I examine myself and take in my reflection – my short stature, heart-shaped face framed by long, dark, wavy (slightly frizzy) hair, and excessive curves – I figuratively weigh myself (I can't face the actual scales) and find myself wanting. I have reached the grand age of thirty-seven and awakened to find myself an overweight, married mother of twin boys, and while I know many people would tell me to suck it up and get on with it, that I'm lucky to have so much, something I can't quite define seems to have clicked inside me. I have an overwhelming sense that it's now or never if I'm going to make any changes for the better in my life. In truth I'm not even sure if it's going to be possible. *Midlife crisis?* I wonder. *Maybe. Maybe I'm already too late?* It's a depressing thought. However, when all is said and done, the only question that really remains is: *if I'm going to do it, what the hell do I do? How do I start to change?*

Several hours later I find myself walking through the doorway of the local gym for an initial assessment with my newly assigned instructor, Stuart. It would be fair to say my considering joining a gym is entirely out of character, as evidenced by my husband Greg's derisive sniggering when I told him over the phone why I was going to be late home from work this evening. However, it feels like it's completely in line with my newfound desire to shake up my world – and frankly, Greg's disapproval provided clear evidence of that. The only thing I could put this particular flash of inspiration down to was too much time spent listening to the loquacious lady on the morning T.V. before my shift at work. She had a lot to answer for, and not just this mad foray into exercise; I have also attempted numerous new recipes at her behest, lured into thinking it would all be so easy, thanks to the overuse of phrases like 'all you have to do' and 'just' strategically placed in front of some improbable task. So once again, for a few brief moments this morning, after my epiphany at the mirror, I had really believed her when she said that I could 'easily make changes to my body and in turn my life', long enough to pick up the phone and make the appointment for after work. *Stupid, really, in retrospect*, I think as I walk into the reception area preoccupied by thoughts of the horror to come. In my distracted state, and in line with my innate tendency towards clumsiness, I manage to trip over the mat which lies just inside the doorway and send myself barrelling forward into some poor unsuspecting soul who just happens to be trying to leave the building as I'm arriving. Instead he ends up with my head in his stomach and emitting a loud "ooof" as I knock all the wind out of him, before finally sprawling in an undignified heap on the floor. I flush bright red as I stagger back to my feet in an uncoordinated scramble, whilst one of the instructors comes running towards us.

"God, James, are you okay?" The object of his concern is still bent double, clearly winded by my unprovoked attack. I'm mortified, mumbling my apologies, as I take in the figure before me, now being supported by the instructor. *I can see why my head still hurts*, I think, absentmindedly rubbing it while simultaneously taking in the visible outline of his firm abs encased in a plain white t-shirt as the person gradually unrolls and tries to return to an upright position. When I finally see his face, my mouth falls open and goes dry. He's the very definition of 'jaw-droppingly gorgeous'; 'made for

T.V.' / model stuff, sporting dark hair combined with sky blue eyes on top of the finest body you could wish to see. He isn't a youth, either; he looks about my own age, judging by the small brushes of grey that pepper the hair by his ears, but he wears it well – far better than I do, if his physical shape is anything to go by. Curiously he also seems somehow familiar. All of this flashes through my mind in the moments of his recovery, while the instructor anxiously hovers beside him. Mr Abs must have seen me staring and clocked my reaction to him because by the time my eyes reach back up to his face, he's returning my stare quite brazenly and making me blush again. On seeing my response, he smirks in a way I find frankly irritating before rolling his eyes and turning to the instructor, saying: "I hope your public liability insurance is all in order?" and casting a meaningful nod back in my direction.

I flush yet again, *God, I hardly ever blush normally*, in part because I'm embarrassed but mostly because I'm pissed off that he didn't have the grace to just leave me to wallow in my humiliation and let me creep away. I mumble final apologies while trying simultaneously to back away from the pair of them:

"Sorry, I'll try not to hurt you again. You've no need to worry really, I normally only take myself out with my clumsiness", before muttering another last "sorry" to no one in particular and staggering my way over to the reception desk to book in. I say 'staggering' because I manage to catch my bag strap round my legs and nearly trip myself again. I force myself to not look around this time in an effort to retain some last shred of dignity, hoping to God they haven't been watching, but I swear I hear two sniggers coming from behind me. My humiliation complete, I feel like turning tail and running for home before I even start. But I take a deep breath when I finally reach the desk and determine, as I have come this far, I really need to see it through. Anyway it would have just meant walking past the pair of them again, as they're still standing by the door talking and casting occasional glances in my direction, which would have just been even more embarrassing. *Anyway, surely there couldn't be any further mishaps to face?* It turns out I was wrong.

My new instructor, Stuart, had to (of course) be the witness to my humiliating entrance debacle. As he walks me to his private room for my initial assessment, I could swear he's deliberately staying a couple of steps away from me, in case I suddenly try to take him out. He begins to take a medical history, looking amused as I catalogue my history of minor sprains and breaks.

"I can be a bit clumsy," I explain a little sheepishly this time.

"I can see that," is all he says, while trying to smother a grin, endeavouring to maintain a professional expression. He asks me questions about where I work, trying to assess my level of daily activity, and when I tell him I work on reception at a doctors' surgery, he can't contain himself. He openly laughs, telling me how 'that must be convenient', in between sniggers. I want to scowl at him, but in the end I can't help joining in and laughing too, admitting how it's something of a standing joke at work. By the end of the interview I realise he is actually just a nice person, despite finding humour in my clumsiness. He even makes the pain of being weighed and measured, and told I am officially overweight (looking far too close to the obese range for my liking), less painful than it might have been because he is so utterly convinced that I can do something to change it. 'All' (*there's one of those words again*) I needed to do was regularly come to the gym and follow the simple programme he has given me, and the weight is bound to fall off, he assures me. So, despite hating the scrutiny of the fellow gym users, I obediently trot around the gym after him as he demonstrates to me how to use the various pieces of equipment. Some of the others surreptitiously watch my progress, but at least I make it through without any further breakages of me or anything (or anyone) else. Stuart is great, and he reassures me all the time it will be a simple job to make the changes I am after. The cynic inside me tells me he is offering the kind of insincere reassurance of someone who can only profit, now he has my membership fee and direct debit details. He shouldn't care, I figure, because either way he wins: if I don't keep up the visits, he still keeps my money, and if I do, then he can lay claim to my miraculous transformation.

"I've seen worse," he assures me at one point. Clearly he believes this small gift of kindness will make me feel better about myself, but I'm not sure it does, really. I just feel like a clumsy oaf surrounded by beautiful people, *like the guy I ran into at the door*, I think, remembering those beautiful blue eyes and losing myself for a second in the memory.

Having said all that, I complete the programme and feel loads better for it, right up until the point that I'm standing in the shower afterwards and catch sight of a twenty-something lovely staring at me through the small gap (where the curtain never quite meets the wall) with an expression of undisguised pity on her face. She's like my complete polar opposite: tall, blonde, thin, pretty and young. I think I might actually hate her for being so perfect. I can feel the endorphins generated by my gym exertions disappearing down the plughole of the shower along with the shampoo bubbles, unidentified hairs and my confidence as I wither under her scrutiny.

Body confidence has never really been my thing. Even at my supposed best, during my late teens and early twenties, I had erred towards oversized cardigans and baggy jumpers, combined with jeans in an effort to mask my perceived body inadequacies. I told everyone else at the time it was because I didn't care about fashion, that I wasn't shallow, but I'm not sure what I said was entirely the truth. In retrospect I probably just made myself look worse than I needed to, but I've never really felt any better over the years, especially after the kids.

I can feel my shoulders hunching further forward in an effort to hide myself from scrutiny, as I endeavour to speed up the washing and rinsing process and escape into the gloomy anonymity of the changing room. On a positive note, I tell myself, at least she had noticed me – that doesn't happen every day. These days it feels unusual to be noticed by anyone at all, unless I'm falling over something. Maybe I'm overly sensitive, but it seems as if I'm reaching an age where people look past me, or through me, to something lovelier or more interesting beyond. I know I shouldn't care so much, that I am being shallow to even be bothered, and I also know my family would never understand how I feel. They think my sole purpose in life is to serve their needs, and (to be fair to them) maybe it is. *Maybe I am being selfish. But I have spent the last 18 years not being selfish*, I decide.

I have reasons to be cheerful today, I remind myself; I have worked every part of my body in a way it has frankly not seen since I did gym at school. Well, not even then, given my tendency at the time to find any excuse I could to avoid all forms of exercise. The problem was the less exercise I did, the worse the problem of my weight (and therefore my confidence) became, because my appetite was never an issue. I'm not entirely stupid, as I think some thin people seem to assume fat and overweight people are. I do know the facts about energy in, energy out and the theory of how to keep yourself thin, but overeating and low self-esteem are a vicious cycle I can't seem to escape. I was constantly told when I was younger that I was 'chubby' or had 'such a pretty face', much to my horror, but I have always considered myself too far gone to feel strong enough to do anything about it. Until now. So anyway, here I am, years later, trying to put right what is possibly beyond saving, as a first step to making changes in my life. For now, though, it is time to return to the real world and Greg, so I pick up my bag with a sigh and make my way out towards the car.

Chapter 2

Greg and I first met at university, when I was barely nineteen. He had been my first (and only) real boyfriend – an 'older' guy of twenty-four who had totally dazzled me. He was tall and thin, with the kind of disregard for fashion and physical appearance that had called to my emotionally scarred self-image. To be honest, with the way I felt about myself after the horror of school, I expected it would be unlikely anyone would like me, let alone find me in any way attractive. It meant that I was pathetically grateful for any attention from the opposite sex. Greg was doing a fine art degree, but he was one of those people who just seemed to know something about everything – a worldly intellectual to my naive eyes who could run rings round me in any argument and made me feel in awe of his greater wisdom. It felt like I fell in love the moment I saw him, hardly daring to believe that someone so magnificent could want anything to do with me, even as a friend. In the end I gave my virginity to him and was happy to do so, despite the fact that, in retrospect, the experience left much to be desired. It certainly bore no relation to the toe-curlingly delightful experiences I had read about in the romance novels I had devoured throughout my adolescence.

I remember a lot of fumbling and pushing, followed by a harder push, until he finally gained the entrance he sought, and

I distinctly remember being shocked that it had really hurt me at first; I suppose I wasn't entirely ready, especially with it being my first time and all, but his lust quickly took over and made him oblivious to my responses, or lack of them. He had started moving quickly in and out of me anyway, caught up in his own rhythm. The initial discomfort eased slightly as my body had caught up. And I recall it had started to generate some nice feelings inside of me, so that I was starting to think I might like it, when he had quite suddenly groaned and collapsed on top of me, crushing me slightly as he lay there panting for a few moments, before swiftly pulling out, rolling over onto the bed beside me and falling asleep virtually instantly.

I was left lying there trying to get a handle on my scattered emotions. On the one hand I remember I felt joy at the loss of my virginity finally, while on the other, a part of me registered that the experience had been completely underwhelming, and somehow even at that stage I couldn't help wondering if there wasn't meant to be slightly more to it.

On reflection, and with the twenty-twenty hindsight of a much older (*and wiser?*) woman, the speed with which I moved in to share a room with him, taking on the role of his washer woman, cleaner, cook and lover should have set off some alarm bells. My best friend at college, Emma, did try to warn me many times, but to be honest I thought I was completely in love by that stage, and therefore blind to any flaws in my new boyfriend. I was happy when he grudgingly let it be known that we were together. I put up with any derogatory comments he made about me when we were with friends, despite Emma telling me in anxious tones that I shouldn't, that he was too controlling, that I was losing my own identity. To be fair to him, at times he could be a model boyfriend – mostly when we were alone. He 'rewarded' me with sex every night, although it always followed a similar routine to that first time, no real foreplay, just functional sex until he came; but despite my lack of sexual fulfilment from the physical relationship, just the fact it was me he wanted to have sex with every night was enough to see me through.

The first fly in the ointment – and it was a massive, bluebottle-sized fly – had come several months into our relationship when Greg had pointed out that I was getting 'even fatter'. We had been out with our main group of friends at the time, and he had made the comment as I had eased back into my seat after having bought a round of drinks for everyone, narrowly avoiding dropping the tray of full glasses as I squeezed back round the table. The comment had hurt a lot, especially seeing Greg laughing along with all the others. I laughed it off, saying it was probably contentment, but something about the remark had niggled, and not just the cruelty coming from someone who supposedly cared about me, made so very publicly about an issue he knew I was sensitive about. I was certain I wasn't eating more; despite a bit more alcohol in my life compared to my pre-university days, there really wasn't any reason for me to be putting on weight – and yet I knew subconsciously I was. Only that morning I had changed into a skirt with an elastic waist because my jeans hadn't fit me. It was the following day, while bemoaning the unfairness of my life, and more particularly my weight, to Emma that she tentatively asked if there could be any other reasons for my weight gain. An emergency rush to the chemist, followed by two pregnancy tests, and the reason was depressingly clear – the rate of colour change on the little stick was indisputable. I was pregnant. Worse was to come when, following a trip to the GP, and then the antenatal clinic, I was found to be almost twenty weeks gone – with twins.

I remember Greg had flipped his lid when I told him. I had never before seen him so incredibly angry. "You stupid bitch," he had yelled, "how the hell did you let that happen?"

"Well, how do you think? We weren't exactly as careful as we could have been. You didn't always use a condom."

It was true, we had often had sex without any sort of protection, like that first time. When I would nervously question it, he would say it felt better without and would promise he'd withdraw in time. Clearly that hadn't happened, or at least not often enough or soon enough in the proceedings to make a difference. He had ranted at me that I was a "stupid cow who didn't know how to take the pill"; I had "ruined his life", and he demanded I have a termination, but in truth it was far too late. I was already nearly 20 weeks by the time I had found out. And besides which, I had seen my babies on the scan – there was no way I could get rid of them when I already loved them.

My parents took it only marginally better than Greg when I finally gathered the courage to tell them. I had all the same "stupid girl" and "ruined your lives" comments, combined with an extra dose of parental disappointment and guilt, finishing with them telling me that if I was old enough to behave like an adult, then I was old enough to face the adult consequences which come along afterwards – like children. After that point they pretty much withdrew all financial and emotional support and have barely had any involvement in our lives beyond the odd Christmas visit to see the kids.

That had all happened eighteen years ago, and now my babies were men themselves, in age if not behaviour. It would be fair to say the intervening years have not been plain sailing. I had to drop out of university, supposedly just for a few years until the children were older, but in truth it just became too hard to go back once the kids arrived. Greg had carried on with his studies, because as he said at the time: 'it was an investment in our future, and it was only a matter of time before his work was 'recognised"; and I stayed home in our bedsit, scraped by on benefits and looked after our babies and Greg.

The first couple of years were really hard, not that I think we were anything special, just that babies are hard work anyway. Make that two babies with colic, teething, insufficient sleep and no money, and it didn't make for a happy mix, but I consoled myself with the fact we were okay as a couple. We were healthy, Greg's studies were going well, he told me, and I adored my babies. While we might not have had any money, we still had each other – we were coping, and Greg had stuck by me when he could have walked away. Greg's sex drive had not diminished at all, kicking in a mere four weeks after the birth of the boys, but this time I was on the pill. We didn't need any more stress in the system, I figured, until we had sorted ourselves out (it never happened). We had finally succumbed to intense societal pressure and got married after five years together, mainly due to the comments from Greg's parents about 'how it looked', which had eventually been too much stress for Greg to handle. Our boys, Adam and Ethan, had been our pageboys, and while it had been a low-key event at the local registry office, I still thought it was a nice party at the time, despite tripping on my grand entrance and Greg rolling his eyes at me. Everyone told me I looked tired and to take care of myself as well as everyone else, but it was hard when there was so little time to do anything but cope.

When the boys finally started full-time school, I managed to get myself my job. At that time Greg had just been finishing his Masters in Art History, so that clearly needed to be his main focus, while I started first in an administrator position at the local doctors' surgery during school hours, before moving on to reception work. Over the course of the years, my effort and loyalty were noticed. Consequently I was rewarded by the practice investing in me: allowing me to do some courses and helping me to move up the ranks, finally taking on some of the business management responsibilities. The increase in money had really helped at home and allowed us to move out of the bedsit and into a very small three-bedroom semi with a very large mortgage (those were the heydays when they leant money to people who couldn't possibly afford to repay it), in what the estate agent had described as an 'up and coming' part of town. In other words, it was a bit of a dive area, but it was a step up from where we had been. At least the kids had a bit of a garden to play in while Greg had a small studio in the garden for his painting. It was actually a large shed with lots of windows, but he was happy, so we all were.

That tended to be the pattern in our married life – if Greg was happy, we were all allowed to be, but if he wasn't, then God help us.

At the same point my career had begun to develop unexpectedly, Greg began to find that life after university was turning into a major disappointment. It seemed there was a surfeit of arts students fighting for positions and recognition, and Greg's lack of willingness to compromise meant he refused to apply for anything which would get his foot in the door if he deemed it unworthy of his skills, regardless of our need for income. He continued to channel his energies into his paintings; convinced people would eventually see his brilliance and rightly reward him with commissions, only to find himself thwarted time and time again. With every knock back, I watched his bitterness seem to grow exponentially, and we all suffered for it at home, creating a toxic environment the family had to live in. In the meantime, I carried a full-time job and parenthood.

If I'm honest I would say Greg was, and is, resentful of any paltry success I may have had despite it being a million miles away from the writing career I had always imagined for myself. What I've found hardest, though, is that eventually his constant belittling of my achievements has rubbed off on my beloved boys. They believe his propaganda: that I have been a bad mother for prioritising my career above their care, making them feel neglected despite the need for income to put food on the table and presents in their stockings at Christmas. The tirade of criticism from Greg has become a chorus, as the boys are now old enough to join in, and I have become just too weary to fight back. The only constants in our married life as the years have ticked by have been sex and criticism, and sometimes (if I am really unlucky) both. Greg still likes sex most nights, and if I dare to suggest I might be tired, he claims it as his right. Most of the time I just let him, as he doesn't need much involvement from me to get what he wants, but sometimes I get angry and resist. On those occasions Greg usually gets off on it. He actually seems to like it more when I put up some resistance; it brings a fire into his eyes which I don't normally see there. The sex is passionate in a way that our sex life usually isn't, and it's on those rare occasions that I have very occasionally orgasmed. The first time had been such a surprise after so many years without that I had cried, partly due to guilt; regretting I had responded physically to such dominant, controlling behaviour and feeling I had failed womankind somehow by enjoying it, and partly because of the immense joy I felt from experiencing such a beautifully intense sensation and release. I don't think Greg even noticed.

I have no idea how much the people around us, our so-called friends, know about the reality of our lives, but I put on a good show and have genuinely tried to do the best I can for all three of them, whatever their criticism of me. To most onlookers, I guess Greg and I seem to have a happy marriage with staying power. In truth, I just don't think I have the energy to go anywhere.

If I think back, I believe it was when the boys had their eighteenth birthday that something inside of me finally clicked. My maternal duty felt like it was done, and somehow it seemed permissible to put myself first again. Hence my awakening: allowing myself to hear and listen to the words spoken by the lady on the T.V., followed by the resulting trip to the gym. While my critical inner demons tell me I am insane to think there is any point in trying to do anything about my life, that it's essentially already over and that I should really just crawl into a corner and sit there quietly for the remainder of my days, there is still a small kernel of hope inside me which tells me to try, that I still have something to offer the world, that I am good at my job and could be good at other things if I tried.

As I head out the door of the gym to get back into my car, having dried and dressed myself back into the anonymous uniform of my daily life, it feels as if the kernel of hope has grown slightly, nourished by the time spent exercising my body, and I resolve to go again. I wave at Stuart, who is just leaving the building as I drive away, and I wince as I graze the hubcap on the kerb due to my lack of attention to the road. I glance in my rear-view mirror, hoping I got away without him seeing anything, only to catch sight of him grinning at my departing car.

Chapter 3

As I push my key into the front door I can hear the sound of raised voices coming from inside, and the positive glow I have been feeling dies a little. Greg is inside – he must have finished his work in the shed for the day – and so too is at least one of the boys, judging from what I can hear. I prefer it when there's no one in when I get home; it's just easier that way.

"Where have you been?" is the instant call to the sound of the front door opening. The gym has pushed my normal routine back by more than an hour, and Greg's generally not good with any sort of change in his life or daily routine – not that it has happened often, to be fair.

"I went to the gym – I told you I was going to. You laughed at me, remember?" I remind him as I haul the bags of groceries I had picked up on my way home onto the side in the kitchen. The house looks a wreck, and despite having been there most of the day, Greg has done little about it, leaving it instead for me to do when I have finished preparing their meal, despite being the only one who has spent any time that day at paying work.

"What a joke!" Ethan says snidely as he walks in behind me, immediately rummaging in the bags to see what I have bought for tea.

"What is this shit?" he asks, pulling out the pasta sauce I had grabbed quickly from the shelf in the supermarket, knowing it could be ready quickly and hoping to head off exactly this sort of confrontation. I can't help myself and sigh loudly in a rare outward sign of dissent, and he glances up at me in surprise.

"It's dinner," I say quietly. "If you don't like it, then feel free to go out to the shop, buy yourself something different and cook it." Ethan looks at me like I've grown horns suddenly, and even Greg looks up from the newspaper.

"What's the matter with you?" Greg growls.

"Nothing. I'm just saying this is what I'm cooking. And if he doesn't like it, then he's old enough to do something about it himself."

"Yeah, well, the stupid little shit managed to lose his job today, so he can't afford to go and buy himself diddly squat," he says scathingly, casting a disapproving parental stare at Ethan.

"It wasn't my fault," Ethan whines, sounding more like eight than eighteen.

"Whose fault was it, then, if you can't manage to get your lazy arse out of bed in time for work? You've already had two warnings about the same thing," Greg comments, warming to his theme, having clearly been round this particular conversational loop several times already, so having anticipated

Ethan's response. I reflect inwardly that it is somewhat ironic to hear Greg criticising others about their work ethic, when he has done precisely nothing over the last 18 years to support the family income; but I know better than to make any comment. Ethan, however, is far less circumspect.

"Oh yeah, that's rich, coming from you!" I flinch at the words as Greg jumps instantly to his feet, years of rejection and resentment blazing in his eyes.

"Who are you, you little shit, to criticise me? You have no idea about what I have achieved in my work, despite everything I've had against me. I work hard every single day, and the fact that my work is not fully appreciated yet is not my fault. But it will happen, I assure you – one day I will see my work recognised for its importance, and you will see I was right."

I roll my eyes before I can help myself, having heard this same tirade more times over the years than I can possibly count. Unfortunately for me, this time Greg catches sight of the expression and his anger ignites further. He lashes out at the bag of shopping, sending the sauce bottle smashing to the floor. "Fuck this," he snarls, grabbing his coat and keys and slamming the front door on his way out. I know he's going to the pub; he always has in times of stress. I also know in my heart that this tirade isn't over, at least not where I'm concerned – he'll be back to punish me later. I sigh again and look at Ethan, who is surveying the mess in the kitchen with a disgusted expression on his face.

"Stupid," he says to no one in particular before walking out, as if this is somehow my fault for buying pasta sauce in the first place. I sigh again before starting the process of clearing up all the mess, reflecting that if my life had a soundtrack these days, the signature sound would be one long sigh.

The noise of my phone beeping with a text from within my bag distracts me from the mess momentarily, as I am just finishing wiping the last of the sauce off the floor tiles. I pause to root around in my bag and find my phone, which as usual has migrated right to the bottom, before I finally get the chance to look at the message. It's from Emma. Emma is one of the few people from college I'm still in contact with, apart from Greg. Time and again, she has shown herself to be a true friend to me over the years; helping with the kids when they were younger every time I felt I had reached a point where I just couldn't go on anymore. The kids called her Aunt Emma when they were little, and to be honest she has done far more for them than either Greg's parents or mine – or Greg, for that matter. Emma was the only one who ever thought to take the kids off to the park just so I could have a bath or sleep for a couple of hours when they were small, after I was at my wits' end having been awake all night with one or both of them.

More recently, now that the boys were older and out doing their own thing, Emma and I have started to enjoy more adult time together again. We meet up in the pub regularly on Tuesday evenings for a couple of drinks and a chance to vent – well, to let me vent, anyway. Emma's life had taken a very different path to my own. She completely managed to avoid any serious distractions from boys while she was at university, gaining her law degree and finally going on to qualify as a solicitor, eventually being taken on by a local practice which specialised in family law. I like to think my example of how you can fuck up your life provided a focus for her and helped her to avoid the usual distractions life tends to throw at you, enabling her to achieve everything she wanted to. She met her husband, a barrister, through work five years ago, married him, and is now pregnant with their first child which is due in January. I really love Emma; she's like the sister I didn't have. She has always been attractive, the sort of friend who, when you're with her, makes you feel all the more aware of your physical failings. She's petite, slim, blonde and perky, and the guys (including Greg) have always just adored her – it seems something about her size brings out the protective side of most men. Her husband, Phil, is gorgeous, and when I first met him she literally had to tell me to close my mouth because I was gawping at him. He's 6 ft 4 and dwarfs her tiny frame, but he has absolutely doted on her right from the beginning, and now their fairy tale is complete because they are having their much-wanted baby. Emma is planning to take a career break for a while in order to stay at home with the baby, made possible because Phil earns enough so they can get by on just the one income. It is all so far removed from my own experiences of love, marriage and parenthood that I would like to scream about the unfairness of it all occasionally, except that Emma is my best friend, and she is a good person and deserves to be happy. *Just because for some reason fate has decreed I don't, that doesn't mean I shouldn't be glad for my friends, does it?*

I look down at the text:

C u later at the Anchor? I'll be there about 8. E x

I quickly text her back:

Yes – can't wait

I get back to my clearing up, throwing away all of the kitchen towels now covered in pasta sauce, before making myself a quick salad that had originally been planned to accompany my pasta, but now, by necessity, had to be the whole meal. I reflect that with my trip to the gym, followed by salad for tea, the weight will indeed soon be falling off me.

Chapter 4

The evening with Emma has been great – the perfect antidote to my shitty evening at home. Emma is absolutely delighted to hear about my trip to the gym, genuinely pleased to know I had been able to do something for myself for the first time in about... well, 18 years. She laughs a lot as I describe my entrance, raising an eyebrow at my description of the guy I took out.

"Are you blushing, Lil?!" she teases me. I am.

"It's just the memory of utter humiliation in a public place yet again," I fudge, *but I don't think it is.* I keep getting flashes of that fine body, those eyes... I haven't had a reaction to a man like that since I first met Greg. Unsurprisingly, that night after I get home, my dreams are filled with people with piercing blue eyes which seem to look straight into my soul.

****

Emma has been so encouraging about the changes I'm trying to make that I feel motivated the next day to go to the gym again. And now after three weeks of regular gym visits, I'm actually beginning to see the impact on my body. It isn't anything anyone else would notice yet, but I can feel the slight loosening of the waistband on my jeans, and there's slightly more muscle tone all over my body.

As I walk in today, taking my usual care to avoid the mat, Stuart waves at me like I'm an old friend. It seems I'm already becoming a regular, and even the thin people have started to greet me now. I consider perhaps I had been wrong about their lack of friendliness in the beginning – it had nothing to do with what I look like and was more based on the fact they were as shy as I was, except that in skinny people it seems to come across as standoffishness, I now realise. With regular attendance and increased familiarity, I'm now becoming one of the gym 'family', and I'm finding I like them more than my own family most of the time. I am thinking those warm and fuzzy thoughts right up until the door to the female changing room is flung open, when I'm directly in front of it, smashing me on the forehead and momentarily stunning me so that my knees give way and I crumple to the floor. The blonde I had seen on my first visit exits the changing rooms with her bag slung over her shoulder, casting me a scathing look as she takes in my crumpled form on the floor.

"Don't sit there, for God's sake! People need to be able to get in and out of the changing room," she asserts in a tone of voice that clearly says: "*how can you be so stupid.*" I'm still too stunned to respond, and by the time I collect myself enough to consider trying to get to my feet, let alone informing her she has just nearly knocked me out, she has already flounced past and out the door.

"Are you okay?" A pair of hands reach under my arms and pull me to my feet. For a moment my knees fold as I try to stand, and it is only the support of my helper which keeps me in place. Gradually I collect myself enough to turn and thank my rescuer. *Of course it had to be*, I think despairingly as I take in the face and body. It can't just be any old person; it has to be the man I've been having dreams about since the last time I humiliated myself in front of him. I just stand there, looking at him blankly and trying to fathom what to say until he finally says: "Are you sure you're okay?" obviously taking my silence as an indicator of some sort of damage to my brain. *Not good*, I think, *I'm coming across as half-witted now.*

"Really, I'm fine. Thank you for helping me, but I can manage." It sounds ridiculously prim and standoffish even to my own ears. He lets go of me, and I instantly miss the feel of his arms upon me. I watch him step back and raise an eyebrow while he takes in my appearance before saying:

"Can you? Really? All the evidence would seem to indicate the contrary. You're going to have quite a bruise there." He points at my forehead. "I suggest you think about putting some ice on it," he says before turning and walking stiffly away into the men's changing rooms. In retrospect I don't think I could have handled the situation worse if I tried, and I regret my ridiculous response as I watch him disappear again. With my mind filled with my latest instalment of hideous embarrassment, I move to finally enter the changing rooms, when Stuart sees me and calls me over. I sigh before walking slowly over, wondering what else could possibly go wrong today.

"Hey, Lily, I was thinking about you today," he says as I approach, before peering at me closely and adding, "Have you done something to your head?"

"You were?" I reply, frankly amazed anyone ever thought about me when I wasn't physically in their face. I choose to ignore the observation about my latest injury.

"Yeah, we're putting together a fundraising event for a family whose five-year-old has been diagnosed with leukaemia, and I thought you might be just the sort of person who'd like to get involved. It's no big deal, really, just a three peaks type challenge, but with big hills rather than huge mountains – we thought we'd go up to the Peak District to do it so it's a bit more of a challenge, but it won't be too hard. I know you've got kids, so I thought you'd be up for it. The added bonus is that it's also great exercise. And since you've been going great guns in here, I thought it might be just your thing."

"Oh, I don't know," I mumble, taken aback at the thought of being included in the challenge. "I'm afraid I'd just hold you back. I'm not really fit enough yet."

"Nonsense, you silly mare," he laughs, "don't worry about that. We already have a real mix of people coming. Some of them are gym regulars, but some are the newbies like you. Pat's coming, and she's much less fit than you are," he adds. "We'll just make sure the group is split so those who want to go fast can go ahead, and those who don't can do it at their own pace. It's only over three days, and we're going to stay in a local house that's near the peaks we're planning to walk, so you'll even get a little holiday while you're at it. It'll be perfect. I'm sure we'll manage to have a giggle in the evenings," he says with a wink which can only be described as naughty. I can't help myself smiling back at him.

"I don't know," I hesitate, mentally listing all the reasons why it would be virtually impossible for me to even think about taking off for a few days on my own like that. I start with the most obvious excuse: "I can't really justify the cost of getting there; we're a bit skint at home at the moment, and I'm spending all my spare cash on gym membership." It's the first of the many reasons that came to mind, and possibly the most socially acceptable, while somewhat embarrassing to admit. I can't imagine telling him any of the other reasons; *my husband would never let me go away with a load of other people, let alone blokes*, or *my husband expects me to be home so I can cook him his meals*. Unfortunately for me, Stuart has clearly anticipated my first excuse and has already prepared a response.

"No, no no, the only thing you need to think about is putting some money towards food and drink while we're there;

the house is free because one of the other members owns it as a holiday rental property. He knows the guy whose kid is ill and offered it to us free of charge as his personal contribution. The place looks amazing, not really a house, more like a mansion – it sleeps over twenty if we double up in rooms. It'll be a right laugh. John has offered us a coach from his company, again at no charge, so it really is just a bit of money for food and drink. And let's face it, you'd need to eat if you were staying at home, so it won't cost you a lot more. Oh and maybe a few quid towards fuel," he adds as an afterthought. He knows he has me, and the smug grin on his face tells me he's confident I can't worm my way out.

"Well, I don't know," I hedge, "it sounds okay, but let me speak to Greg and I'll let you know for sure when I come in again. When is it?" I suddenly think to ask.

"Great, brilliant!" Stuart says emphatically, as if I've already confirmed my attendance. He hands me a sponsorship form, telling me: "All the details are on here. You might as well make a start getting sponsors soon. And I wouldn't bother trying to nobble anyone here – I've already cleaned up – so you'll have to try your other mates." I'm heartened by his assumption I have other mates to "nobble", as he puts it, as I quickly dart across the gym and into the changing room before he can think of anything else.

I finally start to change out of my work clothes and get ready to start my workout, but as I do I catch sight of my reflection in one of the mirrors and groan. A brilliant red line that will soon become a vivid purple bruise marks the middle of my forehead where the door had hit me. Days and days of more embarrassment as I'll be forced to explain what I've done to myself once again lie ahead of me. I sigh as I finish doing up my laces, ignoring the throb of my head as I bend forward.

At the beginning my workout, Stuart makes a point of finding me again and informing me he had taken a quick look at my training regime and adjusted it to help me prepare properly for the challenge. I look at the card and groan inwardly to see the increased resistance weights and gradients he's added to what was already a stretching programme as far as I'm concerned.

"Oh, and I've found you a roommate too," he calls over his shoulder as he walks off to harass some other poor victim.

"Sorry, what?" I ask, momentarily confused, before I realise he meant for the walking trip. "Who?" I call after him, my anxiety about the level of commitment he's already assuming betrayed by my shrill tone.

If he hears my anxiety, he chooses to ignore it, calling back: "Annie. She's over on the cross-trainer, if you want to introduce yourself." And with that he's gone again.

I look over to the cross-trainers and see a couple of women who could possibly be Annie. Summoning all my courage I walk over and tentatively call: "Annie?" to the first lady, who looks to be in her fifties with a plumpish figure like mine and dark hair. She shakes her head and points to a third lady further along the row that I hadn't seen previously, as she'd been hidden by the column. I follow to where she pointed, only to be confronted with a woman who could have easily been a model. She's like some sort of glamazon, at least six feet tall, with dazzling red hair that falls in perfect ringlets, where it has escaped its ponytail around her equally perfectly proportioned face. Think Elle McPherson with red hair. *She basically embodies almost everything I'm not*, I despair inwardly.

She looks up and catches me staring at her, at which point her face breaks into a massive grin as she booms: "You must be Lily! It's lovely to meet you. Stuart mentioned you to me. What on earth have you done to your head?" she says, pointing to my bruised forehead. Annie speaks in the way people do when they are talking and listening to very loud music at the same time and don't realise they are virtually shouting. She sees me flinch, as the heads of all the other gym users shoot up and around like meerkats at such atypical noisiness and stare in our direction. She quickly pulls off her headphones. "Sorry, didn't meant to shout at you," she says, followed by another of her melting smiles. Frankly, her voice isn't much quieter than the first time, but something about her personal magnetism draws me to her, and I can't help but smile back.

"I hear we might be sharing a room," I say, looking up at her shyly. She laughs, a great joyous laugh that draws the attention of the room again and makes me laugh in response this time.

"I can't wait, Lily. I'm so overdue a bit of fun. I don't know about you, but some play time with a bit of walking for a good cause thrown in sounds really good. I think you and I'll hopefully have a great time in between the exercise," she says with a wink. I explain to her I still need to sort out some things at home before I can definitely confirm, but if it's at all possible I will try to make it.

Something about her has me looking forward to going. She grins at me and takes my mobile number, immediately entering it into her phone, insisting we will need to meet up in advance of going to agree who's going to bring what, and that she'll text me to arrange a day and time in case we don't bump into each other again at the gym.

I nod obediently before hesitantly raising my hand in farewell and then scurrying my way over to the first apparatus on my revised programme, surreptitiously watching Annie out of the corner of my eye all the while. She's magnificent, with a body to die for. Not stick-thin, but womanly with legs which stretch on seemingly for miles. She laughs her way around the gym, appearing to know everyone. I watch their faces light up when she pauses to speak to them, especially the men. *Kind of like a red-haired gym version of Princess Diana*, I muse, feeling small and invisible by comparison. I know immediately when she's left because the electric hum that seems to accompany her has gone, and the gym seems just a bit less brightly lit and cheerful, so I buckle down to trying not to fall off the treadmill at the new gradient Stuart had set me.

Chapter 5

By the time I get home that evening, all the boys are already in. They have now adjusted to my new routine of going to the gym after work, happy to wait for food a little later if it means they don't have to cook for themselves. I had been mulling on my way home over how to position the trip away, worrying about how the boys and Greg were likely to react, but it seems as if the fates are smiling on me for once in my life. As I'm serving up plates of chicken with salad and potatoes (the rotisserie in the supermarket has recently become a personal lifesaver and worth the cost of a few of my personal luxuries), Ethan announces that the agency has found him a new job. There are general encouraging noises from around the table as he explains he will be doing silver service waiting on tables at posh events. The agency apparently keep a supply of people trained, whom they then draft in when a client has a big event that they need extra staff for. It seems the job would involve a weekend training course, because apparently there was a certain etiquette and technique which needed to be adhered to. But after that, assuming he passed his assessment, he had been told they tended to be needed most weekends and some weekday evenings too; and the money was excellent. I don't hear much more after he mentions the training weekend is the same weekend as the planned Peak District trip. One down, two to go.

It's like some sort of divine miracle when Adam, who's waiting to start an English degree course at Exeter in October, pipes up. "Well, since Ethan is buggering off and won't be around at weekends, there isn't much point in me hanging around much longer at home. My room in University Halls is available from the middle of September, so if one of you can take me down there, I'll head off the same weekend to give myself a chance to settle in and get the lie of the land before term starts properly." I hold my breath, not daring to show the hope on my face.

Greg grunts before saying, "Well, your mother is too crap a driver to cope with such a long journey, so I'll take you." As if warming to the idea, he adds: "If you let me crash on your floor, we can have a boys' night before I have to drive back, and I'll show you the tricks to being a proper student."

Lost in his moment of reverie, Greg misses the look of horror that flashes over Adam's face, and the smug grin on Ethan's, before Adam politely says, "That would be great, dad, thanks."

Greg smiles warmly at his son, looking excited at the prospect of a weekend away, before turning to me and saying: "So you'll have a weekend to yourself for once. What will you do with the free time?"

"Well," I pause as I feel three pairs of eyes look up at me from their plates, clearly not expecting me to have any plans. "There is a weekend fundraising event in the Peak District for a kid with leukaemia, which the gym has organised. I wasn't going to go, but since you guys are all away and don't need me, I think I'll go and support it... since it's such a good cause." I really emphasise the bit at the end. Deathly silence meets my announcement. Clearly Greg was fine with the idea of him going off for a weekend, but the idea of me doing the same is somewhat less palatable. I hold my breath, waiting for some sort of reaction from Greg.

"Who are you going with?" he asks, seemingly just out of interest, but I know him well enough to recognise the edge to the question. He runs his hand through his hair, another sign of irritation and stress.

"Just some people from the gym. I don't actually know a lot of them. People like me who need the exercise," I say, laughing slightly nervously, knowing I was deliberately painting an image of fat people for some reason. "We'll spend each day walking up a different peak, and the evening recovering," I add.

"Where will you be staying? We can't afford a hotel for you."

I bite back the response I want to make – which is that since I have earned all the money coming in to the house, if anyone deserves a short break at a hotel in the Peaks, it's me –

and calmly reply instead: "Someone's donated a big old house for the group to stay at. It's not going to be comfortable, but it is free, so the only cost will be my food. I'll have to share a room with another girl, but it's all for a good cause." For some reason I can't explain, I know I need to make it sound like it isn't going to be any fun or Greg will kick off about it. I hold my breath again while trying to look like I don't really care.

Greg eventually grunts before looking at me and saying: "Well, it looks like you'll need to arrange someone to feed the cat." I know it's as good as I'm likely to get from him, so I smile and reassure him I'll make some arrangements, while calmly spooning extra chicken onto his plate.

The rest of the meal passes relatively smoothly. I keep the growing excitement inside me firmly harnessed.

****

In the middle of the following week, I receive a text from an unknown number:

Hey babe, how about a drink so we can sort out the details for our trip?

My mind is blank as I gaze at the words on the screen. And then it finally clicks – Annie. Greg has been worryingly quiet about my planned trip. I've made sure all the arrangements are in place for everyone else's plans (I've already got clothes washed and ironed for packing, shopping done, cat feeder recruited, car oil and water topped up), keen to make sure no complaint can be made of me or my plans. For some reason Greg has a habit of ruining any plans that I'm looking forward to, and I still can't quite believe the same won't happen for this trip.

Memories of my 30th birthday flash through my mind. Emma had bought me a weekend trip to London that involved an overnight stay at a cheap hotel and a trip to the theatre. She had planned it as a great girls' weekend, and we'd both been really excited. Unfortunately, about three hours after we got to London on the first day, I received a call from Greg to say he was unwell and not in a position to look after the boys. You could have argued the boys, at age eleven, could have coped for a day with sandwiches and extra T.V. time, but Greg was adamant he needed me home, even if the boys didn't, so I dutifully got back on the train and went home again.

Emma had been fuming. "He's controlling you, Lily. You are allowed a life of your own, you know," she ranted. "You don't have to run back to him immediately when he demands you to. In fact it would do him good to have to stand on his own two feet without you for a bit; it might make him appreciate you a bit more."

I had never heard her quite so angry before, as I sat embarrassed on the train with her home, cringing inwardly at the loudness of her voice in the quiet but packed carriage. "It's not about the money, Lil," she assured me as I apologised profusely for the waste. "I just want you to have a chance to enjoy your life too. You give them everything, and they have absolutely no idea just how lucky they are. Greg is too controlling of you; if he really loved you, he would want you to be happy and do things you enjoy too. Instead, all he ever does is make sure you're there to provide for his own enjoyment." She was building up a head of steam now. "And the one time I think I've finally found a way to spoil you, he even manages to ruin that and drag you home."

I had yet again made excuses for him, same as I always did, and eventually she'd had to let it go, but deep down I knew she was right. Greg had control issues which were getting worse as the years progressed. It was almost as if the more dissatisfied he was with his own life, the more he felt the need to impact on mine.

A part of me still can't believe that he's just going to let me waltz off to the Peak District for three days on my own with a bunch of strangers. For that reason I don't want to talk to him about Annie, let alone introduce her to him. I can only assume Stuart from the gym must have let her know I had confirmed my place, and now she wants to meet for that drink and make our plans.

It's Tuesday and a long shot, but I quickly text her back:

Hi, yes gr8. Don't spose you're free 2nite and can make it to the Anchor in Tudor Street? Other nights are difficult for me. I'll b there at 8, Lily

I wait, not sure what I'm going to do if she can't make it. It takes three whole minutes until my phone bleeps again, and I hurry to look at the message:

Lovely. C u there A x

With huge relief, I send a quick text to Emma, realising she probably needs to be forewarned.

Em, hope u don't mind. Have invited a friend to join us this eve. Will explain when I c u. Lil x

That done, I sit back in my chair and spend some time trying to figure out why I feel guilty, almost like I'm doing something wrong.

Chapter 6

When I walk into the pub just before eight, Emma is already sitting at our preferred table. Brian, the landlord of The Anchor, is perched in my usual seat, having brought her lime and soda directly to the table, rather than making her walk to the bar like everyone else (including me) was made to. Brian grunts at me as he sees me approach and reluctantly rises from the table, casting a longing look in Emma's direction. Emma doesn't even notice, as she's beaming at me.

"Don't get up," I say quickly, as she struggles to gain enough momentum to lift herself and her bump, which seems nearly as big as the rest of her, off the stool to greet me with our customary hug.

"Nonsense," she says with one final rock that rolls her body sufficiently to propel her into my arms. She giggles as we hug, adding: "Bloody hell, Lil, I have absolutely no idea how you managed to do this with twins." I laugh as we both sit back down, and she continues in a whisper, "Glad you're on time. Brian was just telling me about his dog's labour again, the time when she had eight puppies. If it's not bad enough that everyone who has ever had a child wants to tell me about their nightmare labours, or their friend's nightmare labours, if theirs weren't bad enough, I now have Brian's dog's nightmare labour to add to the list. Doesn't anyone ever have an easy birth?"

I laugh again, feeling obliged to reassure her, "You will, Em. You're good at everything you do, and I can't imagine this will be any different. Anyway, if it is hell, then there are always drugs or epidurals. 'Never say never', that's my childbirth motto when it comes to pain relief!"

She laughs. "Thank God for you, the lone voice of childbirth sanity, Lil – actually, I think you might be the only voice of sanity against a tidal wave of natural-childbirth Nazis, judging by the antenatal classes I've attended so far. By the way, what have you done to yourself this time?" she asks, pointing to the remnants of my forehead bruise that is now turning yellowish.

I grimace. "Head-butted a door."

"Oh God, Lil, I'm not sure you're safe to be let out alone." She rolls her eyes before adding, "Do you want a drink?" while looking over at Brian again, who fortunately is already gazing longingly in her direction and ignoring all the other people waving notes over the bar at him.

"Sure, vodka, lime and soda to keep you company... well sort of."

Emma calls over to Brian, somehow managing to be heard over the noise in the pub, "Brian, sweetie, can I have a vodka, lime and soda, please."

Brian's eyebrows nearly rise through the top of his hairline before Emma adds with a giggle: "Not for me, silly, for Lil," pointing at me in case he couldn't hear her, at which point he scowls in my direction before making it, plonking it on the bar and looking at it and then at me meaningfully.

I sigh; clearly I don't warrant any special treatment. I stand up and weave my way through the groups of people until I reach the bar, hand him my note and stand there waiting for my change while he fiddles with the till. As I wait there with my hand out, the door opens and a wave of murmurs ripple through the bar in reaction to the newcomer. I can't immediately see who's arrived, but I guess just from the impact in the bar that it can only be Annie. The first part of her I see is her hair. Out of the ponytail this time, it forms a riotous cascade of red ringlets that frames her face and flows out over her shoulders. She stands a few inches taller than several of the men in the pub and has to duck under the beam as she sees me, waves and makes her way over. Brian, at this point, is now openly staring at Annie – as is the rest of the bar, including Emma, to be fair.

Annie sweeps me up into a huge hug that speaks of years of friendship rather than minutes, then announces loudly: "Lily, at last!" She gives a huge laugh, as if she's just heard the most amusing joke ever. I can feel the room leaning in towards her, as if magnetically pulled towards an orbit where she was the sun, and we were all the planets worshipping her warmth.

"Can I get you a drink?" I stutter. *God, why is it she paralyses me into near incoherence?*

She smiles benevolently at me. "What are you having?"

"Vodka, lime and soda."

She frowns at my response. "God no, not that." She sounds genuinely horrified. "Landlord, please, will you tell me what single malts you have?"

Brian just blinks at her until I prompt: "Brian?"

He starts and visibly comes to before stuttering, much like I had, through a list of Scottish malt whiskies.

"Talisker, please," she says assertively.

Brian nods and tells her he'll bring it over. *Bloody hell, am I the only one who doesn't rate sufficiently highly to warrant personal service from Brian?* I wonder as we make our way to where Emma is sitting. Emma's expression is equally bemused as she takes in the vision that is Annie. However, she seems more amused by the reaction of everyone around us, rather than overwhelmed by the presence of a living goddess. *I guess that's what comes from having confidence in your own beauty*, I reflect.

"Emma, this is Annie; Annie, meet Emma," I introduce. They're shaking hands as Brian comes over, clasping the small malt glass carefully and handing it to Annie. For a moment he looks like a cartoon as his head swings wildly between Emma and Annie, finally settling on Annie as he tells her there's no charge for the first drink in his bar for a new customer.

I nearly snort my vodka over the table, as Annie merely smiles at him beatifically. Brian scowls at me, clearly having heard my snort, before stomping away back behind his bar. Emma lets out a tinkling laugh, saying: "Well, I've never seen Brian quite so overcome that he would give away free drinks, Annie. It seems you have quite an effect on men. When I've had this baby, promise me you'll take me out for a night, please; I think it would be the cheapest night out ever."

Annie smiles her most wicked smile, making Emma laugh again as she says: "You'd better believe it, but only if Lily promises to come too!"

I just grimace.

"So tell me, how on earth did you two meet?" Emma asks.

I open my mouth to speak, but Annie is in there before me. "We are soon to be roommates on a wild and romantic trip to the Peak District," she says overly dramatically.

I wince as Emma raises an eyebrow and looks at me incredulously. "Really?" she enquires, sounding frankly shocked at such atypical behaviour from me.

I giggle nervously and look around, aware that more than one person in the bar is acquainted with Greg, and that with all the attention Annie draws to her, it feels at the moment like there is a hushed silence in the room as they all lean in, awaiting my response.

"We're doing a three peaks weekend to raise money for a kid with leukaemia," I say, more loudly than I need to, fervently hoping that this is the version that will get back to Greg, and not the 'wild and romantic' one.

Emma smiles as the tension bubble in the room seems to burst and normal chatting levels resume, and I add, "Annie and I are sharing a room while we're there. I thought you wouldn't mind us meeting to chat about what we need to take?"

"No, of course not." Emma smiles at Annie before frowning as she turns back to me. "But is Greg okay with you going?"

I glance nervously at Annie, who immediately asks: "Who's Greg?"

"My husband," I answer quickly.

"And why would your husband not be okay with you going?" Annie asks smoothly, in the style of someone who could never imagine another person having that sort of influence over her actions.

I swallow, trying to consider how to respond when Emma chips in, "Because he's a complete control freak who doesn't let Lily out of his sight, except to let her go to work while he sits on his arse and tells her he's an artist, when he really does bugger all." She pauses for a second, looking apologetically at me – as if she thinks she's being disloyal to me, when all she's really doing is telling the truth – before continuing. "He barely lets her come here to meet me, except he has spies in the room who'll report back her every movement," she says, looking around. "He never lets her go anywhere, so I'm frankly amazed she's off to the Peak District without him, and more especially with you," she says, looking meaningfully at Annie.

Jeez, Emma, I think, *why don't you say what you really think?*

"I mean, don't get me wrong, I think it's brilliant," Emma continues, "I've been trying to break my beautiful friend out of her cage for years, so anything you can do to help is much appreciated." She actually looks teary as she finishes, and I just don't know what to say. I've always known she feels anger towards Greg about the way he is with me, and the way I always feel the need to defend him, however outrageous his behaviour, but she's never expressed it so openly before, let alone in front of a virtual stranger.

What is it about this woman? I wonder, looking at Annie again. I reach out for Emma's hand and clasp it in mine as she uses her other hand to point at her bump and mumbles: "hormones", as if her outburst needed some sort of excuse.

Annie just looks at us both and smiles. "Well, it seems I've got here in the nick of time," she laughs, as she necks her whisky before loudly demanding a second from Brian and slamming her glass on the table. "And one for my friend here, please," she adds, indicating me.

Brian immediately moves to fulfil her request, ignoring his other paying guests. I get up to collect the drinks from the bar, managing to knock into a table and topple a glass on my way, so I end up replacing that person's drink too. When I finally get back to the table, I'm sure I didn't imagine Annie exchanging a look with Emma, as if I'd missed a significant part of the evening's conversation. I have the distinct impression there is a conspiracy forming between the two of them, and I'm not sure if I should be worried.

Chapter 7

We spend the rest of the evening discussing what our wardrobe and other accoutrements need to be so we can cope with both the day and the evening exploits in the Peak District. When Annie announces that we need a formal outfit, as the group has planned to have a black-tie evening at the house to celebrate the achievement, albeit only 2/3rds done of our challenge (the final peak would be completed on the last day prior to getting straight back on the coach and heading back home), I nearly die.

"I don't have a dress to wear for that sort of event," I gasp, horrified. *There's no way in hell I could buy myself a dress without Greg knowing, and if I told him I needed a frock to get dressed up, then there would be no way in hell that I would be allowed to go.* Even as the thoughts echo in my head, I know it's pathetic I let him control my life to that extent, but it's just easier than having the conflict.

Emma sees the anxiety on my face and immediately correctly interprets the reason. She calmly asserts: "I'd like to buy you a dress, Lil. We can go out on Thursday to late-night shopping, instead of you going to the gym, and pick one out together. It'll be a belated birthday present or early Christmas present, whatever you'd rather. I can even keep hold of it if you prefer, and then you can collect it from me before you go to get the coach on Friday after work. Or I can drop it off for you there; whatever works for you, really."

It's pathetic, but I nearly sag with relief as Emma neatly solves all my problems without me needing to open my mouth. It's so embarrassing; I wonder just when I became so spineless I was unwilling to take Greg on and challenge him about something that was essentially completely unreasonable behaviour. I'm not doing anything wrong, just getting a dress to wear to a function. I resolve to stand up for myself at home more. *But not this time*, I think, *not 'til after the trip. I don't want him to ruin it for me.*

"Thank you," I whisper, wondering how it was I deserved such a good and loyal friend. Emma just smiles and simply says, "I expect a photo."

Annie assures her she will see to it herself. The rest of the plans include walking boots, raincoats, hats, gloves and plasters. I already have most of it, the product of many a cheap camping holiday with the boys because our money was too tight to do anything else. Annie, on the other hand, seems more used to city life, but she dutifully makes a list on her iPhone of everything she needs, including where she would be most likely to find all the different items, while Emma watches on, bemused by the whole situation.

At the end of the evening, Emma and I say 'goodbye' to Annie. I watch them hug each other like old friends, and then

Annie whispers something in Emma's ear before moving towards her taxi. Emma smiles, and they both turn to look at me, making me feel awkward.

"Stop fidgeting, and get in the car," Emma scolds, having determined that after a vodka and two whiskies I'm very likely beyond the drink-drive limit. I do as I'm told, wondering how the hell I'm going to get the car back tomorrow after work and what time I need to get up in order to get the bus.

"She's great, I really like her," Emma declares after a last wave at Annie as her taxi pulls away. I nod my agreement.

"Thanks again for the dress," I begin.

But Emma just waves her hand vaguely at me and says, "It's my pleasure, really, I mean it. It would give me great joy to see you out enjoying yourself for once, looking as beautiful as you are and letting other people see it for a change. I just wish I could be there to share it with you," she says, sounding a little sad.

"Next time," I whisper. She looks at me intently, as the brake light from the car in front illuminates her face with a red glow, and nods. It feels like she's trying to see right inside me.

"I would really like that," she says emphatically. I look away and let the moment pass, both of us knowing how unlikely a next time was.

As we pulled up in front of the house I'd felt my shoulders tighten as I rehearsed what I was going to say to Greg about why I was in Emma's car and why our car was still at the pub.

Emma grabs my hand as I move to open the door. "You've done nothing wrong," she assures me. I give her a half smile as I ease out of the car seat.

Closing the door behind me, she lowers the window and calls out quietly: "See you Thursday, I'll pick you up at half five. If you have to tell him anything, tell him I need help getting some stuff for the baby. It's true; I could do with your experience in choosing a pram. Phil's mum is hassling me to make a decision about which one we want, as they insist on buying it for us, but I get even more confused every time I go and look at them. So if you will be my baby guru and help me choose a pram, I'll help you choose a dress."

I decide she's a mind reader; it's like she knew I was chickening out of the trip the further I got from Annie and the pub. This way she knows she has me; I could never resist helping her with stuff for the baby. I immediately give in. "Okay, see you Thursday at half five outside work."

She beams at me before waving one last time and pulling away.

I square my shoulders and walk to the door, fumbling the keys in the latch as the cold air combines with my alcohol-fuddled brain and ruins what was left of my already severely lacking hand-eye coordination. The door jerks open from the inside, and Greg stands there sizing me up with a look before glancing at the obviously empty driveway.

"Where's the car?"

"At the pub," is all I say as I make to push past him, feeling unusually bold for once.

"Why?" he asks, blocking my way with an arm.

"Because I had two whiskies and a vodka," I reply. "I'll pick it up tomorrow after work – I'll get the bus in the morning."

"You don't like whisky," he says, still looking at me intently, his arm still blocking my path into the house.

"Well, I did tonight." My voice sounds tired to my own ears, and clearly he hears something in it because he lifts his arm and lets me pass. I hang up my coat and head straight up the stairs to our room, with him following close behind me. The boys are either out or already in bed, most likely the former because they rarely go to bed before midnight these days. He stands there watching me as I take off my makeup and brush my teeth in the bathroom.

"What's up with you?" he mumbles. I turn towards him, and for the first time in a long time I really look at him. I see his angular, still overly slim frame, his square jaw with perfect nose and hair flopping down over his forehead, hiding the green eyes I used to love when I first met him. Now all the small gestures irritate me; every time he runs his hand through his hair to move it out of his face, I wonder why he doesn't just get it cut. There's no denying he's still a handsome man, but I also see the grey in his hair and the lines etched on his face that reflect all the angry and disappointed expressions he has made over the passing years, and I realise I feel virtually nothing of the love for him I had felt in the early days. He sees me weigh him up with my eyes and look away, finding him wanting.

"What's with you?" he says again, angry this time, seeking to reassert control. I move back into the bedroom and reach for my pyjamas.

"Don't bother," he growls, pushing me back onto the bed with one hand while fumbling to undo his shirt with the other. I sigh and sit down on the bed as I begin to slowly undo my own buttons. It isn't fast enough for him, so he grabs it and tears, sending the small buttons flying across the room.

"Shit, Greg, that was my favourite shirt," I complain without thinking.

He just pushes me back against the bed, secures both my hands in one of his and growls: "Shut the fuck up."

He reaches for my skirt and pushes it up, exposing my pants, which he pushes to one side before pushing two fingers straight up inside me hard. I moan at the sensation because the invasion hurts at first, but eventually my body starts betraying me as he moves his fingers, touching my most sensitive places.

I want to hate him for doing this, but my body has other ideas. I can feel a slickness forming as his fingers press within me. I'm responding almost instantly, and he knows it. My nipples harden, exposed through the lace of my bra, and he lowers his head to suckle first one and then the other until I'm whimpering for more, a dull ache forming in my lower stomach that demands his attention.

All the while he holds my hands tight in place in the firm grip of one of his large hands. He withdraws his fingers suddenly and tears off my pants, before fumbling one-handed with the buttons on his jeans to release his erection. His knee forces my thighs apart, and I feel him nudging at my entrance before pushing in hard.

Suddenly, I want him. My back arches, and I push my hips against him, deepening the contact. He only thrusts a few times when I feel the telltale tightening and trembling in his body and he's shouting my name as he comes, finally collapsing onto me, eventually releasing my hands. The whole event must take no more than ten minutes if we're lucky.

We lie there in silence for a while, both breathing heavily, before he stands up, takes off his trousers and shirt and then climbs into the bed. I can tell he's asleep within five minutes of shuffling out of his jeans. I get up, remove what's left of my shirt, my bra and then my skirt, and slowly pull on my pyjamas. As I lie back down on the bed, with the lights turned off, I think about what just happened. *Jesus, all I'm fit for is the bloody Jeremy Kyle show*, I reflect, wondering how it was that my life was turning into the worst kind of car-crash television. *I didn't say no*, I console myself.

Chapter 8

Greg didn't look happy when I told him I was going out with Emma for a second time that week, but after I explain how she needs me to help with the choice of pram, as well as doing a bit of other shopping, there really isn't much he can object to without looking childish and even more controlling than he actually is. I have prepared a lasagne (Greg's favourite) for all three of them, and bought a pre-washed salad. I tell them all they had to do was warm the lasagne through, open the salad and eat it; I will do the washing up when I get home.

Emma is waiting outside the surgery promptly as agreed when I finish work, greeting me with a bright smile and a wave. It's nice to be greeted so warmly, I reflect as I climb into the car. We drive slowly through the rush hour traffic, filled with the crimson glow of brake lights, until we get closer to the centre of town and the traffic lifts slightly. We are going against the flow – with most people heading to their homes and families in the darkening evening as autumn closes in. Emma easily finds a parking place, and we make immediately for the maternity department of John Lewis – *well, really, a girl like Emma was never likely to buy things for her baby from anywhere else, was she?*

"Right, there's only three things that really matter when you're buying a pram," I intone in my most knowledgeable-sounding voice, grabbing a large teddy bear and thrusting it into her slightly startled arms. "Firstly, you have to be able to fold the buggy up single-handed while holding a baby," I say, nodding towards the teddy, which she adjusts until it's perched on one hip. She moves towards the first buggy she most likes the look of (also one of the most expensive) and tries to shift the clasp to unlock it and fold it. Several frustrated minutes and at least one broken nail later, even after the assistant closes in on us (scenting the prospect of an easy sale) and demonstrates the easy closing mechanism three times, the pram stands resolutely upright.

"Well, bloody hell!" Emma exclaims, now disgruntled as she discards her first choice and moves on to her second-favourite. The mechanism on this one is marginally easier, and after only three attempts Emma folds the contraption up with a flourish and steps back with a look of satisfaction on her face.

"Okay, so what's the second thing?" she asks.

"You need to be able to lift it, also while still holding a baby."

"Well, why would I need to do that?" she exclaims indignantly. "Couldn't I just pop the baby in his or her seat in the car?"

"Well, yes, if you are putting it in the car, but what about if you're getting on a bus? I had a caesarean; the only option for me for the first six weeks was to go on the bus if I wanted to go out, and trust me, sometimes you need to get out of the house. If you can't carry it onto the bus, the only alternative is handing your beloved child – or children, in my case – to a complete stranger. Believe me, I know this from experience, and it's not ideal," I add.

"Okay, Okay, you're right again 'oh wise one'," she says with resignation as she attempts to lift the buggy with one arm. The look of relief on her face to know she can lift it is second only to the assistant's, who has already seen the value of her sale diminish.

"Okay, hit me with the final rule," Emma says, slightly nervous now.

"Well, this one's easy, but again a common issue if not thought about beforehand." I pause for dramatic effect, ignoring the eye-rolling assistant. "It needs to fit in the boot of your car. Again, this is one I learnt firsthand, but some of these beasts are huge," I say, looking meaningfully at the contraption in front of her.

Emma looks down with a slightly wobbly lip as she weighs up the size of the pram with the size of the car boot on her little KA. The assistant is waffling about how deceptive these things could be and car boots were made big enough to accommodate prams these days, but we both know the pram is far bigger than her car could fit. The KA had been Emma's pride and joy, bought with her first proper pay packet on qualifying as a solicitor, but is now sadly found wanting, given the expanding needs of her life.

"Sorry, honey," I say, giving her a big hug.

"No, it's fine, really, thank God you saved me from making a very expensive mistake," she says, smiling at me, although her eyes still look sad. We move on to look at the smaller versions, but I can tell her heart isn't really in it when she finally puts a reserve on one and arranges the delivery date, three weeks before the birth. The assistant actually scowls at me as we say 'thank you' and pay.

"Okay," says Emma, visibly brightening as we leave the maternity section, "now it's all about you. How long have we got?" she asks, glancing down at her watch.

"About an hour and a half," I say, knowing that if I'm not home before nine I'll get grief from Greg, and I don't want to start anything with the trip now a mere week away. I look at her anxiously. "Is that long enough?"

"Sure," she says with confidence, "you know how you know everything there is to know about prams and everything to do with babies and children? Well, I'm like the Yoda of shopping for dresses."

I laugh as she pulls me towards the party dresses in the store. It isn't a section I habitually frequent, and one glance at the price tags tells me why. She's all business now.

"Right," she says matter-of-factly, as she begins grabbing dresses from the rails, muttering about the importance of emphasising my legs and bust. The fabrics are luxurious, and the price tags tell me I'm well out of my league.

"You have to be kidding," I say as I catch sight of a red dress she had selected that looked like it was more suited to her than me.

"Trust me," she says, as if she's talking to a difficult child. After about twenty minutes she has about eight dresses for me to try and thrusts them into my arms before manhandling me towards the changing room. She isn't content to just leave me to try them on my own, insisting to the unconcerned attendant that she's required to supervise me and positioning herself on a small chair just outside the changing room.

As I reluctantly peel off my regulation cardigan, shirt and black slacks that had become my staple uniform for work, I'm amazed to see the dresses she chose are all in a size smaller than my usual. Maybe the gym is having an effect after all, if Emma is noticing it. I pull the first item on, a fitted little black dress to the knee with long sleeves and a plunging V-neck. I reach behind to do up the zip, then turn to examine myself in the mirror and gasp. The person standing looking back at me doesn't look like me at all. Once I get beyond my spectacular cleavage, I can't believe I actually have a waist for perhaps the first time in my adult life. I may not be tall, but somehow the work at the gym has started to tone my body and reduce my inches, producing a figure that, while by no means perfect, is well-proportioned and shapely. *Damn*, I think, *I look like a woman. Oh my God, I'm going to start singing Shania Twain songs in a minute.*

My reverie is broken by the grating of the curtain rings on the bar as Emma unceremoniously rips the curtain back.

"What's taking so lo–, bloody hell, Lil, you look fucking fantastic!"

I smile at her, a big mega-watt grin, both at her uncharacteristic use of the 'F' word and because for once I actually agree with her. I do look good. *At least for me*, I auto-correct.

Emma is still talking: "The structure of that dress is great. It gives you lots of support, not that you really need it with your gym efforts. They've really paid off, Lil, I am so proud of you. All we need to do is get you some 'fuck me' shoes and the right underwear, sexy but supportive, and you will be good to go."

"'Fuck me' shoes," I echo faintly.

"Yes, you know, 'bar to car' shoes. Good for looking good in, but totally impossible if you actually have to do much in the way of walking. From what Annie said you'll just be having a party at the house, so you can make your dramatic entrance, look glam for a bit and then kick them off when your feet start to hurt, by which point everyone's past caring anyway!"

"I don't know," I start to say.

"Lily, don't lose your courage now. You're doing brilliantly. Try on the other dresses to compare, but really I think we've struck gold with our first try. You're going to look fab, and with a couple of little accessories, you'll be perfect." She sounds pleased with herself.

Her phone rings and distracts her, so I retreat back behind the curtain, carefully removing the dress. A quick glance at the price tag makes me shudder, but I hang it carefully back up and reach for the red dress. More confident this time I marvel at the ease with which I can do up the zip, and then I turn to inspect myself. Where the black dress had made me look sexy and womanly, this one shouts "strumpet" at me from the mirror. I laugh as I try to manhandle my breasts into the dress so that at least my nipples aren't on display.

Pulling the curtain aside I show the dress to Emma, who's still talking on the phone – to Phil, I guess from the sweet smile that's playing at her lips. She shakes her head emphatically when she looks up and shoos me back into the changing room with her hands. Two more dresses later, and two more negative shakes from Emma, and I'm getting tired of getting in and out of dresses. I've never been much of a girl when it comes to shopping. Unusually for me, though, I'm not disheartened, because while none of the dresses look quite as good as the first, none of them look exactly bad. If ever I needed any encouragement to keep up with my efforts at the gym, then this was it. The positive impact of even just a short six-week period has really made a difference, and I resolve to keep going.

I stick my head out of the cubicle to see if Emma will permit me to go with the first dress and save me having to try any more. She has just finished talking to Phil.

"Is it worth trying on any more?" I ask tentatively. "I really like that first one."

"Me too," she agrees. "Let's go and get underwear and shoes." She reaches into the cubicle and grabs the dress, leaving me to gather up the others and hand them to the poor assistant before rushing to catch up with her as she strides off towards the shoe department.

"Was that Phil?" I ask when I finally catch up with her, as she stands perusing a row of impossibly high black stilettos.

"Yes," she answers, looking a bit sheepish.

"How is he?" I enquire, knowing her well enough to know she has something to get off her chest.

"Oh, fine, I was just telling him about the prams, and not being able to get the one I wanted because it won't fit in the boot of my car." A slightly embarrassed flush passes over her face before she adds, "Phil insists he needs to get me a new car anyway, because mine won't be big enough when the baby comes along, so I can get the bigger pram after all."

She actually looks guilty as she says it, and I rush to reassure her. "Good for Phil. I'm glad for you, Em, you deserve it. You deserve to be happy, and I'm glad you've got a man like Phil who wants to do things for you to make you happy. That makes me happy." I mean it.

"Yeah, but you deserve to be happy too, and you never get breaks like me." It's sweet that it bothers her.

"Please don't ever think you can't tell me the nice things that happen to you, just because they don't happen to me. I want to hear about it – what car are you getting?"

"Not sure, maybe an Audi A3 or a Golf, something that's small enough for round town but big enough for kids, you know?" She's started to sound excited again.

"Absolutely," I agree, "sounds perfect." Emma reaches for a pair of shoes, quickly catching the eye of the assistant and asking for a size 6. I love her all the more for remembering my shoe size.

"Well, I guess we need to order that other pram, then," I say while we wait.

"Yeah," she says, the excited smile back on her face. When the assistant comes back with the shoes and I try them on, we both coo about the wonderful things they do to my calves. I can see now why women wear them, although I'm not sure I would be able to cope for more than about half an hour before needing to kick them off again; plus, given my propensity for clumsiness, I'm frighteningly likely to do either myself or someone else an injury while wearing them. Emma strides over to the till and pays for both the dress and the shoes, before leading me, despite my protests, to the underwear department.

One well-fitted lace bra and matching panties later, and I'm done.

"I've got a clutch bag that'll look perfect, not that you'll need it if you're staying in the house for the evening, but it'll be good to have just in case, or for your lipstick."

"As if!" I laugh, and Emma frowns at me.

"I'll have to have a word with Annie about that," she says. I look at her to see if she's serious but figure she's joking.

As we make our way back to the start of the shopping trip, and the maternity department, I reflect it had been a long time since I had enjoyed shopping so much. The maternity department assistant casts smug expressions in my direction as Emma amends her order, before we make our way back to her car and begin the short drive home. As we pull up in front of the house I lean over to kiss her.

"Thanks, Em. Really, I mean it, thank you. I had a great time, and I love the dress."

"I wish I was going to see you in it," she smiles sadly.

"You never know, maybe there'll be another posh event I get randomly invited to, when I can wear it and take you with me." *Unlikely, though, in reality,* we both think but don't say out loud.

"I'll look after the bags and bring them in to you at work, a week Friday, to put in your bag, and then you won't have a load of stress at home. You are driving straight to the place the coach is leaving from after work, aren't you?"

"Yeah, by taxi, although I'm finishing a little early." Greg and Adam are leaving first thing Friday for Bristol, and Ethan will be off at a bit before lunchtime, while my shift is for a few hours from just before lunch so I can see the others off. The coach is leaving late afternoon, and we won't get there until quite late in the evening, not returning 'til Monday evening after the last walk.

"Well, I want to hear all about it on Tuesday at the pub," she insists as I ease the car door open and get out.

"Thanks again, Em, I really adore the dress."

She just smiles and winks at me before driving off.

Chapter 9

The week passes in a blur, what with getting all the final things sorted for Adam, Greg and Ethan, as well as my own things for the Peaks. I also make sure I go to the gym every day after work, keen to ensure the dress still looks good by the time I get the chance to wear it. By the time we sit down for a rare family dinner on Thursday night, the last night before Adam leaves, I'm both exhausted and excited at the same time. I had prepared a full roast dinner as our family 'last supper'. It is, I suppose as I dish up the plates of lamb, roast potatoes, peas, carrots and gravy, a highly significant night in the Lambert household. With Adam off to uni, who knows when we will next all sit down to dinner together – perhaps Christmas? If my own life is anything to go by, then university will change Adam finally into an adult. With a bit of luck he won't make the same mistakes as his father and I – not that I regret my boys, I just think we made it harder for ourselves than we needed it to be. I had made him a little package of stuff to start university with – basic food provisions, some beer, which no doubt his father would help him with, and a couple of packets of condoms. History has a habit of repeating itself, after all, and while I wouldn't embarrass him by talking about it at his age, I could at least give him a 'not so subtle' hint.

The meal is surprisingly pleasant. It seems the fact that we all have something to look forward to at the weekend makes us enjoy this last dinner together, and there is a lot of laughter for a change. They compliment me on the meal, and Ethan even insists on clearing the plates and serving the apple crumble and custard in the style of a silver service waiter, which makes us all laugh.

Greg and I had decided that we would give both boys a small amount of money I had managed to save to help with university, or whatever they chose to do, and both boys seem genuinely pleased when we present it to them at the end of the meal. Especially Ethan, who I think had always suspected we were disappointed in him for not following in his brother's path. The money won't go far but they know we've done our best, and when both boys take a moment to come into the kitchen and hug me as I wash the dishes, I feel my eyes mist. It's a rare sweet moment.

That night, when Greg pulls me into his arms, I go as willingly as I ever have, wanting the good feeling of the evening to last a little longer. As his fingers trace my thigh and up to my breast I try to lose myself in the sensation, but my mind flickers to checking whether I've packed everything I need for the trip. Whatever he does, however and wherever he touches me, there's just something missing. As he slides inside me I can feel initial friction from the absence of my own arousal, and it takes a few moments until it feels comfortable. I lie there in the traditional style, hating myself as he thrusts into me gently, wishing he would finish quickly, more concerned I'll need to wash my hair again in the morning than about what's happening in bed. I moan in the hope it will persuade him I'm enjoying myself and encourage him to finish, and then immediately feel guilty I'm not getting anything from it, wondering if it is somehow my fault. When he eventually comes it's with the usual groan as he collapses over the top of me, crushing the air from my lungs. I push his body away from my own and quickly slip out of bed to clean myself up. When I finish we lie beside each other, him spooning me. I think I hear him whisper: "I love you" as I drift off to sleep, but I may have imagined it.

****

The morning after is frantic, with the usual family tension returned. It seems I have lost a 'best shirt' for Adam, Ethan has pulled the button off the black trousers he needs for his course, and Greg is pissed because the car only has half a tank of petrol in it. Despite all this I shed a tear as Adam hugs me goodbye, and stand in the road in my dressing gown, waving until they drive off out of sight and a car beeps at me from behind to get out the way.

"Mum, you're so embarrassing," Ethan says with a roll of his eyes as he watches me from the front doorway.

By the time I have showered, redone my hair, and pulled on my jeans and a long sleeved t-shirt top with a hoodie over it to keep me warm on the coach, Ethan is calling from downstairs to let me know he's ready to leave for the course. I run down the stairs, and he looks visibly surprised as he takes in my appearance.

"You look different... you look good!" he amends with a note of surprise to his voice that betrays the compliment as backhanded. He collects himself. "No, I mean it, mum, you look really good, you've lost weight."

I blush and glance down at myself. I guess I'm in more fitted clothes than my usual slouchy cardigans and my weight loss is really beginning to show.

"Oh, thanks," I say, pulling him into a swift hug. "See you Monday night; I hope the course goes well. I love you," I add.

"Yeah, and you," he says, moving away, awkward with the open display of emotion. *He's so like his father*, I think as I watch him struggle to say what he feels. He gives a wave over his shoulder as he walks down the path and away, and with that I'm alone. I feel a shiver of excitement thrill through my body, and I can't really put my finger on what caused it – I'm just a bit demob happy, I guess. I go back upstairs to finish loading my gear into the large backpack I'm taking. The cab arrives perfectly on time to get me to work for my shift, and I leave the house without a backward glance.

Emma arrives at 1pm promptly with my dress, shoes and a sandwich for each of us. I pick at mine as we sit on the bench in the little garden attached to the surgery. I've been trying to avoid bread as part of my weight reduction scheme.

"You're looking good, Lil," she says, looking at me sideways as she tucks into a turkey sandwich.

I really don't know where she puts it all and stays so slim, I think uncharitably as she finishes hers and eats the other untouched half of mine, immediately stopping myself and feeling guilty when I remember just how much this girl has done for me over recent days, weeks, *hell, years, let's be honest! And for God's sake, the woman is having a baby; can't I just be kind when she's gone out of her way for me?*

"Yeah, you're the second person to say that today," I finally acknowledge.

"Don't tell me Greg actually paid you a compliment!"

"Don't be silly," I laugh. "Ethan told me I'd lost weight just before he left. I guess the gym is working."

"It is, Lil, but you were always beautiful anyway, whatever size you were. You just never realised it."

"You're just my best friend and therefore obliged to love me whatever I look like – it's part of the contract," I counter. This is an old conversation, and one which I've always liked to deflect away from as quickly as possible. "So when are you picking up the new car?"

"This weekend," she says, instantly buzzing with excitement. She has already informed me that they've found a car at the local Audi showroom that is second-hand but with really low mileage which she loves. There's only the paperwork and insurance to sort out before it's hers. "How about I come and pick you up in it on Monday evening when the coach gets in? I assume Greg isn't?"

I can't miss the slightly accusatory tone in her voice. She's right, of course. It hadn't crossed Greg's mind to offer. I had been planning to get a taxi from the coach meeting point.

"That would be perfect, although I might be a bit muddy after the walk that day. Are you sure you don't mind me getting into your shiny new car? I might make it dirty."

"Hell no! Hey, I'm going to have a puking baby in the back soon, so I think we can cope with a bit of mud."

I hug her as we say our farewells, and she makes me promise again to send her a photo of me in my dress, before I make my way back inside for the rest of my shift.

The rest of the time 'til 4pm drags at work, as I stare at the clock, watching the minutes tick slowly by. When one of the doctors tries to get me to start a patient search at five to four for anyone who has missed their flu jab, I abruptly and uncharacteristically tell him I don't have time. He looks at me surprised, and I realise this is probably the first time I've ever said no to him. *Why is it people really only notice me, or even look at me, when I do something unexpected? The rest of the time they just take me for granted.* At 4pm prompt my taxi pulls up, and without a word to the others I grab my pack and head out the door.

"Good luck," one of the other receptionists calls as she sees me leave. She had sponsored me, so she knows where I'm going. I've managed to raise £250 in total from other staff and a few of the regular patients, which isn't bad. My family, in typical style, hadn't given a bean. I don't pause to talk to her, instead shouting out my thanks and waving over my shoulder in the same way Ethan had this morning.

I'm nervous in the cab on the short drive to the car park where we're meeting the coach. As we pull in I can see a small crowd already gathered around the door of the coach which is waiting with the engine running. I pay the cab driver, giving him a small tip (I always have, I just think it's the right thing to do, really) and hop out. The driver follows me, insisting he'll carry my bag to the coach. I guess the tip thing pays for itself in the end after all. *It's all about karma.* The coach driver takes the bag from the cabbie and stows it in the hold.

"Thanks," I say again to the cab driver.

"No problem," he says. "Have fun," he adds with wink before walking back to his car. I can't remember the last time a man winked at me. *Has a man ever winked at me before?* I look over to the group standing by the coach door at the same time as Stuart is looking towards me. He waves and beckons me over. This is it, I guess, time to meet some of the other walkers. I take a deep breath to calm my nerves and walk over.

"Lily, great, you made it in perfect time. We're just waiting for one more person, I think, and then we'll be ready to go."

"Annie?" I hazard a guess.

"Ha! Yes, how did you know?"

"Well she's kind of unmissable, and I thought I'd have known if she was here already," I say, squinting to look at the few heads I can see already sitting on the coach. He agrees, turning to the other people who are standing near him and chatting quietly.

"Guys, this is Lily. Lily, do you know anyone?"

I look at the group for the first time properly. There are about six of them. Pat, the only other woman, acknowledges me with a nod as I say,

"Pat and I use the gym a lot at the same time, um." I scan the rest of the faces, who all look familiar, but I don't know any names. "I'm not sure of anyone else's names, sorry," I say, flushing with embarrassment.

Stuart, sensing my discomfort and with the ease of someone who deals with people professionally, steps in quickly and introduces everyone; "This is Pat, as you know, Phil, Colin, Pete and Paul." As he says their names I look at each in turn, and they nod and smile at me. I nod shyly back, wondering how the hell I'll ever remember all the names. They look nice, sort of normal, and Pete particularly gives me a big smile. They don't look like frightening fitness freaks, so with a bit of luck I'm not too out of my depth. I feel hopeful.

"Can we get this show on the road yet? It's a long drive," a voice demands from the top of the steps of the coach. I look up and feel my jaw drop. *Bloody hell, it's him*, is my first thought. I haven't seen him at the gym since the day he picked me up off the floor when the door slammed into my face. It hadn't crossed my mind someone like him would want to spend his time on a walking trip. For the first time I have the chance to really look at him while he's talking to Stuart and the others. I finally realise why he seems familiar. He kind of resembles Rob Lowe, which explains my adolescent physical response to his proximity I suppose, remembering the passion of my teenage crush. A closer look at the guy standing on the steps of the coach, and I can see a few small differences – a narrower jaw, slightly bigger eyes – but he's as near as, damn it. As my gaze reaches his eyes I realise he's looking straight at me, one eyebrow raised in a sort of ironic questioning yet knowing way.

"Well?" he enquires again, his eye still on mine. For a moment I'm not sure if his question is about whether we'll soon be on our way or whether I find him pleasing to stare at. I flush, fearing the latter. His bright blue eyes bore into me, and for a moment I feel again like he can see straight into my soul. He finally looks away, back at Stuart, and I gasp a deep breath – I didn't realise I had been holding it. The paralysis that had held while he looked at me had finally releases. *How long had I been transfixed?* I wonder.

"Nice-looking, isn't he?" Pat whispers in my ear. I nod, flushing bright red again as I realise my gawping has not gone unnoticed.

"Bit like Rob Lowe," I whisper.

"That's what I thought!" Pat shouts with a shrieking laugh that has everyone's heads swinging back round to look at us, including the Rob Lowe look-alike. His gaze fixes upon me again, and I giggle completely uncharacteristically. His eyebrow shoots up again, and I see a twitch of a smile play at the corners of his lips. *His lips*, I find myself gazing at the perfect Cupid's bow. It's only the fact Stuart is still speaking that means I manage to pull my eyes away this time.

"...one more, Annie," I hear Stuart say.

"Is that her?" I hear Mr Abs say, as all our heads swing in the direction he's looking. Sure enough, there she is, striding across the car park, untied hair billowing around her face and over her shoulders, looking more than ever like some catwalk model. Her long legs are encased in tight faded blue jeans, that showed every perfect contour, and a fitted leather jacket finishes the look. A collective sigh rises from the male members of the small group as she waves and hurries over. A quick glance at the Rob Lowe look-alike tells me he too is enjoying the show; the small smile I saw earlier is playing again on his lips. *Stop looking at his lips*, I tell myself crossly, ignoring the small spike of jealousy I felt when I saw him watching Annie. Three different pairs of hands offer to take her bag for her, which she graciously bestows on Stuart. Stuart immediately hands it to the driver, who rolls his eyes and moves to pack it onto the coach.

"Right, all aboard!" says Stuart with a grin, as he puts one arm around Annie's waist and urges her forwards. The object of my crush has already retreated back inside the coach. When I finally mount the steps I find myself worrying who I'm going to sit beside and not paying attention to where I'm going. *Oh my God, this is like school all over again*, I realise, hating the insecurity. I step into the warm coach and scan the available seats. A long arm waves at me from about halfway down – Annie. I focus on her, ignoring anyone else who might be looking, as well as failing to notice a bag that has been left sticking out into the aisle. I trip, of course, and land nearly on Stuart's lap. Of course HE has to be sitting beside Stuart.

"Hello again, Lily," Stuart sniggers as I struggle back to my feet, apologising all the while.

"Do you think she's safe to be on a walking holiday?" I hear the other guy say to Stuart as I move on down the coach. I'm mortified to hear them both chuckling at the prospect.

"Roomie, come and join me," Annie trills loudly, thankfully distracting attention away from my blunder. All the men on the coach look at me with undisguised envy on their faces as I move to join her. There are actually enough seats available that we don't need to share rows at all, but it seems too rude to not sit beside her having been invited, and frankly I'm just glad to finally be sitting down in my own seat.

"Thank God," she whispers conspiratorially as I join her, "I thought I was going to have to fight Stuart off from wanting this seat," she says with a wink. I laugh.

"Would that be so bad?" I wonder out loud.

"Hmm," she says reflectively as she gives it some thought. "I think it's more a case that we can't make it too easy for them, now can we?" I smile, enjoying being included in the girly chat, despite it being well outside of my realm of experience.

"But you do like him?" I press.

"He's not bad. Mr Right Now if not Mr Right, perhaps?" I laugh a little more loudly than usual. In the moment of silence that follows I wonder if perhaps I'm not just a bit relieved Annie seems to have her sights set on Stuart and not the man who looks like Rob Lowe. *Must stop calling him Rob*, I realise, *before I do it to his face.* Now that would be embarrassing. *Nearly as embarrassing as mooning after a man who resembles my teen crush*, I tell myself sternly. *I am a 37-year-old married woman, for God's sake; I need to start acting like it.*

The coach is out of the car park and accelerating up the road as the on-board microphone system crackles to life.

"Ladies and gentlemen, welcome to the start of the Regency Gym three peaks challenge, in aid of the Emily Fisher Fund!" Stuart declares loudly and excitedly. There is a pathetic cheer from within the bus. "Oh come on," he continues, "you can do better than that." There is a slightly louder cheer this time, further enhanced by Annie doing a perfect wolf whistle. Stuart looks at her gratefully and gives her a wink. She blows him a kiss. I really envy that easy flirtatious way she has about her.

"Okay," Stuart speaks again. "Our lovely driver and the kind donor of this coach for the weekend – Mr John James – has suggested we drive for a couple of hours until we get to the M40 and then stop for some food and a break. That should let some of the rush hour traffic die away a bit before we do the last stretch to the house – a donation again by the most benevolent Mr James Lattimer."

I realise with a start that he's looking at Rob Lowe. "James," I breathe under my breath. "James Lattimer." It fits him somehow, sounds upper-class. *He definitely has a look of money to him – the sort of easy elegance that comes from never having had to worry about it*, I think.

"Did you say something?" Annie asks me.

"No," I say quickly, "just sniffing." She looks at me and raises an eyebrow.

"Bloody hell, can everyone do that but me?" I ask, pointing to the offending eyebrow.

She laughs. "Why, who else can do it?"

Not willing to expose my fixation with Mr Lattimer, I mumble, "no one," and she looks at me and laughs loudly again.

Everyone but us is cheering again, with more gusto this time, and John and James are waving their arms in recognition. I realise we're thanking them for their generosity to the cause. After the cheer dies down, Stuart thanks us for our attention and reminds us we have a break in two hours before signing off. The coach quietens, with just a low conversational mumbling resuming around the seats.

"I think you and I are going to have the best time," Annie says, looking at me intently.

"I hope so," I say honestly, "I don't get away much."

"So Emma was telling me."

"Was she! When did you speak to Emma?" I say, slightly surprised my best friend and my newest friend have been talking about me behind my back.

"Oh, we swapped numbers at the pub. We've spoken a couple of times," she says offhandedly.

"Oh really – about what?" I ask, unable to keep the slightly hurt tone out of my voice.

"You," she says brazenly, twisting in her seat to face me. "You're lucky to have a friend like her."

"I know." I also know I sound like a sulky teenager.

"She wants you to be happy."

"I am."

"Are you? Really?"

Before I can answer, she speaks again. "Anyway, this weekend is all about getting you to relax and have a laugh." She's rummaging in her pack by her feet as she's talking to me. "Voila!" she announces with a flourish, producing two cans of ready-mixed Pimms and lemonade. "They were in my freezer for a couple of hours, so they're nice and cold," she says as she hands me one. "I had to consider what was acceptable for your poor deadened palate given all the vodka, lime and sodas you have taken over the years. Still, it'll do the job," she says, swiftly opening the can and taking a long swig. "Ooh, the weekend starts here."

I gingerly open my own can and take a swig. It's nice. The kind of drink you could forget even had alcohol in it. *Probably not good*, I think.

"So I hear you have a magnifico new dress."

"I do." I can't help the grin appearing on my face.

She smiles back. "You're looking good, Lil – you've lost even more weight since I last saw you."

"Oh my God! That is like the first time in my whole life that I've received three compliments in one day," I marvel. "I might just start believing it if I'm not careful."

"Well, you should. Anyway," she says conspiratorially, leaning forward and lowering her voice. I naturally move towards her as she continues, "what are they like?" She nods her head towards the other people in the coach.

"I don't really know. I only got here just before you. Stuart introduced me to a few people, but the only ones I recognised were Stuart and Pat so far. Pat's nice, I've chatted to her a few times at the gym, but I really don't know anyone else at all."

"What about the handsome one who was staring at you?"

"Who?" I say with that kind of false high note which betrays the lie. Annie doesn't even say anything, just looks at me and I crumble. "Look, I don't really know him. I only heard his name a few minutes ago when Stuart just said it."

"So?" she prompts.

"Well, it's silly, really; I saw him the first day I joined the gym when I tripped over the mat and nearly took him out, and then he caught me staring at him just now." Annie is looking at me with a bemused expression on her face, forcing me to continue trying to explain. "I couldn't help myself." I can see a smile forming on her face as I confess, "he looks like Rob Lowe, the object of all my teenage fantasies," hoping to God she's old enough to know and appreciate him.

"Oh yeah, he does a bit, doesn't he!" she says in a tone that implies she had never thought about it before, but that now I said it she could see the resemblance, before adding, "never thought much of him – too thin. I like a bit more to a man, myself."

"Like Stuart?" I tease.

"Sometimes, but that's changing the subject. Let me summarise what I think you're telling me. You were staring at him because he looks like your teen crush," I nod mutely as she continues, "but why then was he staring at you?"

"Really, he wasn't. Don't be silly." I feel obliged to add. Annie just raises one of her perfectly shaped eyebrows at me again. I seek desperately to think of something to change the subject before seizing on: "What are you wearing Sunday night?"

She clearly knows it's a distraction, just looking at me for a moment longer before allowing it to work. Sure enough, Annie delights in describing the two dresses she has brought for the occasion. The conversation moves on to what other clothes she has brought with her, and I marvel she managed to pack it all in one comparatively small bag.

"So what do you do?" I ask her after we've exhausted our discussion of clothes.

"I run an art gallery. It's in Trafalgar Street, the Lord Gallery."

"That's nice," I say, but even to my ears it sounds insincere. It's too close to home for comfort, a sudden reminder of Greg and disappointment. I know her gallery; it's one Greg has spoken about before, moaning as ever about the unfairness that so many inferior artists were getting picked up and featured. I feel guilty for even speaking the thoughts in my head. Disloyal. Annie is looking at me strangely.

"I know your husband's an artist," she says, as if that were all the explanation that was required for my odd response, and in a way it was.

"Emma?" I ask.

"Emma," she confirms. Well at least that saved some of the awkwardness which would have ensued when I finally dropped it into the conversation. "You should show me some of his stuff sometime."

"Oh, you really don't have to." I feel incredibly embarrassed and literally cringe.

"I know, but I'm kind of intrigued to see it. Tell him to bring it in sometime."

"I will, thanks." I say it more to finish a conversation that couldn't feel more awkward if we tried than because I have any intention of mentioning the offer to Greg.

After what seems like far too long a time following our awkward exchange, the coach eventually slows as it pulls off into the services, and I couldn't be more grateful to have the chance to get off and interrupt the direction our conversation was taking. I stand up quickly when the bus stops and manage to move up the aisle before most people have gathered their wits, let alone their belongings. Stepping off the coach into the cooling evening air is a relief.

"Be back in the reception by seven, please, people," I hear Stuart saying as I clutch my bag tighter and stride towards the services. I quickly make my way to the ladies, mostly because I need a reason to explain to Annie why I've just virtually run off the coach. *Get a grip, Lily*, I tell myself sternly, looking at myself in the mirror as I wash my hands in the small white ceramic basin. I plaster a false smile on my face and exit the washrooms in the direction of the restaurant.

Chapter 10

A few of the coach people are already sitting at a table. I can see James sitting with one of the few other girls on the trip – a closer look shows her to be a wiry blonde who couldn't look less like me; as I get nearer I see she's the bitch girl who nearly took me out with the door. *It just had to be her, didn't it?* They're sat slightly apart from some of the others. I look away as his gaze lifts from the girl (I don't know her name yet) and swings to where I'm standing. I feel a surge shoot through my body from just his gaze, and it's connected directly to my groin. *Jesus*, I think as I feel the ache building, *I thought the books lied about that sort of thing.* I need to get a grip; I'm too old to get this sort of reaction from a look. I join the food queue and see Annie and Stuart a couple of people ahead of me.

"Hi," I call, feeling awkward as they both turn to look at me, especially given my undignified exit from the coach, but desperately needing someone to sit with in the canteen. Annie is my only friend to date, and I'm doing my best to ruin that already.

"You okay?" she asks, looking at me intently.

"Yeah, sorry. I just needed the loo. I was kind of desperate – you may have noticed." I laugh at myself, but it's awkward.

"No worries," Stuart says, oblivious to any tension with Annie and me.

"Sure," says Annie, and she looks at me sympathetically. *Bloody Emma*, I think. *What the hell has she been telling her? When I see her on Monday I'm going to be giving her a piece of my mind.* I had been looking forward to being anonymous and reinventing myself with a new group of friends. But, thanks to Emma, my miserable little life is right there with me in Annie's eyes as she's looking at me. I've seen it enough times. I really hate the pity, it's always so judgemental. Resigned to my fate, I do what I'm good at and distract attention away from me and onto the food. Annie seems to have piled huge amounts of everything on her plate. I look at the prices and choose a chicken stir fry with a small bowl of plain rice. It's cheaper and I suppose isn't too bad for my diet efforts.

We pay and sit down at a table beside the others. People are starting to get noisy, as clearly several other people had been tucking into cans of drink on the coach. The effects are beginning to be felt, and the tone of the conversation has turned. With six girls in the group and eleven men, there is likely to be some serious ribbing and male posturing in evidence over the weekend. While I guess most of the group are married, it doesn't seem to stop the constant banter, which has the beginnings of a 'Carry On' tone to it. I feel out of my depth when a few cheeky comments are flung my way.

My anxiety must show on my face because Annie whispers to me: "Don't worry, Lily, they're only teasing."

"Yeah, I know. I'm just not used to it."

"Well you will be by the end of the weekend," Stuart chips in. "It's not likely to improve much. I recommend you just roll with it – it's all fairly harmless, but if anyone bothers you then you let me know and I'll see them off for you." It's sweet, he sounds like a big brother.

"Me too, babe," Annie adds. I give them both a big smile, noting the way Annie is looking at Stuart approvingly.

"Thanks, guys, really. But I think I need to stop being a baby and just enjoy the time I have."

"Quite right," says Annie approvingly, handing me another tin of Pimms from out of her bag to emphasise the point. I take it from her and crack it open, taking a long swig.

By the time we have finished eating, it's nearly time to get back on the coach. We wander towards the meeting point where most of the others are already collecting. James and the blonde are standing next to each other, and I can't help but notice how she keeps touching his arm while they talk to each other, or how she's much younger than he is. He looks to be more around my own age, but still the touches she gives him send a message. Seemingly nothing to the average eye, I know she's marking her territory.

"He's not into her," Annie whispers in my ear.

"How do you know?" I answer unguardedly. "I mean they look good together, she's a good-looking girl, he looks like Rob Lowe..."

Annie laughs. "Sweetie, she is all over him like a rash, but watch his body language. He's not interested, mark my words."

I look closer. Sure enough, every time she moves closer, he moves marginally further away. I laugh, wondering why the thought makes me feel so happy. One of the guys, I think I remember his name is Pete, comes over at the sound.

"Hi," he says, looking a bit awkward. "Some of us are thinking about heading down to the local when we get in if it's not past closing time. There's meant to be one about a mile from the house. Do you fancy joining us?"

For some reason he's looking at me when he says it and not Annie, for once. I feel flustered and don't know what to say.

"Sure," is all I can think of in the end. He looks pleased. I smile at him, letting the unfamiliar expression linger on my face as Pete stands there wittering on about how much fun we're going to have. I nod absently, lifting my eyes to lock straight into familiar piercing blue ones. My breath catches at the intensity of his gaze. He actually looks pissed off. *What the fuck?* I wonder as he scowls at me. The moment only breaks when John announces it's time to get back on the coach and

James quickly turns and slips an arm round the blonde's waist as they saunter back.

I scowl and look round to see where Annie is, only to find her watching me with her arms folded across her chest. She laughs when she sees me blush; "curiouser and curiouser," is all she says.

Chapter 11

The rest of the journey is relatively easy, filled with enjoyable banter with Annie, Pete (as I had since had confirmed) and another guy called Colin, who had moved places to sit across from us on the coach. Annie is such a natural flirt with men; she has them both eating out her hand immediately. It's fun to listen to.

When John announces we are five minutes away, I peer out into the overwhelming darkness, trying to get a glimpse of the area. Barring the occasional house lights I can't see much through the windows. When the coach eventually pulls up it's on a long gravel driveway. I gather my stuff and follow everyone else off the bus to collect my pack from the hold. We then traipse the rest of the way up the gravel drive to the house. I say house... It's huge. Like a proper mansion, built in the Georgian style. It is beautiful, even in the darkness. I can make out a vast red brick frontage and columns around the front door.

"Welcome, everyone," James says as he fumbles with a key. "I hope you like it."

"What's not to like?" Annie mutters beside me.

"Oh my God, I think I've died and gone to heaven," I breathe as I walk into the entrance hall and take in the expansive space and sweeping staircase. Portraits of stiffly formal ladies and gentlemen ascend the walls to the first floor.

"Do we have to do the walks?" Annie grumbles. "I want to stay here and play lady of the manor, please."

"I couldn't agree more – it couldn't be less like home if it tried, well except perhaps for the artwork wherever you look," I amend.

"Oh, does Greg do portraits?" she enquires.

"Not really, I mean, occasionally he's done them of us, and we have some of those up. Mostly he likes more contemporary abstract art; that's what he's doing at the moment."

"I mean it when I say I want to see it," Annie says.

"Please, can we not talk about him?"

"Okay, sorry, subject closed for the rest of the weekend." Annie grins at me, making a zipping motion across her mouth, before grabbing her bag and saying: "Come on, let's nab a decent room before they're all gone." We run up the stairs giggling like girls.

The house is massive, and to be fair there isn't a bad room in the place. Annie and I find a beautiful room, with a large open fireplace and a small en-suite, that we bag. It has one large double bed we'll have to share, which is why some of the guys are a bit more squeamish about it, but we don't care. We quickly unpack our clothes, Annie cooing over my new dress and shoes, before leaving the room to find our way back downstairs to the others. I only realise my handbag is still in the room, with all my money I would need if we were going to the pub, when I get back down to the bottom of the stairs.

We can hear the noise of excited chatter coming from one of the sitting rooms.

"I'll join you in a sec, Annie," I say, nodding in the direction of the parlour. "I've forgotten my bag," I call over my shoulder, sprinting back up the stairs. I run into the room, retrieving the bag quickly and exiting without a look, smashing instantly into a solid object and bouncing off it onto the wall and then the floor in a little heap.

"Bloody hell!" a familiar arrogant and slightly exasperated voice intones. I look up, embarrassed as I inelegantly scramble back to my feet, ignoring the hand he held out to help me.

"Sorry," I mutter, squirming with awkwardness, only enhanced by the physical reaction my body is having at his proximity.

"We seem to continually meet like this, Lily. Where's the fire this time?" he enquires.

"We're going to the pub, and I forgot my bag," I say by way of explanation, feeling like I needed to offer an excuse for why I was running in the halls.

"Are 'we'?" he questions pointedly.

"Well," I stutter, "Pete asked Annie and me, and I think Colin is coming, probably a few of the others too. I'm sure you'd be welcome if you wanted to join us," I add, feeling obliged to make the offer. I both want him to come and don't at the same time.

"No, that's quite alright, thank you," he replies in clipped formal tones. "I was just retiring to my room." To my horror he indicates the room next to ours. "There's a spare front door key on the hook in the kitchen you can use to let yourselves in with when you get back. Just remember to put it back up there, won't you?"

"Oh. Of course. Thank you, I mean, sorry." *Oh my God, what the hell am I saying? Why do I lose the power of rational speech when he looks at me? I am a 37-year-old woman, for God's sake, not a teenager.* He's looking at me with that arrogant but curiously entertained expression on his face, and I feel a flush of embarrassment yet again. I back away down the hall for a few steps before turning and running the rest of the way. I could swear I hear laughter behind me as I flee – I really hope I've imagined it. This was becoming a humiliating recurring theme.

I detour until I find the kitchen and have collected the key, before making my way back to one of the parlour rooms, where Annie in true 'Georgian lady of the house' style is holding court. While everyone else looks dishevelled following the long drive with barely a moment to do more than run a brush through their hair, Annie still looks like she just stepped off a photo shoot, standing and laughing in the middle of Pete,

Colin, Arthur and Stuart. The blonde, whose name I've learned is Sarah, is sitting in the corner with another girl, Rachel, whispering and casting looks like daggers in Annie's direction.

"Lily, at last!" Annie exclaims when she sees me at the doorway. "What took you so long?"

"I had to get the key," I say, dangling it in front of them from my finger. "I bumped into James," I say, flushing at the mention of his name and the memory of the accuracy of that statement, "and he told me where to find it."

"Oh, is he coming?" Sarah enquires from the corner, suddenly brightening visibly.

"Um, no – he said he was going to retire for the night." The oddly antiquated phrase sounds funny coming from my mouth. Annie smirks. Sarah scowls.

"Come on then, troops," Annie calls, collecting us all together, and we dutifully march the mile down the road to The Hope and Glory.

It's small but cosy, and I drink more than my usual in a relatively short space of time, as do most people, so the walk home is all the more entertaining for the meandering route we take zigzagging across the quiet country road. *Thank God there's no traffic*, I think as I stagger a little for the umpteenth time.

"Steady there, girly," Pete says, grasping my hand to pull me back to the verge. I giggle when he doesn't immediately let go of it again once I've re-stabilised myself. We walk that way, hand in hand, following the group surrounding Annie until we get back to the house, where I push to the front of the group, brandishing the key. After a couple of attempts I unlock the door and we all pile through. Annie immediately makes for the stairs and our room, ignoring the protestations of her entourage.

"I just need to put the key back," I stage-whisper to her, the image of James' stern expression immediately coming to mind, and stagger off in the direction of the kitchen. Key replaced, I return to the now dark entrance hall and make my way carefully up the stairs and along the corridor to our room. When Pete lurches out from a dark doorway and puts an arm out to stop me going any further, I actually squeal like a small piglet.

"Where are you going?" he asks, breathing alcohol fumes at me. I know he's drunk too.

"To bed," I say assertively.

"Oh don't, please," he wheedles, trying to put his other arm around my waist. "What happens on tour stays on tour," he whispers, moving closer.

"No, I'm not interested," I say, more loudly this time as my anxiety level rises. The sound of a door opening causes Pete to jump back from me. In the dark hallway I can see the light reflecting off two bright eyes.

"I think the lady said no," a voice drawls quietly but assertively.

"Yeah, right," Pete says, backing away and looking embarrassed. "Sorry," he says, looking at me. I just nod at him and watch him depart.

"Thank you," I whisper, lurching back towards where James had been standing, but he's already gone and all I hear is the click of his door closing.

Chapter 12

In the morning the light wakes me early because neither Annie nor I had thought to close the curtains in our drunken stupor, and anyway I've always tended to be an early riser ever since I had the boys. I creep to the shower before pulling on some fresh clothes, trying all the while not to wake Annie. I needn't have worried; it seems she sleeps like the proverbial dead. A glance at my watch tells me it's 6.30am, and I'm gasping for a cup of tea – fortunately the only symptom of my excesses from the night before. Thank God I don't tend to get hangovers. I make my way down the now familiar route to the kitchen, find the kettle, mugs and tea and make myself a cup. The house is silent. I wander from room to room, discovering two more sitting rooms, a games room which included a snooker table, a formal dining room and a library. I return to the prettiest sitting room and stand at the picture window, admiring the view out over the countryside. The theme tune to the James Herriott All Creatures Great and Small vet T.V. programme (I had watched when I was a kid) starts playing in my mind, and I start humming it as I stand there drinking my tea.

"Wrong county," a voice from behind startles me.

"Sorry?"

"All Creatures Great and Small. It was filmed in North Yorkshire, and we're in Derbyshire."

"Oh," I say faintly as he walks further into the room, embarrassed again. *Why do I always feel so stupid around him?* I wonder. He's wearing jeans, faded by years of wear rather than fashion, and a fleecy jumper. He manages to look sexy and yet dressed for the elements. *How does he do that? What is it about rich people that they always have just the right outfit for any occasion?*

"How are you feeling?" he enquires. "Hungover?"

"No," I say a tad defensively. An image of him seeing Pete off the night before flashes to mind. "Sorry for disturbing you last night," I say, blushing slightly.

"I wasn't asleep."

"Oh, well thank you anyway." *Why does every conversation feel so awkward with him?* I wonder. I move to the fireplace and pick up the photo of him with his arm around a striking blonde. She looks vaguely familiar. I recognise the location as the top of the staircase in the house.

"My partner," he says before I ask.

"She's beautiful," I force. *Entirely perfect for someone as perfect as him.* I feel a spike of jealousy. *What right do I have to feel jealous?*

"We're separated," he adds. My heart leaps. *What the hell am I thinking? I'm married, for God's sake!*

"You need to be careful, Lily." He has stepped up behind me now, and I can feel heat rolling off his body and his warm breath tickling the back of my neck.

"Why?" I whisper, my mouth suddenly dry, but not from the alcohol.

"You stand there, a naturally beautiful woman, looking luscious and sweet with your kissable lips and big innocent brown eyes, and I want to eat you up."

His breath is brushing my cheek now, and I have to will myself not to lean back against his firm chest. I can't look at him, or I know I would be lost. My mouth opens slightly, and I feel my nipples tighten at his proximity. *Oh my God, he hasn't even touched me yet*, I think in despair.

"And so do most of the other men on the trip, it seems to me," he says, stepping away again, his voice sounding less intimate. "What was your husband thinking letting you out alone, I wonder?" Is that censure I can hear in his voice?

"Hellooo," a voice calls from the hallway. It's Stuart. "Ah," he says on finding us, "I thought the kettle was hot so someone must be up." He's totally oblivious to the overt sexual tension in the room, or at least he's choosing to ignore it. "Need to wake up those others in a minute if we're going to get this show on the road by 9.30. Some of them are going to need breakfast, rehydration and paracetamol before any walking can happen, I expect." He looks at me before adding meaningfully, "you okay?"

"Yes!" I say it a tad more defensively than necessary, perhaps, given the state of me last night. "I didn't drink that much." Both James and Stuart snort. I choose to ignore them. "Want me to knock on some doors?" I ask. "I'm used to waking teenagers up, so how hard can a few hikers be?" I say it for effect, to emphasise my family – judging by the smile on James' face, he sees straight through the tactic.

"Oh would you, sweetie, that's great. Face like an angel and the personality to match – your husband is one lucky guy, eh, James?" Stuart smiles at me before looking at James.

"Indeed he is," says James, eyes on my lips.

I literally scuttle out of the room and up the stairs, wondering what the hell just happened there – *did I imagine it? Had he just made a sort of pass at me? Men like James don't notice me. My newfound freedom must be going to my head*, I tell myself sternly. *Focus on the task at hand before you make a fool of yourself.*

An hour and a half later, and everyone is up and gathered in the kitchen drinking coffee and orange juice. The fact it can accommodate us all gives an indication of its size. A large oak table with benches running along either side is the centrepiece. Porridge, croissants, bacon and toast are all available to eat, although a couple of the group seemed a little too fragile for food. I hear James explaining to Arthur that his housekeeper Mrs Edge had got in some supplies in advance of our visit.

"She even got some food in for this evening, but I told her we wouldn't need her to prepare or serve it, so I hope someone here knows how to cook a roast chicken with all the trimmings."

"I'm hopeless in a kitchen," Sarah whines before continuing, "and I can't bear to get food under my nails – plus," she's warming to her theme now; "these extensions cost a fortune. And if any break, I don't want to look tacky for the do tomorrow night." James turns to her, and she withers under his look of disapproval.

"I can cook," I say in a small voice.

"Good, well that's sorted, then. You can be head chef, and I will be your sous chef. The kitchen is the only place I take orders." His tone is light, but I hear the teasing underneath it.

Oh my God, I am starting to see sex everywhere, I despair. Now I have the prospect of an evening of trying to avoid him in the kitchen to look forward to, endeavouring not to embarrass and humiliate myself any further. I look around at the group, but no one seems concerned now the decision has been made about who's cooking. Only Sarah is looking at me with a scowl spoiling her pretty face.

"Morning, Peeps!" a lyrical voice announces, and Annie floats in looking like a vision of loveliness in her skinny jeans and t-shirt. She grabs a croissant and a coffee before turning to me and asking, "What did I miss?"

I blush, and she laughs. *Curse my blushing,* I think angrily, *what am I feeling so guilty about? I haven't done anything wrong…Yet.* And that right there is the problem, really.

By half past nine we're all on the coach again, with packed lunches made and cagoules packed. Countryside this beautiful doesn't get this green and lush without plenty of rain. I'm glad for my waterproof walking boots but still feeling a bit nervous about how I'll manage with the pace the group has set, considering how new I am to the whole exercise thing. Some of these guys have been working out for years. When I raise my worries with Annie, she just shrugs and says that lifting weights does not necessarily mean you are good at walking hills. I hope she's right and I'm not about to humiliate myself yet again. Still, judging by the state of some of the team, not everyone will be operating at their best.

We're heading for the first peak, called Kinder Scout. The coach stops in the village of Edale, and the initial part through the village and the first part of the moor makes me more hopeful I can actually cope. We're following the brook upstream, and the gradual gradient is relentless, but I can manage. People have naturally begun to split into different-paced walking groups, and I find myself walking with Pat, Pete and Colin. Annie is with the lead group, with Sarah desperately trying to keep pace with her from the looks of things. It seems Sarah has decided Annie is her competition for the title of top girl, *or top bitch in Sarah's case. Jeez, where is all this girly animosity coming from?* I wonder. James is in the middle with Stuart, the pair of them continually checking behind to see we're still with them. Or at least that's what Stuart is doing; James just seems to look at me, *or am I imagining things now and just seeing what I want to see? What had that all meant this morning?* I need to talk to Annie about it, I realise – I need a second perspective.

The ground has become boggy, so much so that in places it's almost bouncy where there's a firm top layer over wetter parts. Everyone enjoys springing about on it until the earth gives way on Stuart and he finishes up ankle-deep in bog, at which point everyone focuses back on getting through it without any more mishaps. It's a relief when we get onto the firmer ground for the last part of the climb. It's steeper here, but I keep up well.

In fact everything's okay until I trip over a rock and land hard on one knee. It hurts briefly, but my pride takes a bigger hit. Pete is beside me in an instant and offers me his hand, which I gratefully take, giving myself a moment to rub my knee. As I stand up I scan the group to see who had noticed; only one pair of eyes seems to be watching me as ever, and they actually look pissed off for some reason. Pete has taken up position beside me and continues to reach out to help me over trickier parts, and I just try to ignore any dirty looks I'm getting from James. It's hard work, and I barely look up from my feet until we reach the high ridge. When I do, the view is spectacular: out towards Snowdonia one way and the distant smog of what we think is a city – in all likelihood Manchester – in the other. We pause for our lunch huddled down on the side facing away from the wind. I'm sitting with Annie, but Pete comes to sit behind me. His perpetual presence around me is becoming slightly concerning. *Oh shit, now I'm going to have to say something. That's just great*, I think. *How much more embarrassing can things get?*

"Look, Lily, I just wanted to say sorry," he starts, sounding awkward, "for last night, I mean," he stutters. "I shouldn't have been so in your face. You're a lovely girl, but I knew you were married and I shouldn't have pushed like I did – I drank too much. Will you forgive me?" He looks sincere and genuinely sorry, and I figure what the hell, he's a nice guy the rest of the time. I want us to be friends; I don't have that many of them.

"Sure," I decide, "I'll give you a second chance." He smiles with relief, and I smile back at him.

"Well, well, well, and what have I been missing, please?" Annie demands. Pete looks sheepish as he describes the pass he made at me the night before. When he comes to the part where James appeared, I see Annie's eyes widen slightly. At the end of his rendition Annie ribs him mercilessly, and to his credit he takes it, until Stuart announces it was time to make tracks again. Pete springs to his feet with a look of relief on his face and moves off to join some of the other guys in the group. There was obviously only so much he could take.

The descent is, if anything, at least as hard as the ascent, which is a bit of a shock to me. My knees are killing me as we travel along the ridge and down Jacob's Ladder. Annie is walking with me this time, mostly in silence, with the occasional comment about the scenery which is astoundingly beautiful.

"I think he wants you," Annie suddenly says out of nowhere.

"Who? Pete? Maybe last night when he had his beer goggles on, but he knows the score now. He doesn't really want me, he just wants someone. He's not married so he's got nothing to lose," I excuse him.

"No, not Pete, my dear." I stop in my tracks and look at her.

"Then who?"

"James."

My pulse leaps at the mention of his name. I hadn't imagined it, and here was the confirmation I was after. I pause before answering, asking carefully: "What makes you think that?"

"So you don't deny it, then?"

"I didn't say that. I asked why *you* would think he wants me. I mean look at me!" I say dismissively, pointing at myself.

"Don't be silly, Lily, you're a beautiful girl who is completely oblivious to both your inner and outer beauty. Better to ask how could he not want you? You're like a butterfly emerging at the moment, Lily. You just can't see it yourself yet. Or won't – I'm not sure which. Anyway, the fact remains the man wants you; it's written all over his face every time he looks at you – which is often, by the way. My question to you is what are you planning to do about it?"

"I can't quite believe it's true," I say frankly. "This sort of thing doesn't happen to me. People look past me, not at me. People look at people like you, not people like me, especially people like him," I say, nodding towards James, who's about fifty metres ahead of us.

"That's a lot of people," she nods sagely.

"It is," I grin.

"But just say this time it was different, that people like him," she says, nodding in James' direction, "did want people like you this time – what would you do?"

"I'm married."

"I know. You might still want to give it some thought, though. Lily, I sense you're at a crossroads here. You need to be sure you take the right path for *you*, honey. Choose what you want rather than making bad, quick decisions in the moment. I'll say no more, but I'm here if you want to talk to me, anytime," and she grasps my arm firmly. "No judgement," she adds.

"Thanks Annie, I really appreciate it," I say, hugging her swiftly.

We return to our companionable silence as we continue with our descent. The group has done well, completing the walk in four hours, with another hour for lunch. The weather has been unusually kind too. I'm proud I have managed it with apparent ease, and I take a moment to bask in a sense of personal achievement on the coach back.

We are back at the house by 4.30pm, so I have a bit of time to kill before I need to start the dinner. I nip into the bathroom first to luxuriate in a bubble bath, using the cooking card to trump Annie, whose face looked alight having just been asked to meet Stuart for a drink before dinner. As I wallow in the warm waters I feel my joints relax and the aching parts of me ease slightly. Hair washed and legs and armpits freshly shaved, I make my way back into the room where Annie is lounging on the bed reading, waiting for her turn in the bathroom. I marvel at how glamorous she managed to look with absolutely no effort, even when she was filthy. I grab my clean jeans, an old shabby t-shirt and one of my favourite cardigans and begin to dress when Annie suddenly says, "No, no, no, Lily!"

"Sorry?" I say, looking at her to see what's wrong.

"No, Lily, I am not going to allow you to leave the room looking like that. You dress like you are 67 and not 37 for God's sake, woman. No wonder you have no idea how lovely you are. Show me all your other clothes, and we'll try and salvage a decent outfit from it. Maybe I have something that might work," she adds thoughtfully. She proceeds to rifle through my possessions, choosing my best jeans and handing me a black capped-sleeve shirt of hers to try.

"This won't fit me," I protest, trying to hand it back.

"It will! It's stretchy, and my back is broader than yours – I'm bigger than you seem to think. And you are certainly smaller than you seem to think. Just try it – please? For me?"

I give in and put the shirt on. It's tight, and feels revealing compared to what I'm used to wearing, but when I look in the mirror I'm pleasantly surprised by what I see.

"Lovely!" Annie claps her hands together, pleased with herself. "Now you may leave the room."

A quick look at my watch tells me I'm already late. "Shit!" I worry as I sprint to the kitchen.

Chapter 13

James has turned the oven on to warm and is already there setting ingredients out on the sides when I walk in, trying desperately not to look like I've been running or am in any way flustered.

"At last," he says as he hears the door. "Thought you were going to stand me up and leave me to fathom out how to cook for all these peop–" His words stop as he turns from the worktop to look at me. He takes me in, eyes raking up and down my body but resting longest on my cleavage which must have been made all the more apparent by the shirt's plunging V-neck. "Wow!" is all he says as he stalks towards me. My heart thumps so loudly I'm sure he must be able to hear it as he stops directly in front of me.

"If we're going to get any cooking done, I need you to wear one of these," he says, his voice darker sounding than I've heard it before. He reaches past me to the back of the door and unhooks an apron, swiftly putting it over my head before placing his hands on my hips and turning me on the spot. I swear I can feel my skin burning at his touch, even through my jeans. As he swiftly ties a bow, pulling the apron tight over my hips and emphasising my newly slimmed waist, I try to gather what remains of my wits and focus on the task at hand. Cooking for seventeen people is a stretch, considering the most

I've ever cooked for previously was eight, when both sets of parents had once come for Christmas. What a miserable experience that had been for everyone. I don't think it was coincidence that both my parents and Greg's tended to go away now over Christmas – a pattern that had started pretty much from the same year. *Still, the principles must be the same*, I reassure myself. It's just the quantities that are different, and space might be a challenge. Although a quick glance around the modern-styled kitchen, complete with a massive range cooker plenty big enough for two chickens and some roast spuds, puts that concern to bed. Now it's all about the timings. While I've been checking it all out, James has been pouring us both large glasses of wine.

"One of the fringe benefits of offering to cook for everyone," he says, handing me one of the glasses.

"Thank you," I say, automatically taking a sip and trying to collect myself. "Okay," I say, looking directly at James, "find the potatoes and start peeling, please."

"Yes chef," he replies crisply in the manner of the people I've seen in the T.V. chef programmes. He dutifully finds all the accoutrements he needs and sets to his task, while I prepare the chickens and get them into the oven, sipping my wine as I go about my work. When I look over to see how he's getting on, I'm pleasantly surprised. He's actually very proficient; this is clearly not the first time he's peeled a potato. I put the water on to parboil them once he was done with the peeling, and then move to find the other vegetables that had been bought to accompany the meal. Purple sprouting broccoli with baby carrots and mangetout seem to be the vegetables du jour – *wow, posh vegetables.* Even better, they take virtually no time to prepare or cook, so we can leave them until the last minute.

"What do I do with these?" James asks, looking at the pile of potatoes in front of him, all freshly peeled and cut.

"Put them in the pan of water on the cooker, please." He proceeds to deftly do as I ask – I'm beginning to suspect he's at least as well qualified as I am to be cooking this meal. Once done he wanders to the fridge and retrieves the bottle of white wine before collecting our now empty glasses, sitting down beside me at the big oak table and pouring us each another large glassful.

"You must let us know how much we owe you for all this," I say as I reach for my glass, sipping nervously. My mouth feels dry from the proximity of his body to mine. I know if I just flexed my knee we would be touching. I keep sipping my wine to give myself something to do. At this rate I'm going to be legless before the chicken is cooked.

"What?" he says, sounding mystified.

"All the food and drink," I say, indicating the purple sprouting broccoli and wine, "it must be costing a fortune, and you're already providing the house – which is amazing, by the way."

"Glad you like it," he says, looking genuinely pleased.

"It's stunning. I don't know how you could ever leave it, although I guess when you rent it out it must feel less like home, and you probably have somewhere equally gorgeous at home."

"Can I tell you a secret?"

"Yes," I say slowly, wondering what I'm about to hear as I take a large, undignified gulp of the rather fine wine.

"I don't actually rent it out," he whispers. "It just stands waiting for when I, or anyone else in the family, want to come and use it. The housekeeper, Mrs Edge, looks after everything while the family aren't here. She's the one who got all the food in."

"Why did you say you rent it, then?" I ask, genuinely bemused.

"Because, in my experience, people feel uncomfortable when you rub their face in your wealth. I thought the group would be more relaxed if they thought it was a rental house. So, really my contribution is only the food and drink because the house would be here anyway and it's a waste not to make use of it when people are trying to raise money for a good cause."

"That is actually surprisingly sweet of you," I say, the alcohol starting to make me bold. It's hit my bloodstream fast thanks to my empty stomach, all evidence of my half a sandwich at lunch having disappeared long since. "So just what is it that you do, James, that has made you wealthy enough to have a house like this standing waiting for you, all fitted out with the latest mod cons and dining out on purple sprouting broccoli every day?"

He laughs, hesitating before answering,

"I was totally unaware purple sprouting broccoli was an indicator of wealth. Whatever made you think I wasn't sweet, by the way?"

"I don't know. Men like you don't have to be, maybe?"

"Men like me, Lily? We are so going to have to explore what you mean by that sometime soon." I'm beginning to wish I weren't drinking quite so freely as he continues, "you asked what I do – nothing special, I'm just an investor. I came into some money a while ago and I've used it to invest in various things – a few films, a couple of good innovations, some of the dot-com businesses a few years back which I got out of in good time. It's made me enough that I'm okay."

"More than okay, I would say, judging by all this," I say, indicating the space around us.

"I guess. Look, I know it's a cliché, but money really doesn't make you happy, you know, Lily." The way he keeps using my name feels strangely intimate. I need to distract myself away from the physical response I have from hearing my name on his lips.

"Oh my God, I didn't expect you to play the 'poor little rich boy' card," I say before I can stop myself, once again rueing my runaway tongue.

He raises his eyebrow at that. "Why don't you say what you really think, Lily?" he says drily.

"Well, okay I will, and while I'm at it, stop with the ironic eyebrow thing. It's doing my head in," I say, indicating the offending feature. *Oh my God, what is the matter with me!* "Sorry I'm being incredibly rude. You really shouldn't have let me drink so much; it tends to make me frighteningly honest."

"Don't be sorry, I like it," he says, his eyes softening. "Too many people tend to tell me what they think I want to hear."

"Look, no disrespect…"

"Which is always the precursor to a disrespectful comment," he interrupts, laughing.

"Touché," I smile. "But I can't feel sorry for your apparent wealth. What you choose to do with it might not make you happy, but surely that's your own choice. Trust me, *not* having money can make you unhappy. Not having to worry about money can only be a good thing."

"Voice of experience?" He's really looking at me intently now – like I'm some sort of curiosity.

"Yes, sadly very experienced."

"What does your husband do?"

"He's an artist – how very traditional of you to assume my husband should take care of me."

"Why wouldn't he want to if you're his wife?" He actually sounds genuinely surprised. "I take it he's not a tremendously successful artist, then?"

"Not so far," I say, depressed by the topic now. "Look, can we change the subject? I think we need to move the potatoes from the water to the oil to roast now anyway." I'm already moving across the kitchen and away from his scrutiny.

"Do you work?" he calls over to me.

"Yes."

"So... as what? Why are you being evasive, Lily?" There it is, my name again. It sounds strange coming from his lips, kind of refined and less dowdy. Almost like a caress.

"I'm not being evasive; it's just not very interesting when you work as a receptionist."

"What about your children, then? Does he look after them?"

"No, I looked after them until they went to school, and then worked during school hours. I'm pretty much full-time now they're eighteen and they don't need looking after anymore. Adam has just left for university."

"Eighteen! Bloody hell, how old were you when you had them, then, twelve?" I guess there was a compliment there if I really looked for it, but this was a conversation I've had too many times in my life to take any pleasure from.

"I was nineteen, and no, they weren't planned, but I got on with it – that's life." I really hope this will be the end to the whole conversation. All these reminders of home are killing my buzz.

"So let me summarise what I've heard. You fell pregnant at nineteen, married the father," he makes this sound like a question, as if I may have got pregnant by one man and married another – *Jeez, he must have a low opinion of me* – I just nod as he continues: "brought up the children and have supported their father while he has struggled to make a career as an artist?"

"Yeah, sounds about right," I respond, fiddling with the food, while he sits there gazing at me as if I were some strange exotic creature he had never seen before. He gets up from the table and moves to where I'm standing.

"And what about what you wanted?"

"What do you mean?"

"Well, I can see how everyone else has benefitted, but I'm not sure what you got from it all."

"Husband, children?"

"So you're happy?" he says, piercing me with those blue eyes which when he focused them on me seemed to delve straight into my soul. *Was I happy?* I know I should just say 'yes' and be done with the conversation, that if I do he'll back off and leave me alone. I just can't seem to form the word. My deafening silence, it seems, is an answer in itself for him, and I watch his expression move from questioning intensity to pleasure. The final expression before I turn away is almost predatory. I force myself to move, trying to escape from a situation I'm not ready to face. I feel afraid, unsure what just happened, cold fingers of fear grasping at my chest and making my breathing become shallower. *What have I done?* I think, before turning to face him.

We stand there just looking at each other for a few seconds from opposite sides of the room, and then suddenly he's moving with purpose towards me, his hands reaching to cup my face, his face moving towards mine until our lips touch. It is beautiful and gentle and like no other kiss I've received before. When he pulls away my legs feel like jelly, and I stand there looking at him for a moment before my limbs seem to work again and I can stagger away to the safety of the oven.

"So this is where the party is," Sarah's voice cuts into the silence. She's dressed to the nines in skinny black jeans tucked into high-heeled boots, showing off acres of long, lean legs and topped with a tight t-shirt. She goes straight over to place a hand possessively on James' chest, calling over her shoulder to me: "Is dinner ready?" She actually sounds a lot like Ethan and Adam do at home. To be fair she is probably far closer to their age than my own. But I catch the look of disgust that passes over James' features as she says it, as does she. He moves away from her, suddenly keen to be checking the food. The vitriolic look she sends my way indicates she thinks I'm entirely to blame for his sudden lack of interest.

"About forty minutes, if you could let the others know?" I say as politely as I'm able, not wanting to stir the situation any further than I already have. She mutters something I don't quite catch as she flounces out the room.

"What did she say?" I ask James, mystified.

"I think it was 'whatever'," he says, and we both fall about laughing at how the slang phrase sounds in his refined tones. It takes me a few minutes to compose myself again. I'm immensely grateful to Sarah for the break in the tension she inadvertently caused, because for the rest of the time as we set the table, finish the vegetables and make some gravy, the silence is just companionable, as other guests drift into the room ready to eat what we had prepared.

The dinner is a resounding success, no doubt helped by James, who acts as a perfect host, and the copious bottles of wine that are flowing throughout the meal. I've eased off drinking, anxious about getting too inebriated to think straight when every instinct I have is telling me I'm in danger. When everyone toasts the chef I blush, until Sarah asks if I will be cooking again tomorrow evening. The thought of cooking in my new dress is horrific, but before I can answer James announces he has asked Mrs Edge to come and prepare the food, with some support from a couple of locals, so we could all enjoy the evening. His eyes linger on me as he says it.

With the meal completed, and Arthur, Colin and Pat agreeing to washing up duty, most of us move into the sitting room, with a few people heading for the pub. Annie and Stuart curl up in a chair together, and I can see the body language become more intimate as they talk. When Sarah comes in and sits on James' lap, and he places an arm around her, she throws me a triumphant look. I'm tired, I realise, ignoring the jealous surge that washes through me, so I quietly stand, slip out of the room and make my way alone to bed.

Chapter 14

The next morning I deliberately stay in bed later, until I know others will be up and about, despite having woken early and heard James' door open and someone leave his room. My greatest fear, if I'm honest with myself, is that it's Sarah leaving after a night of sex with James. I hate the thought.

I dress in my walking gear and make my way to the kitchen, where almost everyone is already sitting and having breakfast. Annie had not returned to the room the night before, and one look at her sitting beside Stuart tells me where she'd spent it. She gives me a radiant smile, and I can't help grinning back at her.

"Details later," she giggles as we make our way out to the coach.

The weather is far less kind to us on this walk with almost continual rain, and the beautiful scenery shrouded in mist. Despite the waterproof items I'm wearing, rain seems to seep in everywhere, even my underwear. Lunch is a miserable affair, soggy sandwiches not holding much appeal, with the group keen to finish swiftly so we press on after a short break and finish the walk nearly an hour earlier than anticipated.

"You can't avoid me forever," a quiet voice at my side informs me. I turn to find James at my elbow.

"I didn't know I was," I say as nonchalantly as I'm able, given the fact my heart rate has just accelerated to 100 miles an hour. His eyebrow tells me I haven't got away with it. "Again with the eyebrow," I say, pissed off now, and he laughs, which just makes me even more irritated. I flounce onto the bus and flop down next to Annie.

"So he has the most enormous penis," is the first thing she says. I turn in my seat to look at her, taking a second to work out she's talking about Stuart.

"Well that's good," is all I can think to say.

"Yes, yes it is," she replies, and we both fall about laughing, trying to compose ourselves only to lose it again when both Stuart and James turn round to scowl at us.

Back at the house, Annie insists on taking care of my beauty preparations for the evening. We spend an enjoyable rest of the afternoon, after our baths, with her doing manicures and pedicures for the both of us while she regales me with stories of her night's exploits with Stuart. Turns out he has natural staying power, and a taste for locational variety, so they had spent the night shagging in as many of the rooms in the house they could find that were unoccupied, including the oak table in the kitchen, before retiring to his room, which he was fortunately not sharing with anyone. *Thank God tonight's dinner was being served in the formal dining room,* I think, concerned there was no way I would be able to eat off the oak table again.

She looks horrified when I tell her I'm not planning to do anything special with my hair and makeup, sitting me down in a chair while she plucks my eyebrows and then powders and brushes my face with every conceivable type of makeup, before straightening my hair.

"I went to a religious school, Lily," she tells me at one point. "Most of the girls found God, while I just found GHD," she titters, waving her straighteners at me. "Girl, you so need to get yourself a pair of these to manage that unruly mop of yours. I promise you they will change your life." She won't let the subject drop until I have 'crossed my heart and hoped to die' if I don't purchase myself a pair when I get home. I haven't had so much girly fun since I had been at university and before I had hooked up with Greg, and even then I had carried so much teenage angst about myself and my body I hadn't been able to enjoy it as much. When I put on the underwear Emma had made me buy, and realise she had got me stockings to wear rather than tights, I feel a thrill of excitement. As I slip the dress and shoes on and finally turn to look at the complete ensemble in the mirror, I nearly cry.

"Oh my God, Lily, you look stunning," Annie breathes as she takes in my appearance. "Wait, let me take a photo. I promised Emma I would." She fumbles in her bag for her phone while I stand staring at the vision in front of me. Annie had made the makeup enhance my eyes, bringing out their rich chocolate colour and making them look huge, while my skin looks flawless and the light gloss on my lips shows off their natural fullness. My straightened hair falls further down my back, looking sleek and glossy, while the dress enhances my curves as before, flattered further by the well-fitting underwear. Finally the shoes make even my little legs look long. I look like a different person, and even I can see that I look beautiful. More importantly, I feel it.

I turn to look at Annie. "Thank you so much. You and Emma. I don't know what I would have done without you. I feel like you have helped me find myself again, as if I've been asleep for ages and I've finally woken up."

"I told you, Lil, you're like a butterfly. Promise me you won't let yourself go back to sleep again; this is your moment, darling. Life is so very short, so you have to grab it with both hands." We spend a few fun minutes taking various photos of me, while I pretend to be a model, and then she emails them to Emma. The response is almost instantaneous:

Lil, your outer beauty has finally been allowed to shine and reflects your beautiful personality. You look so very wonderful, and I am very jealous not to be sharing it with you. Make sure you enjoy every moment, and then I want a repeat performance that I get to share when you get home, please. Love you, babe. Have an amazing evening. E x

While I read the email Annie slips into her silver sparkly sheath dress. It's short, and her legs look amazing. She has put her hair up so that ringlets cascade around her face. She looks dazzling, and together we make quite a sight. I suddenly feel nervous.

"Ready?" Annie asks, sensing my sudden reluctance to leave the room. "Come on, babe, you can't get all dressed up like that and then stay in your room all night. Shoulders back, head high, let's go and show them what we're made of. Oh, and try not to trip over anything," she sniggers.

With that she grabs my hand and pulls me from the room. Arm in arm we descend the stairs and walk into the room where drinks are being served. Most people are already standing in small groups, chatting and drinking, but the conversation stops as we enter. Stuart and James are standing and talking, dressed in their black tie, but pause when they see us. Stuart moves swiftly to Annie's side, puts his arm around her, kisses her cheek and whispers something in her ear that makes her laugh. I envy her the easiness of her singledom. I want someone to embrace me that way, and yet there's no way I could ever imagine Greg in this situation, moving to my side to tell me I looked lovely. I couldn't remember the last time we had even gone out anywhere together. When I look over to where James had been standing he's gone, no longer standing at the fireplace. I feel a moment of disappointment. I don't know what reaction I had expected, but I had at least expected something.

"You look fabulous, Lily," Stuart leans over to include me in their conversation, and I'm pathetically grateful to him for noticing me standing there awkwardly on my own. "I am totally getting a photo of you looking like that to use in our advertising at the gym. Have you got a photo of yourself before I brought about such amazing changes to your body, so I can do a before and after?"

I laugh and tell him he has completely fulfilled all the preconceived ideas I'd had about him when I first met him when I joined the gym. Pete comes over with Pat to join us and hands me a glass of champagne. I smile at him gratefully, glad he has carried on being a good friend despite our earlier awkward moments.

"Lily, you look amazing," he said, as Pat agrees. "I'm not sure I can ever get over the fact you're already married," he adds with a sad little puppy dog smile. He looks so sweet and sincere when he says it that I lean over and kiss him on the cheek by way of a thank you. As I pull away from him I feel

James' presence behind me even before he says anything, as if a magnetic force were pulling me towards him.

"You take my breath away, Lily Lambert," he whispers in my ear while the others are chatting about the walk tomorrow. I turn to face him, drowning in the blueness of his eyes for a moment. "And it would seem you have the same effect on most of the other poor men here too," he says, casting a stare in Pete's direction, "judging by the looks you're getting. It's killing me, Lily, to have you here so close and not be able to touch you as I want to," he breathes. Pete turns to me at that point as if to ask me something, touching my arm as he does so, but steps back a pace under the weight of James' glare, uncertain what he might have done.

"Dinner is served," a lady in serving attire announces to the room, breaking the tension between the two men and giving me a chance to calm my breathing a little. I couldn't feel less like eating if I tried.

"Come," James announces, offering me his arm to escort me into the dining room. It would be churlish to say no, so I hook my arm around his and lightly place my fingers onto his arm. He looks at them and smiles – so it wasn't just me who felt the connection every time we touched.

The dining room is laid out formally; it appears we are having several courses, despite the fact my appetite has run for the hills due to the nervous fluttering that had filled my belly. James sits at the head of the table and places me to his right. Pete fills the place to my right, with Pat beside him. The only dark spot is when Sarah sits to the left of James, opposite me. She gives me a complete once-over, her eyes taking in my appearance before commenting, "It's nice to see you make a bit of effort for once, Lily."

"Thank you, Sarah, and you look lovely as ever," I say, completely ignoring her snide tone and the childish comment. She actually does, and I'm in far too good a mood to let her spoil it. The conversation moves on, flowing from the exploits of the walks to holiday plans for the summer. I sit there quietly listening to the ebb and flow of people's voices, enjoying the camaraderie that had built amongst the group over such a short time. I can't actually believe that tomorrow evening I will be back at home with Greg and Ethan. Home feels a million miles away, and it's going to be hard to go back.

Several times during the meal I feel James' thigh brush mine and I find myself waiting after each occasion for the next time it would happen – hoping it would, and that it would be soon. Even such a brief contact would send an electric thrill through my skin which seemed to be hardwired straight to my groin, leaving me in a state of acute arousal which did little for my appetite for food. The meal slowly weaves its way through three excellently prepared and served courses that I could only really pick at. When the last course is finally cleared I'm relieved.

Stuart takes the opportunity before people start to drift off to say a few words to the group, standing and tapping his glass with a spoon to get people's attention; "I just want to thank you for making the effort to come all this way in order to raise some money for little Emily. I know her mum and dad, who many of you know from the gym, are hugely touched at what you've done. I'm delighted and proud to say that the collective sponsorship efforts of the group have raised nearly £4000." The group cheers and applauds while Stuart continues, "But even better than that, in addition to the amount we raised, our benevolent host James has agreed, as he told me just a little earlier this evening, to match our total himself! So Emily and her family will have £8000 to help with treatment or support for the family."

There are huge cheers this time, including from me. James holds his hands up, and the group instantly quietens.

"Someone I know once told me it's what you do with your money that makes you happy, not the money itself, so apparently I'm getting more pleasure from this than anyone." Everyone laughs. He looks around at all the people in the room, lingering on me before continuing, "As Stuart said, you've done an amazing job with what you've raised, seriously, and I just wanted to do my bit too. So, enough of the talk, I hope you enjoy the rest of the evening and make the most of the house. We've laid some coffee out in the other room if you want to go through, with a little bit of dancing if you wish, or there's a games room down the hall that you're of course welcome to make use of. Enjoy; Mrs Edge will show you where everything is." The group gradually gets to their feet and starts moving towards the room Mrs Edge is indicating, where I can hear some music is now playing. I sit gazing at James; it just seems too good to be true that so many qualities could reside within one person.

"That was a wonderful thing you did, James," I say softly. He smiles. "Almost Buddhist," I continue. "I think they believe, among other things, the path to happiness is to do things for others. I would say you just helped yourself to a little bit of happiness right there."

"You gave me the idea," he says, gently placing his hand in the small of my back as we get to our feet. It's a small gesture, but my body reacts instantly to his touch. I gasp and look at him, my mouth opening slightly, eyes widening – I have a feeling we're both remembering that kiss. He stares back at me, feeling the same magnetic pull to just keep touching each other somehow.

"Dance with me," he insists, taking my hand and leading me to a room with an area where the floor has been cleared and music is playing from an iPod through speakers. A few other couples, including Annie and Stuart, are already there. I know it isn't a good idea, but I can't resist as he finally puts his arms around me, finding myself leaning in against his body as we sway together in time to the unknown piece of music. He rests his cheek on the top of my head and I feel cocooned within his protective arms. We don't speak at all until the track finishes all too soon, when he looks intensely into my eyes and whispers, "This is too public, and I'm not saying that on my behalf but to protect you." He casts a meaningful look around the room at several people who are surreptitiously watching us with interest from the corners. "I need to be alone with you, Lily, and I think, or at least I hope, you feel the same way." He doesn't wait for me to answer. "Come to my room later, please," he breathes, before moving apart from me and walking away to get a drink and talk to some of the others. I stand there for a moment, feeling bereft at the absence of his touch, before collecting my wits enough to walk into the other room and find myself a drink. My head is in pieces. The ball is firmly in my court now, and I'm in complete turmoil. This is indeed the crossroads Annie had warned me about, and I'm clueless what I'm going to do. Aware it would look strange if I just stood there in the middle of the room on my own, I join the edge of a group who are talking happily and animatedly about something, making sure I smile at all the same times as they seem to. All the while, however, my thoughts are flitting between reasons to go and reasons not to. *Could I ever live with myself again if I go? Could I ever live with the regret if I didn't? What could the consequences be of going? What about Greg, what about my marriage vows?* I'm afraid my face might look like Edvard Munch's "The Scream" painting if I saw myself in a mirror. I don't see James for the rest of the evening.

After midnight I find myself drifting out of the room and up the stairs. I'm not conscious of the decision I've made until I pass my room and softly knock on his door. When it opens almost instantly, I step inside without hesitation, and he closes it softly behind me.

"I wasn't sure you'd come," he says honestly.

"I wasn't either," I reply, walking towards him. As we stand there looking at each other, less than an inch apart, I can feel every fibre of my body reaching out to his, yearning for him. He reaches out and pulls me to him, pressing his lips to mine, softly at first and then with increasing fervour, and my body explodes with joy as I kiss him back this time. I can't get close enough to him now, pressing my body hard against the firmness of his own until he groans. His tongue pushes past my lips, probing gently into my mouth, dancing with my own erotically, while his hands run all over my body; first my waist, then my thighs and finally my breasts. I can feel his erection already pressing into my belly, and my body responds in kind, a creamy wetness forming in my panties. All I know is I need to feel him, the touch of his skin close to mine, as even his clothes are too much distance for me now. With fumbling fingers I start to undo the buttons on his shirt, while he reaches behind for my zip. I pause my efforts to let him peel my dress down my body, standing there while his gaze rakes over me, from heels to suspenders and bra, my breath coming in small pants now as I see the naked lust in his eyes and know it mirrors my own. He quickly removes his shirt, and my hungry gaze roams all over his chest and abdomen. He is as toned and sleekly muscled as I had imagined him to be, no evidence of any middle-aged spread in sight, and unable to stop myself, I tentatively reach out to touch him. As I do he closes his eyes and leans his head back, his mouth opening slightly. I touch one of his nipples with a fingernail, seeing the corresponding twitch in his groin and enjoying the feeling of power it gives me. I step closer and place my lips over his nipple, first sucking, then flicking it with my tongue before gently using my teeth to tease it until he groans again. In one swift move he sweeps my legs out from under me and carries me over to the bed, where he lays me down gently. We lie there for a moment before he unhooks my bra with deft fingers and tears my panties from me in one swift move, leaving me there in just my suspenders and heels.

"Fuck, you're beautiful," he says as his eyes take in every part of my nakedness. He touches me then; first my breasts, taking each by turn, playing with the nipple with his fingers until they're so sensitive each touch makes me moan, then lowering his mouth and sucking and teasing them until my body arches off the bed to help him take more. When his hand reaches down between my thighs and he feels how wet I am for him, he can only moan his appreciation before positioning himself further down the bed, spreading my thighs wide and lowering his head to taste me. I have never received oral sex before, only given it. The touch of his tongue playing on and around my clit, teasing, before it finally thrusts up inside me is more than my already sensitive body can handle, and I cry out all too soon as wave after wave of beautiful orgasm crash through me. As my senses finally return, I realise James has removed the rest of his clothes and is now kneeling between my parted thighs, his red, engorged cock glistening with anticipation as he positions himself at my opening. He looks straight into my eyes with an intensity of emotion as he slowly presses himself into me, pausing after the first inch, the delicious sensation teasing and thrilling me until I can't take it anymore and need to feel all of him.

"Please, James," I beg him, watching the look of the male predator take over, seeing him enjoying the control he has over my pleasure, dominating me, as he slides himself the rest of the way inside. He fills me completely, and for a moment I can only marvel at my sense of fulfilment at having him there, as close to me as it's possible to be. Then he begins to move again, slowly at first, withdrawing completely and then thrusting back to the hilt, building faster and faster until my mind is lost once more in the cacophony of sensations coursing through my body as I tip finally over into a second orgasm, only to feel his own body tense and then relax moments after as he calls my name and spills himself within me.

Chapter 15

I slowly come back to my senses enough to become aware of a bright pair of blue eyes gazing down at me. He's still lying on top of me, still inside me, propping his chest up with his elbows.

"Hello," he says, and he smiles the sweetest smile I think I have ever seen.

"Hello," I say, smiling back but suddenly feeling shy. I feel tears begin to well in my eyes.

"Hey," he says, looking instantly anxious, "please don't regret it."

"I don't, I'm not. I'm just a bit overwhelmed. It's never been like that for me," I try to explain. He looks instantly relieved, and just a little bit pleased with himself. "Best ever, eh?" I smile and nod but feel the need to take him down a peg or two.

"Of course I only had a sample of one before tonight, and it could just have been a one-off..."

"You cheeky miss," he says, grinding his groin into mine. I can feel him hardening again inside me. "Now look what you've gone and done," he murmurs, lowering his face to kiss me again. He is gentle and sensual this time, the connection deeper than I have ever felt before, as he fills me completely again. He pulls me up so that I'm sitting on his lap with him on his knees, and we rock there together, unwilling to pull apart even for a moment. The sensation builds as we move until James whispers: "Now, baby," and my body obeys, fracturing into little pieces of sensation with a gravitational pull centred around him as he rocks into me twice more and comes with a groan, burying his face into my neck as I hold him tight until our breathing and heart rates both return to normal.

Eventually, sometime later James remembers he has a bottle of champagne in an ice bucket he had brought up for us to share in the hope I would come to his room.

"Was I that much of a foregone conclusion?" I worry out loud.

"No, never – I hoped, that's all," he says, removing the cork and pouring us both a glass as I pull his spare bathrobe around me.

"Why?" I can't help asking.

"What do you mean 'why'?" he asks, sounding genuinely bemused.

"Okay," I said, taking a gulp of champagne to give me confidence, "I'm going to just say it like it is. What I mean is I am a married, 37-year-old mother of twins, with the body to match, while you are a gorgeous, single, wealthy Rob Lowe look-alike who, just so you know, in my opinion is probably one of the sexiest men alive. You could have virtually any woman you wanted, including several in this house right now, and yet here you are with me, and frankly I have no idea why."

"Wow," he says, blinking at me, "wow, where do I start? Firstly, Rob Lowe, should I be jealous? Don't answer that," he adds quickly, pretending to look worried, and I laugh. "Secondly, your body is beautiful. I don't think you see yourself properly when you look in a mirror, and for the record, you have the best pair of natural breasts I have seen on any woman ever, and I have to admit I've seen a few." I feel a flush of pleasure followed by a little spike of jealousy at the thought of all his other women as he continues. "You do things to me, baby, just by looking at me. I haven't seen another woman since I clapped eyes on you at the gym, but it's more than that. They say the eyes are the window to the soul, and yours is the most beautiful soul I've ever seen. What you've done for your family, how generous you are with people – I've seen it even in the time you've been here. You're the whole package, Lily, and any man would fight to have you." A little sob escapes my lips as I move into his arms and he holds me there, stroking my hair and pressing little kisses to the side of my face.

We spend the rest of the night touching each other, kissing and making love. It's as if I can't get enough and need to store up as much physical contact with him as possible. We don't sleep. At one point James asks me what my dreams are. I don't know at first what he means.

"For life, Lily, what do you want for yourself? What will make you happy? What do you want to achieve?"

"I don't know," I'm ashamed to say. "I think it might be a bit late for me. I started at the gym because I was trying to change myself and my life, but beyond that I don't know what else I can do."

"You can do anything you want to; it's never too late," he insists. "What did you want to do before you met Greg and fell pregnant?"

I think about it for a moment before saying, "I was an English degree student; my dream was always to write, I suppose, but I never finished it."

"You could always go back to university to finish if you wanted to."

"No, it's too late. I'd feel stupid with all the kids there. My own kids would be horrified," I laugh.

"Well, why don't you just write?"

"What do you mean?"

"You don't have to have a degree to write. Just write something and see what happens. What have you got to lose? I bet you'll be brilliant at it."

I think about it for a few moments. He's right. There is no reason why I couldn't just start to write something. It wouldn't matter if it never got published if it gave me pleasure to do it. The more I think about it, the more excited I feel about the prospect.

"So will you do it?" he prompts me.

"I will!" I say shyly.

"Good girl," he says approvingly, giving me a big kiss that soon turns into a lot more.

When the light begins to appear outside the windows I stand and watch while James takes a shower, a sense of dread beginning to fill me at the thought of our imminent separation. It's too soon; I've only just found him, and now I have to let him go again. Worse, the time we've spent together has only served to emphasise what's missing in the rest of my life. James must sense me emotionally pulling away from him when he comes back into the room, moving to where I stand to wrap his arms around me.

"It will be okay," he says.

"How?"

"I don't know yet, but I just know this can't be all we have. I need you too much."

I want to feel hopeful at his words, but I can't see how. We both have our own worlds to go back to and get on with. This is just a beautiful bubble, and I need to accept that, as does he. I turn to face him, kiss him and then pull out of his arms.

"I need to go back to my room. I need to be there before all the others get up," I say sadly.

"Lily, don't act like this is finished, because it isn't," he insists.

I can't think what to say, can't speak. In the end I just smile at him, my eyes full of sorrow, gather my clothes and slip out the door and back into my own room.

It's empty, as I expected. Annie must have spent the night with Stuart again. I'm glad; I didn't want to have to explain. I run myself a bath and lie there soaking my body and trying to order my thoughts, but all I can think about is now I can't smell him on my skin anymore – his musky scent combined with his shower gel that I so love. I'm a little sore down below, but it's a good feeling. I know we should have used condoms. Although I'm still on the pill I have no doubt he has been with a number of other women. Somehow, though, the thought of his essence inside me is comforting, a small piece of him that I could keep as my own. I wash the makeup from my face but leave my hair straight, wondering what Greg will make of it when I get home.

Greg, I know the thought of him should make me feel guilty, but I really don't. *I must be a really bad person*, I think.

This weekend has been a little selfish moment for me in a lifetime of service to my family, and I just couldn't regret it, however I looked at it.

I gather my belongings back into my pack and do what I can to assemble Annie's, leaving her bag on the bed, and make my way downstairs to where others are beginning to gather.

Stuart had told us we were planning to complete the walk today by lunchtime so that we could get on the road home relatively early and be back by early evening. It meant we needed to be off early, which, after a big night, is proving challenging to some people, judging by how few are around. I dump my pack by the coach and wander back into the kitchen to see what there is to eat. Two croissants, a glass of orange juice and a coffee later, I'm feeling like a new woman until James walks in to the kitchen with Stuart. His eyes go straight to mine, a look of pure intensity there that has my body responding instantly and my mind recalling moments of our time together. I lick my lips and swallow to moisten my suddenly dry mouth, while my hands grip the sides of my chair to stop my body automatically gravitating towards him. I try desperately not to keep looking at him as he gets himself some breakfast, focusing intently on my mug. When I eventually can't resist any longer I look up from my coffee to find his gaze upon me again, except this time he looks pissed off. I can see a muscle twitching in his jaw and sense had we not been surrounded by other people, he would have been across the room in a flash. I stand up, wash my plate and cup and quickly leave the room. I need to gain a bit of space and perspective. Annie is wandering down with her bag as I reach the entrance hall. She looks beautiful but tired.

"Good night?" I ask with a smile.

"The best," she says and smiles the smile of a woman who has enjoyed a night of great sex, winking, before looking right at me and asking, "You okay? You look different."

Trust her to notice.

"I'm fine, just a bit tired. It was a late night." This seems to satisfy her as she wanders off to find Stuart and a coffee. I stand there for a moment wondering where to put myself, as it's too soon to get on the coach but I don't want any more awkwardness. The sound of a fast-paced walk down the corridor behind me makes me turn, only to see James marching towards me. He grabs my hand and pulls me into one of the rooms, closing the door behind us. He pushes me up against the wall with his hands on either side of my body, trapping me.

"Stop pushing me away, Lily," is all he says before he kisses me possessively, his tongue pressing into my mouth, his body hard against mine. My lips are tender when he finally, reluctantly releases me. "This is not over," he promises again before he opens the door to let me out. Most people are already in the entrance hall now, moving out towards the coach, and if they notice us emerging from the room together, no one says anything. As we join them, my head is in pieces: I'm befuddled from lack of sleep, that kiss and general confusion over how James seemed to think there was any way our relationship could continue beyond this beautiful weekend.

****

Somehow I complete the walk, although my limbs are aching from the previous two days' walking as well as my night of passion and sleep deprivation. By general agreement the coach is quiet for the return journey as everyone takes separate rows to spread out and catch up on some sleep. The only break is a quick fifteen-minute one for toilets, but otherwise we just crack on, as everyone in the group appears keen to be home now. Everyone apart from me, it seems. I haven't seen much of James all day except from a distance, which I can only consider is a good thing because I long to touch him and be held by him, my fingers continually returning to touch my lips in memory of that last kiss. I sleep almost the entire way back, so the journey passes all too quickly, with me waking just in time to text Emma and let her know what time we're expecting to be back at the car park. I get a swift response:

Can't wait to see you and hear all about it babe, E x

It begs the question, *what the hell am I going to tell her?* Even worse: *What the hell am I going to tell Greg?*

Chapter 16

As the coach approaches the car park, James suddenly gets up from his seat and comes to sit down beside me.

"You arrived in a cab," he says. "How are you getting home? Will he be here?" He looks and sounds angry.

"No," I say quickly, "my friend, Emma is picking me up." I'm thankful for once that Greg is too thoughtless to come and collect me; it would not have been a good idea to have had Greg and James near each other while we were both so tired and emotions were running high.

"Why? Couldn't he be bothered?" James asks, his anger still evident. I don't answer, as it won't help anything even though it's true. We don't speak any more, just sit there side by side until he reaches down finally and takes hold of my hand, entwining his fingers with my own.

People are collecting their things and making their way to the front as soon as the coach stops. I don't even want to leave the seat, but eventually it's unavoidable. The group spends a few minutes muttering farewells to each other, in that awkward way people do when they have formed new and close relationships but are now being watched by their old world and are suddenly feeling uncomfortable and unwilling to explain what transpired while they were away. I hug Stuart and thank him for making me go, promising to be in to the gym soon before turning to Annie and giving her an enormous hug too.

"Keep in touch," I plead.

"Don't be daft, you silly mare. Emma invited me to the pub tomorrow night, so you'll see me tomorrow."

"Bloody Emma," I mutter, looking over towards the pretty A3 I can see parked a short distance away, and she laughs, but secretly I'm pleased Annie is going to continue to be a part of my life, and she knows it. We give each other another brief hug before I turn to look at James, who I can sense is beside my shoulder.

"I don't know what to say," I whisper, hoping my eyes can tell him what I want to say. He catches hold of my hands briefly and gives them a squeeze before reluctantly letting them go, finally saying, "Don't forget to start writing."

I nod and shoulder my pack, turning quickly towards the waiting car while I still have the strength to walk away from him. Emma gets out as I approach, helps me put my bag in the boot and, sensing I need it, gives me a big hug. It's sweet with her baby bump poking into me and I smile gratefully at her as we get into the car.

"Nice motor," I say smiling as we climb in. It still has that lovely new car smell.

"I know," she says, grinning, before looking more serious: "Is everything okay, Lil?"

"Yeah, fine," I say quickly, "just a bit tired – too much exercise and a long drive." She seems to accept that as she puts the car into gear and slowly drives towards the exit.

"Who's that?" she suddenly asks. Just the impressed tone to her voice tells me she can only be talking about James. I turn to look towards where she's pointing, and sure enough he's standing there watching us. As we pass he raises his hand in a half wave. I try to smile, but it feels small and sad.

"Just one of the group, James," I say, by way of explanation before turning to look out my window so she doesn't see the tears that are filling my eyes and threatening to spill out over my cheeks.

"So, was it good? Are you glad you went?" she asks.

I pull myself together to answer her. "Absolutely," I say emphatically, "It was wonderful."

She turns and looks at me as if she can hear something in my voice.

"Your hair looks great."

"Annie straightened it for me last night for the dinner. She made me promise I would buy myself a pair of straighteners to get rid of my frizz."

"I can see why; it looks loads longer. I wonder what Greg will think," she says impishly.

"I know! I bet he hates it," I laugh. "By the way, you and Annie seem to have been doing lots of plotting behind my back, young lady," I say with a mock-serious tone to my voice.

She giggles. "I love her!" she says emphatically.

"I know, me too," I laugh. "I hear you've invited her to the pub tomorrow."

"You don't mind, do you?" She sounds anxious for a moment.

"Of course not. It'll be fun."

"So you will be there?"

"Why wouldn't I?"

"I don't know, I was just worried how Greg will be with you having been away, I thought he might not let you go."

"Don't be silly. Why would he do that?"

"Oh, I don't know. Ignore me, I'm just being silly and worrying about nothing. I blame the hormones." She has slowed the car to a stop outside the house and is peering at the windows anxiously. We both see the curtains twitch. He's waiting for me.

"Don't get out," I say to Emma, reaching for my door handle. "Thanks so much for picking me up, Em; you have a beautiful car." I get out and go to get my pack from the boot. "Nice boot, by the way," I call to her, "perfect for that buggy." She smiles at me as I blow her a kiss and make my way up the path. It takes me a few seconds to find my key which has, as ever, migrated to the bottom of my bag, and then let myself in. When I do Greg is waiting in the hall.

"Hi," I say, trying to calm my racing heart. "How did it go with Adam? Did you have fun?"

"It was alright. He's settled fine now. He didn't really want me there, though. I came back early."

"Oh, that's a shame," I say, although I'm not really surprised. "Was the drive okay?"

"It was crap. I had a flat on the way back." This isn't sounding good.

"How's Ethan? Did the course go well?"

"He's fine. He passed okay, and he's working tonight already."

"Well, that's good." That's the pleasantries done, and I'm running out of things to say.

"Whose car was that?"

"What car?" I say, momentarily confused. "Oh, you mean Emma's new car! She picked me up from the coach. Phil bought her a new car for when the baby comes because the other one was a bit small. She couldn't fit a buggy in the boot." I smile, but he doesn't return it, so I pick up my pack and head up the stairs with it.

When I get into the bedroom I start to sort the washing from the things that need to be put away. I'm slightly startled when Greg, who I hadn't realised had followed me up to the room, suddenly says, "What have you done to your hair?"

My hand rises up to touch it before I answer, "Oh, my roommate Annie had some straighteners. She insisted she show me what they can do, so she did and this is the result. Do you like it? She thinks I should get some; what do you think?" I'm aware my voice is sounding falsely bright – wrong somehow, forced.

"I don't really care. So what did you do?" His voice is so flat when he asks that my first thought is he knows I'm guilty about something, somehow he knows about me and James and is asking about it. Images of our night together flash through my mind. Then my logic clicks in and I realise he means what did we do on the trip generally. I realise he's still waiting for me to answer him, leaning against the wall with his arms crossed across his chest.

"Oh, you know, we walked up three different hills over the three days and managed to collect over £4000 for the little girl, Emily. The house was nice, I think it was Georgian or something, but it was big. The people were nice. We had a nice time."

"Sounds 'nice'," he says sarcastically. I ignore him.

"It was," I say a tad defensively as I finish putting my things away. "Look, I'm really tired; it was a long journey after an even longer walk this morning. I'm just going to have a shower and hit the sack. I'll see you in the morning if you don't mind," I say, grabbing my wash bag and heading for the bathroom.

As I stand there under the shower, letting the water run over my body, I pray he leaves me alone tonight. I can't face the thought of sex with him. Not tonight, so soon after James. To my relief when I come out of the shower, Greg has gone back downstairs, I can't hear the noise of the T.V. from the front room, so I assume he must have gone back out to the shed to paint as he sometimes does. I climb into my pyjamas and get into bed quickly, turning out the lamp before pulling the covers up to my chin. When Greg finally comes to bed an hour or so later, I lie very still with my eyes closed, pretending to be asleep. I don't relax until I eventually hear his breathing slow into the pattern of sleep, and even then it's some time before I finally let my body relax enough to fall into unsettled dreams haunted by blue eyes.

Chapter 17

When I awake Greg is already up. It's later than usual for me; my disrupted sleep seems to be impacting on my ability to wake up at the normal time. Ethan is still in bed, having got in late from work, so Greg and I sit in silence over the breakfast table as I quickly spoon my muesli down.

Eventually I break the silence. "It's Tuesday. I'm meant to be meeting Emma tonight at The Anchor." Greg just looks at me for a moment before standing up and walking out the back door, making his way down to the shed again. It seems an odd reaction; I'm more used to managing his anger than this odd sort of silence. As I travel to work and sit behind reception, I try to fathom out what was niggling me about the exchange at breakfast. Eventually as I'm eating my sandwich, enjoying a rare moment of late autumn sunshine on the bench in the surgery garden, I finally realise what it was. He had looked sad. I'm so used to seeing him looking angry or disappointed that it's not an emotion I'm used to seeing on his face. On the spur of the moment I send a text to Emma and Annie:

Ladies, not going to be able to make it tonight. Really sorry. Can we do it next week instead? L x

Emma is quickest to respond:

Everything ok? E x

I respond just as quickly:

Yes, fine, just got a few things to catch up with.

I'm touched by her concern. I don't hear from Annie until much later:

Emma and I are going to have to spend the evening talking about you then.

I laugh as I read it.

Never doubted it. You would have done that anyway, have fun x.

It's kind of weird to know they're becoming such good friends because of me.

I don't go to the gym after work, figuring I'm still on credit after all the walking at the weekend, and instead buy the ingredients for a steak and salad dinner, grabbing a bottle of wine at the last minute.

Am I feeling guilty? I wonder as I go about preparing things at home. *I should do; I've been unfaithful.* It crosses my mind I should tell Greg. *What would he do if I did?* I honestly don't know. I'm not sure if he would actually even care. *How would I feel if the shoe was on the other foot?* Again, I'm not really sure. *Not all that bothered, really, if it meant he didn't want sex all the time,* I think. I didn't always feel like that, I realise. Not in the beginning. I would have been devastated if Greg had gone elsewhere. Somehow, over the course of the eighteen years and in the midst of child care responsibilities, I've stopped caring. *Has Greg too?* I honestly don't know. We never speak about 'us', we have always just got on with it, really, like most people do – *don't they?*

James, on the other hand... the thought of him with other women makes me surge with jealousy. I have no right to expect anything from him after three days of albeit intense relationship (on my part). *It could have been anyone*, I reassure myself. *It has just woken me up to what's missing in my marriage, and any feelings are better than no feelings. I need to concentrate on that and work out what I can do to improve my relationship with Greg before I start condemning my last eighteen years of marriage*, I realise. With renewed focus I go about dinner preparations. Greg comes in as I'm pouring a glass of wine for us both. He pauses for a moment, looking at me.

"What's all this for?" *Am I really that obvious? Do I so rarely make an effort that when I do it's noteworthy?*

"Nothing, really. I just thought it might be nice to have a glass of red with our steak," I say brightly. Greg just shrugs and sits down without washing his hands. That bugs me, but I hold back from commenting. He would call it nagging. He doesn't wait for me to sit down before he starts, inhaling the food at his usual rate – he can rival a dog at times. I watch him for a moment before sitting down and starting to pick at my own serving. My appetite really isn't there these days, and Greg wolfing down his food with so little regard for how it tastes only makes it worse.

"You should eat," Greg eventually comments, as he pauses from eating for a moment to sip at his wine. "You're losing too much weight." I'm genuinely surprised; I didn't know he'd even noticed. "I prefer you bigger," he shrugs. I smile; it's nice he wasn't bothered about my larger size. He used to be – *I wonder when that changed?*

"I'm just trying to be a bit healthier, you know – lose some weight, do some exercise. It's not good for me to be carrying the excess now I'm getting older," I try to explain. He looks straight at me as he holds his glass in front of him, elbows on the table. His expression says he doesn't believe me. *Does he think I'm doing it to attract other men?* I wonder. *Am I? Well, I did, but I wasn't expecting to – I didn't set out with that in mind. I just wanted to improve myself, my life.... my marriage? Maybe, if I'm being really honest with myself.* I look down at my plate and cut some steak, deliberately taking time in the movements and chewing slowly to break the intensity of his stare. *Does he know about James?* I suddenly wonder. *Maybe one of the other members of the group saw me with him, maybe they knew Greg and told him? No,* I decide, *he wouldn't be this calm.* I feel at the same time reassured and anxious at the thought. *What would he do if he did find out?*

I'm not sure I want to know, and for the first time I feel anxiety about the potential storm I've sewn into my life.

By the time we have both finished and I've cleared, washed and put everything away it's gone nine. Greg is already in the lounge watching T.V. He looks up as I enter.

"Thought you were going out?"

"I put it off 'til next week."

"Why?"

"Thought I'd been out enough recently, and I'd stay in with you for a change." It's nonsense, really. I hardly ever go out; the last few weeks have been a complete exception. We spend nearly every night sitting side by side on the sofa watching crap T.V. exactly as we're doing now. I'm behaving weirdly, I know, but I don't seem able to stop myself. *At this rate I'm going to be blurting out I'd fucked someone else in the Peak District before we get to the weather on the news at ten.*

In the end we sit there in silence, as we always do. After the weather I brush my teeth and get into bed. Greg is a few minutes behind me. We both read our books for a few minutes, although actually I just lie there holding my book and staring at the page, my mind whirring over what I know is about to happen. Eventually I can delay the inevitable no longer. I put the book down, lean over and turn off my lamp. Greg holds out for another couple of minutes and then does the same. I hold my breath in the darkness, wondering for a second whether Greg is going to leave me alone for a second night when I feel the tentative brush of his fingers against my thigh.

This is it, I think as I feel him move towards me. I try to relax my body and disconnect my mind in an effort to give myself over to the sensations and the moment, but every touch feels intrusive. *What is wrong with me?* I want to cry out. He touches my breast, teasing the nipple until it's erect before kissing it. In the dim light cast into the room from the street I watch his head bobbing over my breast dispassionately, my body ramrod-straight. I can feel his erection already nudging my side. It's a routine I'm well familiar with – breast, kissing, clit (if I was lucky), penetration – we would be done in 10 minutes. I roll towards him, grasping his length in my hand and beginning to jerk him off, hoping to speed up the inevitable process. I can feel him swell and harden further under my touch, a small groan escaping his lips. After several minutes he pushes my hand away as he nears his limit, wanting to come inside me. He rolls me onto my back and pulls himself over me, uncaring that I'm nowhere near as aroused as he is, his knees pushing my thighs wider when, at first, they resist. I can feel I'm dry as a bone as he pushes inside me. Greg is too far gone to notice my lack of involvement as his body presses heavily over mine, thrusting into me. I hate it, I realise as I lie there. I hate how he continues relentlessly, despite my obvious lack of participation, I hate feeling used – like a whore must feel. I especially hate that he will remove the last traces of James from my body. At the moment when he finally comes I feel a tear run down the side of my cheek and into my hair as he fills me, immediately withdrawing to the other side of the bed when he's done. I lie there long after his snores start, wondering what I'm going to do. *Could I return myself to the stupor of the last eighteen years and be happy with that? Now I had experienced the difference in what life could offer, would I really be able to accept my lot?* I don't know. I fear not.

In the morning after my shower I look at myself in the mirror – watching my hair return to its habitual frizz, and realise whether I like it or not my life is sucking me back in.

Chapter 18

The rest of the week is exactly the same as my life has always been with a couple of small exceptions. With Adam away at university and Ethan working most evenings, Greg and I are alone together most nights until Ethan gets home in the early hours. The silence between Greg and me is intense, emphasising the fact that most of the noise in our family has been centred around the kids and not each other. It exacerbates the gulf I feel has emerged between us. I'm not sure if Greg feels it when he's with me or not. He is spending even more time painting than usual, often waking me up when he comes to bed to have sex. Each time follows the same pattern as the first night of my return. As the week wears on, though, Greg seems to relax a little, back into his more usual miserable self. It's almost a relief compared to the silent, tense Greg I observed at first on my return.

The second thing which has changed is that I'm starting to write. In those quiet moments when Greg is painting and I'm not at work, I will pull up Adam's old laptop and write. It's amazing how many hours I can lose in the process, and how resentful I feel when forced to stop and attend to either Greg's or Ethan's needs. I don't fool myself it's any good – it's a crime thriller with a strong female lead – but I love the sense of fulfilment as the story comes together in my mind and I struggle to capture its essence on the page.

My hours of writing have come at the cost of the gym, and while I'm still eating sensibly I know I need the exercise. In part I wonder if I'm avoiding going for some reason – *because of James?* On Saturday morning I decide it can't wait any longer, and I gather my things. Greg is already in the shed painting, so I leave him a note before getting in the car and driving the short distance to the gym.

As I walk into reception Stuart's beaming smile greets me. "She's alive!" he says in the style of Dr Frankenstein in the movie.

I smile. "How are you?"

"Good. More to the point, how are you? We haven't seen you in ages. I thought we may have put you off exercise forever."

"Not at all," I grin, "just busy at home."

He looks at me closely as if searching for something in my face, before saying in a more serious tone, "Everything okay? People were actually worried about you." He doesn't say who, and I don't ask.

"Of course, I'm fine," I say in my usual bland tones before heading off to the changing rooms quickly to prevent the conversation going further.

Pete is in the gym when I re-emerge, and he greets me with a warm hug. It's nice to feel like he's a good friend now. He mentions having seen Annie a couple of times over the week at the gym and that she had said she was seeing me at The Anchor on Tuesday.

"You should come," I say more out of politeness than because I was really thinking he would want to. I certainly don't expect him to accept.

"Sounds great, that'll be fun. Like old times," he says with a wink before heading off to complete his workout. Before he leaves, as he's walking out the door he calls out, "See you Tuesday."

I see Stuart look straight at me, and I blush. My thoughts are distracted during the rest of my session while I wonder how I'm going to yet again explain to Emma the additional person at our pub on Tuesday. As I shower and change I decide advanced warning is probably best, and I send both her and Annie a text.

Pete from the gym just invited himself to the pub on Tuesday – hope you don't mind? L x

As ever, Emma replies almost instantly – she must sit constantly by her phone!

It will be nice to meet 'Pete from the gym'. Good to hear from you, by the way, I've been worried.

She's silly the way she worries about me, but it's nice to know someone does. Annie's response is more direct:

When will you learn! C u there x

She's right, I have to learn to say no, I think, as I exit the gym and head towards the car park. I'm distracted by the potential awkwardness of the evening to come and don't notice the sound of steps behind me until a hand grabs my arm and pulls me round. I squeal like a girl with the shock until I come face to face with an angry pair of blue eyes. James stands there holding my arm as if he's afraid I'm going to run away, looking mightily pissed off as he glares down at me, his body shaking with tension. My heart does a little hop, skip and a jump as I hungrily gaze at his beautiful face. It seems impossible, but I have almost underestimated his beauty in my memories of him. He stands there in jeans and a polo shirt, with trainers, looking impossibly handsome and fit with his toned body, the muscles on his arm taut with tension as he holds me.

"Where the fuck have you been?" he says angrily.

I'm taken aback. "What do you mean, where have I been? I've been at home," I say somewhat obviously, completely bewildered by his anger.

"Get in the car," he says, seeming even more pissed off if possible. I look to see which car he means to find him indicating a sleek Mercedes. Of course, I think. What else?

"I'm meant to be going home," I say anxiously, looking at my watch before looking back at James. He looks like he's going to explode, literally. His voice is frighteningly quiet when he finally says,

"Get in the fucking car, Lily, or so help me God I am going to throw you in there myself, and I don't care who sees me." He means it, he actually means it, and while a part of my mind is terrified by the raw power and aggression coming from him, another part of me is thrilled to be the focus of such emotion. With one last look in the direction of my own car, I obediently follow him to his, where he opens the passenger door, sees me in and closes it behind me as if afraid I might run off on him. He then stalks round to his own side, gets in, starts the car and begins to drive. I have no idea where we are going, and he seems in no mood to tell me.

We eventually drive for about thirty minutes along the coast to Seaford which has a quiet undeveloped seafront, a rare treasure on the south coast of England. It's quiet where he pulls the car in, just a few people exercising on the promenade and a couple of dog walkers. No one I recognise. I chuckle as I look at the pair of us sitting there gazing out to sea. He turns to look at me when he hears the noise.

"What's so funny?" he growls, trying to maintain his angry tone.

"We are," I say, "sat here like all the old folk do on their weekend days out, gazing out to sea."

He smiles at last, acknowledging the truth, before taking a breath and saying, "I was so worried," I frown to hear it as he continues: "no one had seen you or spoken to you after we got back, you cancelled seeing Annie at the pub on Tuesday, and you haven't been to the gym all week."

My mouth drops open, as I am astounded how much he knows about my week. "Stuart told me when you normally work out – I've been there every day waiting for you. Bloody hell, I've never been to the gym so much in my life!" He sounds grumpy again now. "Then I get a call from Stuart to tell me you're there today, completely out of character. I dropped everything and ran, terrified you would vanish again before I got a chance to see you... to talk to you." My eyes feel huge in my face as I listen to him. "Do you know how close I came to coming to the house?" he says quietly.

"No!" I whisper, horrified at the prospect of Greg meeting James face to face.

"Yes," he says. "I didn't know what he might do to you if you told him anything. You could have been hurt." He stops then to catch his breath and compose himself. My heart is beating like a jackrabbit. It had never really crossed my mind James would be worried about me, looking for me, wanting anything more of me than the night we had had together despite what he had said. I look at him, his brow furrowed as he rests his head against the headrest, and I am filled with an overwhelming urge to ease the distress that is written all over his face. I reach over with my hand and cup his cheek gently. He turns his face, at the same time as bringing his hand up to capture my hand which is now pressed against his lips, and kisses my palm. The sensation sends a thrill straight through to my groin, as ever. He sees it in my face, the slight widening of my pupils and shortening of my breath. Instant desire is written all over me. I think I see a flash of relief in his eyes as he moves towards me, pressing his lips to mine, first gently and then with urgency until we are both panting. I eventually pull away before we end up being done for indecent exposure, but he keeps his hand on my thigh as if now he has me there he is unable to stop touching me.

"I want you, Lily," he says, his eyes smoking at me now. I feel as if the desire in his gaze could ignite my body and turn me to ashes. I want him too. I know I do, but real life is calling, and if nothing else, I have always had a sensible head on my shoulders. I turn back, away from him, to look at the sea.

"I need to get back, I need to get home," I murmur, unable to look away from him. He is instantly angry again. "He'll be wondering where I am," I try to explain.

"I don't give a fuck!"

"He's done nothing wrong."

"Hasn't he?" The way he says it implies he thinks he has. I wonder how much he knows about Greg beyond what I have told him.

"I have to get home," I say again, more assertively this time. He hears the difference in me.

"Okay," he says, resigned, "but first promise me two things."

"What?" I say, wary now.

"First, give me your phone number. I promise I'll be careful, but I need a way to talk to you when I can't see you. I need to know you're okay." I'm still thinking about it when he says: "Secondly, I need to know when I can see you. Properly. I don't care when, but I want some time with you."

The air leaves my body with a whoosh. This feels like a major tipping point, a shift from a simple one-night stand to a full-blown affair. I feel like I'm gasping for air, and I can't think straight. I go for delay tactics.

"I'll give you my number, but I can't give you a day yet. I need to check my shifts and commitments at home." It's a fib, but I realise I need to think carefully before I embark on this. I think he knows my inner turmoil too.

He stares at me. "This will happen," he says with complete certainty. "You can run for now, but you will come to me in the end. We're meant to be, you and I. I've never been so certain of something in my life." I don't know what to say, *what can I say to that?* "Number?" he demands. I tell him, and he programmes it into his phone. Then he calls me, and I hear my phone ringing from within the confines of my gym bag. "Now you have mine too," he says simply, before turning on the engine and heading back to town.

We're mostly silent on the journey back. His hand reaches and clasps my own. It stays like that for the majority of the journey, a precious connection for a few minutes. As we pull into the car park I remember something I had wanted to tell him that had flown out of my mind until now.

"I'm writing," I suddenly say. He beams at me, clearly delighted with the news. I smile back, equally pleased with his response. The car park has filled up now, and I'm nervous to be seen getting out of his car – it's the kind of car that draws people's attention to it without really trying because it's so pretty. Even I think that, and I don't give a toss about cars. I glance quickly around to see if there is anyone I know before grabbing my bag and moving to open the door. I can feel he wants to kiss me again, but I know I can't let him. I stand up quickly before my resistance fades and almost run to my car, slamming his car door behind me. As I get in I collapse against the seat, trying to compose myself enough to drive home. I have no idea yet how I am going to explain my extended absence to Greg. I know James is still sitting in his car watching me, waiting for me to go first, so I start the engine and pull away slowly, aware almost immediately of the sleek shape of the Mercedes following on behind. He follows me all the way home, slowing as I pull into the driveway before speeding up again. *So now he knows where I live, if he didn't already.* I'm not sure what I feel about that as I make my way in to Greg.

Chapter 19

I needn't have worried – Greg is still locked in his shed painting when I get home. I have spent the rest of the day writing and thinking about James. After I got in and realised my hastily made-up excuses were not required, I had unpacked my gym stuff to wash it and looked at my phone. I had agonised about what name to save James' number under. In the end I decided in this instance honesty was the best policy, so I left it as 'James'. The first text came in as I was saving the contact. It simply said,

Don't forget to check your schedule and let me know. J x

It felt weird, looking at a text from another man in this house, knowing what it was talking about even though it seemed innocuous enough at face value. It felt more deceitful somehow and I felt guilty for the first time. I had replied simply: *ok*, afraid that if I didn't at least acknowledge it he would be at my doorstep banging on the door.

When Greg finally emerges from the shed towards tea time he is distracted in the way he gets when his art has taken him over. I have always loved that about him – that he can become so involved in his creation that his ability to interact with anything outside of his art is completely reduced to nothing. Unfortunately it also makes him difficult company. He is short-tempered, dissatisfied with the delay until food is ready because he wants to get back down to his painting. Ethan arrives home and immediately winds his father up over something relatively minor, and before I know it there are raised voices and doors slamming. They both insult me over my choice for dinner. By the time I finally take myself off for a bath and bed, I am wondering what possible reason I could have for hesitating about spending time with a man who enjoys my company and is caring towards me. *It would make a pleasant change*, I think. Before I can change my mind again I text him:

Wednesday afternoon is free, from 12.30 until 6 if that is any good for you?

The response is almost instantaneous.

Yes. Thank you. I will make sure you don't regret it.

My stomach clenches at his words, wondering what he has in mind for us as I drift off to sleep.

I don't know what time Greg came to bed that night as, for once, he didn't wake me. It must have been very late. He's already up again and painting when I finally get out of bed, so I decide to go straight to the gym and then spend the rest of the day writing. I feel trepidation as I walk into the gym, but no one I know is there, not even Stuart, so I move efficiently around the equipment before showering and returning home to my book. My creative juices are flowing, as the words run from my head to the page easily. Ethan is out all day serving at a posh society wedding somewhere in the country, so I have the house to myself, and I only pause to make a sandwich at lunchtime. It seems pointless to prepare a roast just for Greg and me, so I decide we can have Chinese takeaway for once, which gives me more time to focus on the book. When Greg finally finds me, it is gone eight and he's wondering where his dinner is.

"Oh, I thought we'd have Chinese," I say, taken aback by the time and standing up quickly to rifle through the hall cupboard in order to find the menu.

"What were you doing?" he asks, peering at the text still up on the screen.

"Oh, nothing, really," I say dismissively, feeling embarrassed. He looks at me expectantly, waiting for more details. "I'm trying to write a book." It feels silly when I say it to him, not like it did when I talked to James about it. He just laughs, completely feeding my insecurities.

"What brought that on?" he finally says.

"Oh, I don't know. I just wanted to have a go. It probably won't come to anything, but I won't know unless I try. I just never intended to be a receptionist all my life, so I thought I would see if I could write. It's what I wanted to do when I was at uni," I try to explain, floundering in my efforts to find the right words. He's looking at me again as if I have grown horns.

"I never knew that," he says, genuinely surprised, and it's true – he didn't, because he never asked me; in nearly nineteen years we never talked about it. We spent most of our early days together talking about him and what he wanted, his hopes and dreams and his views on life, the universe and everything, and then I got pregnant and we just talked about the children. My wants and needs by that point had been far too low down on the priority list to ever get around to worrying about.

"So why now?" he asks. I actually blush as I think about James and hope to God he hasn't noticed.

"I don't know," I mumble, "with the boys being older I just figured I had a bit more time to do something for myself that wasn't work. You have your art that you love, and I can't really say I feel the same way about my job. I don't expect it will come to anything," I emphasise again, "I'm just enjoying doing it."

"Can I read it?"

"No!" I say quickly, embarrassed again.

"What's the point of a book you won't let anyone read?"

"I will let people read it, just not yet. It's too soon. It's a crime thriller, so you wouldn't like it anyway," I say, knowing full well that he only reads art books and sci-fi. He grunts acceptance, and I distract him with the menu for the Chinese.

Monday arrives all too soon, and I am resentful of work interfering with my writing. It's all I seem to want to do at the moment. Reception is busy with all the people who have stored up their complaints over the weekend, so I don't have much time for anything until late morning. When I do finally look at my phone, there is another text waiting for me.

R u working today?

Yes, I reply, wondering why he's asking. His response is swift:

I had forgotten just how beautiful your big brown eyes are until I saw you again on Saturday. I can't wait until Wednesday...

I'm taken aback; it seems my being at work has given him license to flirt. It still amazes me that someone like him is, in any way, interested in me.

Not as nice as your blue, I can't resist replying.

I must look guilty as hell as I look over my shoulder before sending it. I don't think I'm very good at this having-an-affair business. *God, is that what I'm doing now? Having an affair?* I wonder briefly what he might have planned for Wednesday – *will he just take me somewhere to have sex? Will it be seedy? Will I feel cheap?* I start to feel anxious. Another text buzzes its arrival in my pocket:

I am completely distracted with thoughts about you. I'm meant to be listening to a presentation, but all I can do is look at my phone, hoping to hear from you. What are you doing to me?

What am I doing to him? I think, amazed; *more like what is he doing to me?* I hear coughing and look up to realise a queue has formed in front of reception while I've been gazing at my phone. The elderly gentleman in front is tutting at me – *I never get tutted at!* I feel like a guilty teenager as I put my phone down to check the patients in and find them their prescriptions. As soon as it's quiet again I can't resist another text:

You just got me tutted at by a patient. I pride myself on my professionalism at work – what are you doing to me, more like?

The response this time is even faster,

I can tell you what I want to do to you... but even thinking about it is making it difficult for me to stand up and leave this meeting room.

I can't believe what just thinking about him with an erection does to me. Even worse, it's visible to others, as one of the doctors comes out and mentions I look a bit flushed, concerned that I'm not well. I blush even more. *I am behaving like a hormonal adolescent, for God's sake!* It's ridiculous how quickly he gets a reaction from me. I send a one-word text because I can't take feeling like this in a public place.

Stop! And he does; and then I feel gutted and wish he hadn't.

Chapter 20

As I make my way to the pub on Tuesday evening, I can't wait to see Emma and Annie. When I get there I am the last to arrive, and there is already quite a crowd at the table. It seems Pete did decide to come and has already introduced himself to Emma, chatting away to her happily – and Stuart has accompanied Annie too. They are by far the noisiest group in our little local, and I see a few of the regulars peering over at the newcomers looking disgruntled. Brian the barman is positively surly when I walk in, clearly blaming me for the intrusion. In truth I imagine he's upset to see two other men sitting with Annie and Emma, given the evil eyes he's casting in their direction.

Pete jumps up when he sees me walk in and rushes over to offer to get me a drink, reassuring me everyone else has only just got one in and so have no need for a refill. I give him a peck on the cheek as a hello as we wait for my drink to arrive. I can feel Emma watching me from the table. Pete makes a big fuss about pulling over a chair for me and putting me next to him, and I know a couple of the locals have clocked him with me, so I'm glad when we are finally all sitting down at the table. Emma is looking even bonnier than when I last saw her, and I tell her so.

"I feel it," she laughs, "only eight weeks to go now, and I can't wait." I smile at her in the superior way that only someone does who knows about a week after the birth she'll be wondering why she didn't make the most of those last eight weeks: when she's sleep-deprived, leaking from orifices she never expected to leak from and bewildered by the varied demands of a new baby. *Knowing Emma and her luck, though, the baby won't even cry*, I reflect.

Pete is chatting away to her now about the baby and all her plans, while Annie leans over to me and whispers, "And how are you really? Everything okay at home?"

"Yes, fine," I say automatically, and then when she just keeps looking at me I add: "Greg's painting a lot at the moment so I'm hardly seeing him, and I've started to write a bit."

Emma overhears and is delighted. "Really, Lil, that's fantastic! You always wanted to be a writer at college – I'm so glad you're finally doing it. What made you decide to start?"

I'm touched she remembers my college dream; it's nice to know someone knew me back then, but I can't really tell her that James suggested I should. I'm kind of lost for words for a moment, and then I finally fall back on the same reasoning I gave Greg about the boys being off our hands now and me having a bit more time. It's based on the truth, so I'm not lying, just omitting some of the facts. I'm getting a bit sick of all the lies I seem to be telling – it's not good karma.

Annie then changes the subject by asking about Greg's painting and what he's doing at the moment, but I have to confess I haven't been down to his shed to look at it recently, so I don't really know. It sounds a bit tragic when I say it, like we live separate lives, which I suppose we do, really. The chat eventually gets on to the trip to the Peaks. Emma is shown loads of photos of the various walks and all of us dressed up for the evening. She exclaims again about the photos that Annie took of me dressed up. I blush and she takes it as being because I'm embarrassed by the compliments, when in fact it's because I remember how the rest of the evening unfolded and exactly where that dress ended up. Pete puts his arm round me and tells me I was the 'belle of the ball'; it's really sweet how kind he is to me still despite my rebuff to him, so I lean in to the hug and enjoy it for a moment. It's only Emma's eyes turning huge in her face and colour fading as she looks towards the door that has me sitting up and turning in my seat to see what has freaked her out. Greg has just walked in.

The rest of the group catch Emma's and my stunned silence and turn to see who we are looking at, while I swallow to try and moisten my suddenly dry mouth. Greg is walking straight towards us, and he looks mega-pissed. I cringe, fearing just how embarrassing the next few moments of my life are likely to be. Pete is still woefully unaware beside me with his arm around my shoulder until Greg marches straight up to him and says: "Who the fuck is this?" He's talking to me but staring straight at Pete, who still has no idea what the hell is going on.

His mouth is opening and closing like a goldfish. I hurry to make introductions. "Oh hi, Greg, everyone, this is Greg – my husband, obviously." I know I'm sounding jumpy, but I just don't know how to stop it. "Greg, this is Pete, Stuart and Annie. They're all friends from the walk the other week. We were just showing Emma some photos if you want to see? Can I get you a drink?"

I speak so fast I'm surprised anyone can understand a word of what I'm saying. Greg's still looking at Pete, and I know we aren't out the woods yet. Actually it's Annie who saves the day. She stands up and puts her hand out to shake Greg's, forcing him to turn away from Pete to finally look at her. I see the same gobsmacked expression pass over his face as every other man that sees Annie tends to get as he takes in her appearance. It helps that they're eyeball to eyeball. I take all this in as Annie begins speaking.

"Hi Greg, it's nice to finally meet you and put a face to the name. We were just talking about you. Lily was telling us you have been painting lots recently – I'd love to see some of it sometime. I run a gallery in town; my name's Annie Lord." Now she really has his attention.

"Oh really, which one?" he says, finally taking the offered hand.

"The *Lord* gallery in Trafalgar Street," she answers in a way that says, *did you not think it might be, after I introduced myself as Annie Lord?*

Greg has the grace to look embarrassed as he slaps his hand against his forehead and smiles, at last breaking the tension. Stuart is already pulling him up a chair as Greg sits down next to the pair of them. I can hear Greg saying something about a recent exhibition Annie had had on that he liked, and the two of them get lost discussing the merits of different local artists. Stuart is just watching Greg all the while, his eyes occasionally flicking back to me. Pete, on the other hand, still looks tense by my side. He swiftly finishes his pint and starts making some apology about having an early start in the morning and needing to leave. I know it's a lie, but I can't really blame him for wanting to get away. Everyone makes the usual half-hearted protests as he stands to go, but I can tell there's relief all round. Greg doesn't even pretend to smile; he just glowers at him as Pete puts his coat on before then turning and glowering at me. *Shit*, I think. *I'm not out of the woods yet.* Annie distracts Greg with another question about his work, so he turns back to her while I glance apologetically up at Pete.

He gives me a small smile but it doesn't meet his eyes, and I can tell he can't wait to get away from me. I feel tears prick in my eyes as I watch yet another friend walk out of my life, chased away by my beloved husband. It's been a bit of a recurring theme over the years.

"You okay?" I hear Emma whisper, trying to keep below Greg's hearing.

"Yeah," I say, but I'm not. I look round the room, wondering which of the local shit stirrers decided to text my husband to let him know his wife was in the local with a couple of blokes. No one meets my eye. I'm fuming now at the ongoing humiliation my life seems to be.

"He saw Pete's arm around you," Emma whispers again, "his face was horrible. Are you going to be okay later?"

I can see she's worried. So am I if I'm honest. The irony is that I am actually planning to meet another man tomorrow if not have an actual affair, but not with Pete. *This can be like a dry run for if he ever finds out about James. God help me*, I think.

"I'll be fine," I try to reassure her, but she knows me too well and her worried expression doesn't lift.

"What are you two whispering about?" Greg's voice pierces our conversation; clearly the art discussion has ended. I can tell he knows exactly what we're talking about – him – but Emma does a brave job of improvising.

"I scratched my new car; I've been worrying about telling Phil. Lil was just suggesting how to break the news." She tries to laugh it off, but it sounds hollow.

Greg looks at me, and it says, *you'll tell me later.* I actually feel afraid for a moment.

"So where are these photos, then?" Greg demands, and suddenly everyone is reaching for their phones to show him. I hate the idea of him looking at them. I desperately cast my mind back to think if I saw any with blokes' arms round me. I don't think I did, but I can't be sure, and even if they were completely harmlessly meant, I know he'll make a big deal about it. I can see the muscle twitching in his jaw, which is a sure sign of irritation, as he scrolls through. I know exactly the moment he sees the picture of me in the evening dress because he freezes and looks up at me.

His eyes look dark as he stares at me, "Nice dress. I haven't seen you in that before, have I?" I swallow, catching Annie looking aghast realising what she's done by showing him the photo.

"It was mine," she says smoothly, "but it was a bit short for me. I always take a few dresses with me, and none of Lily's clothes were dressy enough for the night, so I insisted she borrow one of mine and that she let me do her hair and makeup on the night. She looked stunning, don't you think?"

Greg is still looking straight at me. I can't believe now everyone is telling lies to protect me.

"My wife's more a cardigan sort of woman, but you did a good job on her," he says, putting me firmly back into the dowdy box I've been living in for the last eighteen years. I see pure anger flash over Annie's face at that, and I pray inwardly she lets it go. Stuart must see something in my expression because he suddenly moves to hug Annie and suggest they should make a move. Everything about the way he does it suggests he can't wait to get her home to bed, but I suspect he just wants to get her away from Greg before she says something we'll all regret. I could kiss him, but that would only make matters even worse. We spend a few minutes saying goodbyes; Greg promises to bring some pieces in to show Annie while I exchange hugs with them both. Annie says, "I'll call you," to me. I can tell she wants to say more but doesn't know how to in front of Greg, and then we're left with just Greg, Emma and me. I can tell Emma doesn't want to leave me with him, but I know I have to get this over with.

I reach for his hand, which seems to surprise him, before saying, "Do you want another, or shall we head home? I'm tired. You must be shattered, Em, carrying that baby around all day." She nods and smiles thinly at us.

"Oh, I think we should go home, love," is all he says, and it sounds completely innocuous, but I know there is an implied threat in there, and so does Emma. By the time we are hugging our goodbyes in the car park she is almost crying. She seems reluctant to let me go.

"I'll call," she promises before whispering, "if you need me, you know where I am – anytime. I mean it, Lil, you've done nothing wrong."

But that right there's the problem, isn't it? Because I have. With a heavy heart I wave to her again before heading to our car where Greg has already positioned himself in the driving seat.

Chapter 21

We don't speak at all until we're inside the house standing in the kitchen together as I put my bag on the side. The first thing he says surprises me: "I didn't know you were friends with Annie Lord." Maybe the lure of a chance with a gallery, now that I am friends with the owner, is going to outweigh how pissed off he is with me for being in the pub with an unknown couple of guys.

"Well, it's only been a few weeks, really, we were put together as roommates for the trip, but we just really got on. She's met Emma and me a few times now at the pub. She gets on really well with Emma, too, although most people do, I suppose."

"Was that bloke she was with her boyfriend or husband?"

"Boyfriend. He's one of the instructors at the gym, the one who organised the trip."

"And the other bloke? Did you fuck him?" I roll my eyes, thinking *here we go*.

"No, Greg. No, I didn't 'fuck' him." I've already mentally decided that I am going to answer his questions honestly – if he asks if I fucked anyone else, I will tell him the truth. I hate all the compounded lies that are filling my life now.

"Did you want to?" he persists.

"No, I didn't want to." I answer honestly. "He's a friend, that's all. Or I thought he was going to be a good friend, but after your little performance tonight I'll be lucky if he even says hello next time I see him at the gym."

"So you like him, then?"

"Yes, I told you…as a friend. That's all."

"So who was that performance with the dress for, then?" I have to give it to him, he doesn't miss much. I think about how to answer him as honestly as I am able.

"I got dressed up first and foremost for myself." It's true – I was planning to wear the dress before I'd even met James. "I wanted to feel good about myself and the weight I'd lost – the dress, hair and makeup did that. Annie helped me feel attractive for the first time since, well, ever. Everyone was getting dressed up, and I just wanted to do the same – be the same as everyone else. Is that such a big deal? Really?"

"I've never seen you look like that." He sounds so sad the way he says it that for a moment I can't reply. It's sad we would never do that sort of thing for each other.

"No," I agree, "we haven't really ever made time to do that sort of thing. Maybe we should." He moves to me and wraps his arms round me in an unusually gentle way. I lean in to him.

"I saw the way he was looking at you, Lil. He wants you." He breathes into my hair.

"Who?" I say confused, momentarily losing the flow of the conversation as this rare tender moment overwhelms my senses. If only it could always be like this.

"That guy in the pub, Pete." And so quickly I'm back in the real world, and I can feel the tension radiating off Greg again. I don't speak. I can't be bothered to keep repeating the same things, and he's not listening to me anyway. Typical Greg, he's made his mind up, and now nothing will change it. His touch on me has changed, his grip on my arms tighter, as he pushes me back towards the table. I stumble, but he doesn't slow at all, half dragging me until I can feel the table edge pressing against my arse. He pushes me down so I'm sitting on the table and reaches for the button on my jeans, yanking both my jeans and pants off in a couple of pulls. I start to protest:

"What about Ethan? We can't do this here."

But he's not listening; instead he's pressing my thighs wide open now and unzipping his fly, pulling out his cock. I realise what's happening here – this has nothing to do with love; this is about possession. He couldn't make it clearer if he pissed on me. He shoves into me, heedless of my lack of readiness, as ever, grabbing my arse and pulling me closer, pressing deeper into me, bruising my thighs. A part of me tells me to fight him, that another person should not do this without me wanting him to, but a bigger part of me that has developed a coping mechanism for this over the last eighteen years tells me just to lie there and let it happen, that it will be over sooner if I do. And that's what I do in the end. I look up into his lust-crazed face as he thrusts into me, just willing it to be over soon, hating the anger I see there.

He sees me looking and doesn't like what my expressions must be telling him, withdrawing from me before flipping me onto my stomach. When he plunges back into me, it's with a renewed vigour. His balls slap against me with each move he makes. It's taking him longer than normal, but my body isn't responding this time – it's like it's finally learnt sex doesn't have to be like this, plus I'm terrified of Ethan coming home and seeing this. No kid should have to see his mother like this, however old he is. Eventually, after what seems like an age of him using my body like one of those blow-up sex dolls, he grunts and pours himself into me. Immediately after he's done he pulls out, wipes himself on one of the tea towels and leaves the room. My legs feel like jelly as I try to stand; the circulation has been cut off while I was pressed against the table. I gather my pants and jeans and shuffle back into them, grabbing the soiled tea towel and pushing it into the washing machine. Once all that is done and I can relax for a second, I collapse heavily onto a chair. My body has started to shake, and I no longer have the strength to stand.

I don't know how long I sit there, but the noise of a text coming in eventually rouses me to find my bag. I know Emma must be worrying about me. When I eventually dig my phone out from the depths of my bag, there are five unread texts. The first two are from Annie and Emma, just checking I'm okay. I reply quickly to them both, reassuring them I'm fine. The other three are from James. I read them in the order they arrived, the first obviously having come in while I was at the pub with the others. I just hadn't checked my phone all night.

Shall I pick you up from work about 12.30 tomorrow?

I decide to read the others before replying.

I heard about the pub tonight. Are you ok?

Good news sure travels fast in this town, I reflect. I can only think Stuart spoke to him about what happened. I scroll down to the last message.

Jesus, Lil, if you don't let me know you're ok I'm going to come and get you.

I think my heart actually stops beating for a moment as I wonder how long it was from when he sent the message to now. The very last thing I need right now is James hammering on the door, however well-meant his intentions. I reckon it's been no more than ten minutes. I quickly reply,

I'm ok, don't do anything silly. I'll see you in the surgery car park at 12.30

I wait holding my breath until the response comes back:

OK, but just call if you need me – any time day or night

For some reason the thought of everyone, especially James, worrying about me makes me cry. I sit there sobbing into my sleeve until I hear Ethan quietly opening the front door and letting himself in. I quickly rinse my face, knowing full well my puffy red eyes will be evidence enough of my tears, before letting myself out the kitchen.

"Oh, hi mum," he says, surprised to see me still up. "You okay?" he asks, sounding concerned and peering closer at me.

"Yeah, fine," I reassure him as I pat his arm. "Think I'm getting a cold, and it's making my eyes and nose run. Your shift okay?" I don't think he buys the cold comment, but he's happy to be distracted off an awkward emotional topic to talking about his shift and the famous people who were at the tables this evening.

I nod and smile at the appropriate times until he's done, before we wish each other goodnight. He surprises me by reaching out and giving me a quick hug, it's kind of stilted and awkward, like he's not used to doing it, but I'm touched by the gesture and feel tears pricking my eyes again. I quickly wish him sweet dreams and scurry up the stairs, before he spots my renewed tears.

Greg is already asleep when I let myself into the room, thank the gods. I have no more energy tonight for conflict. I move as silently as I am able, getting ready for bed, before slipping under the duvet beside him. Once there I lie rigidly, waiting for sleep to enfold me, only to still be there an hour later. My mind is restless, flitting between the events of the evening and thoughts of James. At about 2am I suddenly have the thought that I don't actually have to put up with any of Greg's crap anymore. I could actually leave if I wanted to. *Do I want to?* I ask myself. I'm not certain. *If I break up the family, would the boys mind?* They are older now. *But if I left where would I go, what would I do? What would Greg do without me to look after him?*

The thoughts buzz around in my head until the early hours of the morning. I eventually fall into an exhausted sleep where I dream I am cowering in the kitchen from an angry crowd, with Greg and the boys at the front, all shouting at me and calling me a whore.

It's actually the silence of the house which eventually wakes me. I have slept through my alarm and only have the minimum time to get ready for work. I shower, trembling as I wash the dried come from my legs, hating the tenderness I feel between my thighs as I notice a couple of bruises. I half contemplate cancelling James given my fragile emotional state, but I figure it will likely cause even more stress if he's determined to talk to me. I resolve to see him and finish it. It was a decision I came to last night: if I was going to leave my husband, it was a decision I needed to make based on our relationship (or lack of it), and not to just run into the arms of another man, however lovely those arms, chest and face may be. Having made the decision I am somewhat disturbed to find myself putting significantly more care and attention into my dressing preparations for the day. I wear a skirt for once that has a plaid design, with opaque tights and a fitted V-neck black jumper. It shows off my curves in the right way. I even add a little mascara for a change. *For someone who is breaking up with a guy today, I sure am making a lot of effort*, I reflect as I look at myself in the mirror before grabbing my bag and coat and heading out the door. I don't have time for breakfast, and I don't bother calling out to Greg to let him know I'm leaving.

Chapter 22

The new look at work has caused quite a stir, and I feel uncomfortable about all the attention I've drawn to myself. Several of the patients even comment about how lovely I'm looking, and I guess the fitted outfit has shown my weight loss off because most of the practice staff remark on it and tell me how great my figure is now and how well I appear. Well, my body is, but I see big, dark bags under my eyes as I look at my reflection in the staff toilet's mirror. The time actually flies for once, maybe because of how apprehensive I'm feeling about seeing James and telling him what I've decided. At dead-on 12.30 I walk out of the surgery and into the car park. I can't see the Mercedes as I scan the car park, but the door to a new model Range Rover with darkened windows opens and I see James step out and wave at me before moving round the car. I quickly step over to where he's waiting, holding the passenger door open for me, and climb in. He closes the door behind me before moving back round to the driver's side and climbing in beside me. For a moment he just looks at me – I see his happy smile fade as he takes in my appearance and sombre expression.

"What the fuck did he do to you?" he growls at me, evidently furious at what he sees in my face.

"Nothing, it doesn't matter. We can't talk here," I say, looking anxiously around at the other cars. His jaw tenses, and

I see his grip tighten on the steering wheel before he nods and starts the ignition.

I have no idea what his plans are for the afternoon. Didn't even think to ask. *Is he taking me somewhere planning to have sex?* I wonder. *If he is, what am I going to do? I really don't know.* Now I'm sitting beside him, looking at his profile as he silently grips the steering wheel driving us to our unknown destination, and I feel the same magnetism I always feel around him. I want to lean against his shoulder, I want to feel his arms around me again, I want him to make love to me until the orgasms tremor through my body. Something of what I'm feeling must transmit to him because the next time he looks at me his expression softens and he reaches out to clasp my hand in his own. We stay that way until we pull into a small pub in the middle of the Ashdown forest. It's beautiful here, especially in the autumn when all the leaves on the trees are changing colour to rich gold and red before they fall to the ground at the onset of winter. The pub is tiny, with just one main sitting room area where we find an alcove to sit in. We order drinks and a bowl of soup each before settling in and finally turning to really look at each other. Before I can say a word he is pulling me towards him and crushing my lips to his own. All my protests are silenced as his lips begin to move against mine, and rational thought is lost to sensation as I respond enthusiastically. I move closer to him, wanting to press myself against him and feel that same urgent press from him against me. It's only the slightly embarrassed coughing of the waitress bringing our soup over that breaks us apart.

Jesus, we were nearly dry humping in a pub, I realise, flushing with embarrassment while James murmurs our thanks to her. She gives him a coquettish smile, clearly not put off James in any way, having seen him making out with me. I want to growl at her. He laughs when he looks at me and sees my expression.

"I only have eyes for you, Lily," he says, kissing me again. I have to grip the chair to stop myself falling into his arms once more. He's looking at me intently now, and I can see the tension in his face before he finally asks me: "What happened last night?"

I deflect the question by asking my own, "How did you know something happened?"

He looks guilty for a moment before admitting: "Stuart told me he was meeting you and Annie at the pub last night, and I just texted him to find out how it was, how you were. He knows I like you and worry about you – it seems I'm not the only one. He told me Greg turned up at the pub and was pissed at seeing everyone, but especially Pete. He said he looked really angry with you." He looks at me hard before asking in a cold flat voice: "Did he hurt you, Lily?"

I can't speak immediately; I just shake my head mutely. It won't help to tell him what happened in the kitchen, and it won't change anything. Physically I'm okay, anyway, even if emotionally I'm a mess.

"If he ever hurts you, Lily, I swear I'll kill him." I have no doubt when he looks at me that he means every word he says.

"I'm okay, really," I reassure him, wanting to diffuse the anger. It works, as he reaches out to brush the back of his hand down the side of my face. I automatically close my eyes and lean in to the touch.

"I couldn't stand anything to happen to you," he says fiercely, "he doesn't deserve you."

"He doesn't deserve a wife who is unfaithful," I say sadly.

"If he was good to you, if he treated you as you should be treated, you wouldn't have looked at me in the first place."

I have to smile at that. "I think I would always have looked at you, James," I say with a grin, "I just might not have done anything else but look."

He smiles back at me and reaches for my hand again. "I'm so glad I met you. I've never met a woman like you. You're all I can think about – I've never been like this with a woman before."

"It's just because you can't see me all the time. I haven't had the chance to annoy you yet. If you were with me all the time you'd soon get bored with me."

"No," he says adamantly, "I wouldn't."

"How do you know, though? We barely know each other." It's true; we haven't exactly spent much time with each other just talking. It's always ended up becoming physical.

"Well, I'm going to put that right this afternoon," he says. "We're going to stay here and talk about our views on life, the universe and everything until I convince you we *are* meant to be together."

And so we do. We talk about everything – where he grew up (his parents are titled but relatively cash-poor while land-rich), went to school (a minor boarding school from the age of eight, followed by Durham University), made his first money (an early investment in a low-budget British rom com that did really well and which I happen to have seen and loved) and how he ended up in the same town as me – he's a little evasive but seems to have ended up here because a partner had property here.

I tell him in turn all about my life pre- and post-Greg, the boys, work. It all sounds so dull in comparison to him and the things he has done. When we share our likes and dislikes there's a frightening amount in common. He gives me a smug 'I told you so' look. Before long he's moved the conversation to sex, wanting to know what I like and don't like.

We're leaning in close to each other again now as I answer him in a whisper, "I don't really know. You're only the second person I've ever slept with. I like what you did," I say shyly.

He looks at me like he could eat me before gently asking, "What about with Greg, what are the things you like to do with him?" I don't want to think about Greg or our sex life. A flash of me spread open on the kitchen table as he forces into me comes to mind.

"Not much; it's just pretty straightforward, really. I never really orgasm," I add, knowing this will be bound to distract him.

"You never orgasm! That's terrible, Lily," he says, truly aghast. His voice drops as he adds, "I can see I have a lot of work to do to make up for the last eighteen years." And he moves even closer to me.

"I am going to show you just how much pleasure you've been missing," he says suggestively, and suddenly my body is already responding to him without him even touching me. He senses the change in me, and his eyes become dark and intense before he says, "I want you right now, Lily, and if I didn't think it would put you at any personal risk I would be booking us into a hotel for the night this very minute. The things I want to do to you, Lily, and the pleasure I want to show you..."

He trails off as we both lose ourselves in thoughts of what we're missing. "When can I see you again?" he asks, and the words are heavy with suggestion. The next time I am certain won't be spent in a pub all afternoon... *if there is a next time.* I remember suddenly that I planned to end this today. I don't know if I can. I look at my watch, and we really need to be heading back.

"James..." I begin.

"No, Lily," he interrupts immediately.

"You have no idea what I was going to say," I say, indignant now that he didn't wait to let me finish.

"I know exactly what you were going to say, Lily. You were going to tell me we shouldn't see each other anymore, but I won't let you do it. You need me, Lily. And more to the point, I need you. And while I know this is difficult, it is meant to be. We were meant to find each other. I will not let you cut me out of your life, no matter what." I should feel terrified by his words, this intense, beautiful man telling me he won't let me leave him, but I can't. I'm not afraid of him; I'm thrilled, and I know I want him as much as he wants me. He's still waiting for me to speak.

"Friday," I whisper. "I'll call in sick, and we can have the whole day."

He smiles then, and it's beautiful how it lights his face up. I feel my own responding. He quickly moves to the bar and pays the bill before reaching a hand out to me, saying: "Come, Lily," and I do, without hesitation.

In the car I tease him about just how many houses and cars he owns, and he just shrugs, muttering: "It's just stuff; it means nothing." I love that he cares so little for 'things'. He drops me back at the surgery, where I see my car is one of the last in the car park. There is no one around, so he pulls me to him for one last sweet kiss.

"Friday," he says as he holds my face between his hands, and I nod.

"I'll text you where to meet me; you can't leave your car here if you're dialling in sick," he adds sensibly. I can only nod again.

He lets me go, and I force myself to climb out the car without looking back and drive home lost all the while in thoughts of Friday, and wondering how it is my life seems to be so very complicated suddenly.

Chapter 23

Greg spends so much of his time painting, building up to the appointment he has made to see Annie on Saturday, that we barely see each other except over meals. He doesn't even seem to sleep for more than a couple of hours at a time. It is a blessed relief for me, as it means no sex. As Friday dawns I am in a state of fevered excitement about the day ahead with James. I spend more time than usual getting myself ready once Greg is safely entrenched in his shed for the day. I shave all the bits of me that need shaving and take time doing my hair and makeup. I still don't have any straighteners, but my hair doesn't look quite such a frizzy mess as normal. I choose my best black skinny jeans to wear with a pink top, and I'm pleased with the result when I'm finished. I'm feeling nervous, wondering if I should bring anything with me. I'm wearing the underwear that Emma got me, as it's the only set I can show publicly, but I can't imagine what else I might need. With all the nervous anticipation my appetite has fled completely. When I stand on the scales I can't believe how light I am now compared to when I started. I can see the difference clearly now in my body and face. I get into the car without saying goodbye to Greg. We haven't really spoken at all since the kitchen table incident; he's just back to being surly and making snide comments about the things I do wrong as far as he's concerned, I'm getting better at ignoring him, but it just seems to encourage him to be worse.

James has texted me the address of a hotel near Gatwick, and as I pull into the car park it is still fairly quiet. For a horrible moment I think James hasn't bothered to come, but then I see the Range Rover parked in the far corner and move my car over to where he is. I get out and run to the driver's door which he opens quickly. He jumps out and pulls me into a fierce hug. "I'm sorry not to pick you up closer to home, but the fewer people who see us together the better for you, I think," he says, sounding apologetic.

I hug him again, just intoxicated by his presence as he grasps my hand and leads us towards the hotel reception. For the first time I take in my surroundings and realise I am surrounded by luxury. This is a magnificent hotel with beautiful grounds, and as we walk into the reception I am overwhelmed by its opulence. I cower behind James as he marches up to the desk, announcing his name and collecting the key to our room. I feel as if everyone must be looking at us and knowing we are here to conduct an affair. My cheeks heat with embarrassment as I feel the scrutiny of the receptionist upon me, but on reflection maybe she is just wondering what the hell I am doing here with a bloke like James, judging by the way she is devouring him with her eyes. I'm pissed, and the jealous streak rears its head in me again. I possessively stroke

James' arm as he signs for the room. He looks down at my hand, and I know he knows what I'm doing. He smiles at me before leaning down and kissing me so sweetly on the lips.

Take that, bitch, I think, as the receptionist purses her lips and swiftly processes his payment before handing him the key.

As we move towards the lift James whispers in my ear, "I like it that you're possessive about me."

"I don't know what you're talking about," I reply impishly.

"I think you do," he says, grabbing my hand and pulling me into the lift. I suddenly feel shy as we stand on opposite sides of the lift looking at each other. He's got that predatory look in his eye again, and I'm feeling nervous as we stand there and devour each other with our eyes. I'm relieved when the lift stops and the doors open. James takes hold of my hand again and leads me to our door. I guess I should have expected it, from what I already know of him, but when we walk into the room I am again speechless. It's enormous, not a room like I was expecting, more like an apartment.

"James, you didn't need to do all this," I mutter, overwhelmed by his overt display of affluence.

"It's just stuff, Lily; it means nothing. What matters is that you are here with me. I just want you to feel comfortable, and since we're spending all day in here I wanted it to be somewhere you would be happy to be."

"I would be happy in a cardboard box with you, James. You really don't need to spend money on me."

"I know that, Lily, and it's one of the things I love about you, but I want to look after you. You deserve to be spoiled a bit."

My eyes fill; *God, what is it with all this crying?* It's been so long since someone wanted to look after me, I feel pathetic that at the first sign of kindness I have crumbled into a snivelling mess.

"No, baby, don't cry," he says, pulling me into his arms. "Let me do this, please."

I stand there within the protection of his arms, just breathing in the smell of him, and for the first time since I was in the Peaks I relax completely, submitting to him entirely. James must sense it as he gently puts his hand under my chin and lifts my face, bringing his lips down to claim my own. The kiss is so sweet and gentle, a caress that goes beyond just the physical contact, feeling like it touches my very soul. I feel myself respond, encouraging him as his tongue presses gently into my mouth and entwines with my own. I don't know how long we just stand there kissing. We're like teenagers again who can't seem to stop ourselves. I just want to touch him however I am able, but I defer to him entirely and wait for him to take the lead. Eventually he pulls away from me and takes my hand, leading me to the king-size bed that takes pride of place in the largest room. We stand in front of it for a minute as he pulls my jumper off over my head and pushes my jeans down, until I am standing there in just my underwear, before removing his own shirt and jeans. We just look at each other, and I see my own desire reflected in his eyes. I'm already wet for him; he barely has to touch me, and my body is ready for him. I know I am being completely wanton, but at the moment the only thing I care about is the need to feel him touch me, press his skin against me, push himself inside me. He gently lays me back onto the bed whilst all the while he is touching me; on my face, my neck, my breasts, abdomen, thighs. No part of me goes without his attention. I whimper, wanting to spread myself wide and pull him into me, just needing to relieve the ache that has taken hold of me.

"Ssh, baby," he tells me. "Patience. We have all day, so no need to rush." I groan as I feel his hand move to the place at the top of my thighs. He can feel the wetness there now, and I hear him groan in response, feel the jerk in his already solid erection that is pressing hard into my side. "God, you feel amazing. So wet. I want you so much," he whispers. His fingers trail lightly over my clitoris, playing there until my body begins to thrum with sensation, and I am lost to it. When he presses two fingers up inside me, my body spills over into a shattering orgasm that has me calling his name. As I try to recover my senses, he is already kissing me again, on my lips, my breasts, whispering that I'm beautiful – and I feel it with him. I want him again already. The release was only momentary, and already my body needs him again, this time wanting him deep inside me. He senses the shift in my emotions, and his response is swift. I can feel the urgency in him now to claim me. He rolls me over onto my front, lifting my hips so my butt is in the air while my elbows are pressed into the mattress, my face on the pillow. I feel him nudging my entrance, slipping and sliding as our juices combine. He enters me an inch and then withdraws, and I can't help but groan at the loss of him until he presses into me again. I try to push against him, wanting him deeper, but he resists, enjoying the control he has over me. It is the sweetest agony I have ever felt. He begins to press deeper, each time pulling back just when I think he is finally going to push home and claim me. I can hear small mewling sounds, and I realise it is me keening the loss of him each time he pulls away, I want him so badly now I actually sob as I try to draw a breath.

"Ssh, baby, I'm here," he soothes, and the sound of him whispering in my ear calms me as I feel him press into me once more, as I feel the weight of him when he leans over my back. This time he doesn't withdraw; he pushes into me fully, and it feels sublime. My body tightens at his presence; my nipples become hard, and I arch my back to allow him to press deeper into me. "Oh God," I hear him moan. He kneels behind me, his hands on my hips as he holds me in place and begins to thrust, slowly at first but gradually increasing his speed until we are slamming hard against each other. I want it so much, and all I can think is that I want all of him, my body is his to do with as he pleases, I would deny him nothing. The pressure is building again, deeper this time with the pressure of him pushing inside me. I can feel the same urgency in him as we hurtle together towards our climax. And then I'm falling over the edge into blissful release as I distantly hear him call my name and feel the warm pulse of him spilling inside me. We collapse together, his body over my back, still joined. I feel boneless, unable to move even had I wanted to, even if he weren't surrounding me within his protective embrace as we lie there, breathless.

Eventually, after an unknown amount of time, I feel James start to kiss the back of my neck, and we pull apart as he turns me to face him. The gentle look in his eyes is so tender as he gently traces the outline of my body with his fingers that my heart flip-flops inside my chest. *Oh my God*, I worry, *I am lost to this man.* I know it is already too late, that I will do anything, risk anything, to keep this man in my life. His mouth is now trailing behind the path of his fingers, teasing and tantalising as my body once more responds to him.

He moves down the bed, pushing his face into the top of my thighs and breathing deeply. "I love the scent of me on you," he murmurs, "the combination is intoxicating. I want to possess you completely, Lily," he says, and his words are so erotic they have my thighs parting again to give him access. The gasp I hear in response is not a gasp of erotic pleasure but a sound of shock. I push myself up onto my elbows to discover the source of his surprise, only to find him staring at the bruises on my inner thighs, now purple and yellow.

"Did he do this?" he literally growls at me, sounding furious. I grab the bedclothes and pull them over my body, feeling ashamed. "I asked if he did this," he says again, his voice quietly menacing this time but no less angry.

"Just leave it," I try to say, not wanting to talk about it.

"No Lily, I need to know what he did to you."

"Why? Why do you need to know?" My voice sounds small; I just want the conflict and thoughts of Greg to go away. I want to return to my erotic bubble of a few minutes ago.

"Does he hurt you like this often, Lily?" he asks, his voice softer now.

"No," I try to reassure him, "he was just angry after the pub." I see his hand clench and his eyes close as he seeks to control himself.

"Did he force you?"

"No, not really, he was just angry, like I said." I can't bring myself to say any more. I am so ashamed to be talking about this with him. I feel disloyal to the pair of them now, and I look at his face expecting to see disgust.

His face looks frozen for a moment, "Did you enjoy it?" he asks at last.

"No" I whisper, and I can't miss the look of relief that's written all over his face.

"I know he's your husband, Lily, but I swear to God if he hurts you like this again, or forces you to do anything you don't want to do, I will kill him." It all sounds so melodramatic a part of me wants to burst out laughing, but one look at his face and the clench of his jaw and fist tells me he's serious, and the laughter fades before it has a chance to emerge.

He pulls me into his lap and cradles me, gently stroking my hair before he continues: "I am struggling to share you, Lily. I hate that he has so much of you when I want all of you, that he even gets to touch you, let alone sleep with you. The idea he hurts you just rubs salt in the wound. The fucker doesn't have any idea just how lucky he is," he says, angry again now.

I want to distract him, but I don't know how. All I can think to do is kiss him. He's startled at first, but then he's kissing me back at first aggressively, like he's trying to make a point. But then he calms himself, and it becomes sweet and sincere. His hands move to touch me again, stroking gently, and my body responds by pushing against his touches, I'm desperate to show him how much I want his caress. When he enters me this time, with me wrapped around him, he doesn't take his eyes from mine. We connect like that, gently loving each other until we reach our release, with him coming a few strokes after me. I can't say the words yet, but I fear my feelings are written all over my face as we lie there with our limbs wrapped around each other, perfectly sated. I have no idea what the future will hold for us. We only have the present, but what I do know is I love him already, with a depth that is frankly terrifying.

Chapter 24

The rest of the day passes in a haze of love-making. We order food in the room and feed it to each other, sitting in bathrobes on the bed. He runs me a bath and insists on washing me himself all over my body, finally caressing me intimately until I orgasm again. I can't believe it can be like this. My body feels loved and beautiful. I want to return some of what he has given me, so when it is his turn to bathe I can't resist washing him too. I relish the chance to touch his beautiful body all over as he lies back and closes his eyes, lost in the sensation. As I reach to touch and caress his cock, he opens one blue eye and raises an eyebrow.

"Why, Mrs Lambert, I do believe I've created a monster," he says with a small smile playing on his lips. I only smile as I lean over him to take him in my mouth. I allow my tongue to play with his tip and run along the underside until he groans in ecstasy. I move to take him fully in my mouth, unable to take his full length given his generous size, and gently suck while one hand wraps around his base and the other tickles his balls. I know he's close when I can feel his control slipping as his hips pump more rapidly.

"Fuck, Lily," he says as he finally tips over the edge and shoots into my throat. It tastes warm and salty as I swallow it down. I watch him, delighting in the way he looks so sated, lying there in the warm bath water, before standing and leaving him to go and get myself dressed.

****

We haven't left the room all day, so when we finally emerge it's a shock to encounter other people in the lobby. We have to give up our feeling of intimacy and return to a state of paranoia, always wondering who might be looking at us, ready to report our misdemeanours.

James is quiet as we walk to the cars, before finally turning to me: "You don't have to go back to him", is all he says, his eyes intense as he looks for my response.

"Don't I?" I wonder out loud. He was only verbalising thoughts that had been running through my own head all day. "So what would I do? Live with you?" I see the look of discomfort that flashes over his face, and a little part of me dies inside. "Thought so," is all I say, as I move to open my car door.

"Lily, he doesn't deserve you," he says forlornly.

"Maybe or maybe not, but he is my husband, and he does need me. I don't think he could cope without me," I say honestly and realise it's true, he can't. I do everything for him. I sigh before adding, "I made my bed so to speak eighteen years ago, and now I should be lying in it." I know I sound harsh, and he looks desolate for a moment which makes me soften. "I've had a wonderful day, James; it's been like nothing

I've ever had before. Thank you for showing me how it can be," I say from the bottom of my heart.

"I need to see you again," he says.

"I don't know," I hedge. "I can't call in sick all the time, even given my accident-prone nature." He at least manages to smile at that. "Let's just see what happens, shall we?" I say, unwilling or unable to break it off entirely. He kisses me again, and we get into our respective cars. I let him drive off first, because I need to wait until my eyes are less blurry from the tears that have filled them along with the feeling of hopelessness which has washed all through my body. *He doesn't want me*, I think sadly as I remember his reaction to my suggestion of coming to live with him. *Thank God I didn't tell him I love him.*

****

It's a shock to be back home and cooking the evening meal after such a momentous day in my life. Greg and Ethan are thankfully oblivious to me and my strange mood. Ethan has met a new girl he seems to really like and is spending every evening he has with her, unless he is needed for work. He goes out half an hour after we finish dinner. Greg is frantically preparing for his meeting with Annie tomorrow, agonising over his selections. I'm not going with him; it would just be too awkward, and I don't want to mix business and pleasure and lose a perfectly good friend over it. I have seen this routine a number of times over the years now, and I know from bitter experience that Greg's descent into depression and despair after each knock back is longer and harder to recover from. I'm not sure I have the strength to pull us through another, given my own emotionally fragile state at the moment. Greg is back in the shed after dinner, so once I have cleared up I get out my laptop and write. It's bliss to forget my own life for a few short hours and lose myself in the fictional lives of others. It stops me dwelling on James and our day together, although I am slightly sore from all our activities, so he is never far from my mind. I have turned my phone to silent to allow myself to focus on the book, so it's not until I move to take myself to bed, having reached the halfway point in my novel, that I notice the texts waiting for me. I know without looking they are from James. There are three.

Thank you for everything. I can't stop thinking about you.

I am surprised to see he is becoming less cautious with his messages, quickly pressing delete before moving on to the next.

I'm sorry. I know I disappointed you when we spoke by the car. Believe me when I say I'm working on it. I want us to be together

Again, I'm surprised by how unguarded he is becoming. I don't understand what he means about working on us being together. He knows my predicament, so I can't think what he's working on. I scroll quickly to the last text:

I can't forget the feel of you under my hands and around me, the taste of you on my tongue. Don't cut me off Lily J x

I am shocked at the explicit nature of the text and the instant images of us together from this afternoon that form in my mind. The sound of Greg coming back into the house makes me drop my phone, and I am scrambling to retrieve it when he walks into the room.

He senses my discomfort instantly. "You okay? You look funny."

I realise my face is flushed with guilt, and worse, I am aroused. "Yes, fine," I say more sharply than I intend. I try to soften my voice, while palming my phone from sight. "I was just working on my book. I'm at a difficult bit, I need to concentrate."

As an artist, he understands this. "Well I'm heading up to bed now. I want to be fresh for the morning." He looks bright, even hopeful, and my heart sinks to think what another knock back will do to him – to us.

"Okay, see you in the morning. What time are you off?"

"About ten. I want to park, and then I'll have to make a couple of trips with the canvasses." He's given this a lot of thought.

"I hope it goes well," I say softly, and I mean it. He looks at me from the doorway for a moment, and his vulnerability is written all over his face. My instinct is to want to reassure him that it will be okay, that he will be great and they will be bound to want him, but I can't do it. We've been here too many times before, and for his own sake I can't give him false hope. It hurts too much when we have to pick ourselves up off the floor again.

"Thanks," he says, before closing the door as he leaves the room. I sit there feeling sad for a few moments and wonder what is the matter with me before I realise it's probably the most meaningful exchange we've had in weeks. More because of what wasn't said than what was. I look back down at my phone and James' text, wondering how on earth to respond before finally sending my message:

Today was beautiful – it meant the world to me. But I think we have to stop

I turn my phone off, unwilling to talk further, knowing how little it will take for me to cave to him again. And then I sit there and cry for a long time.

Chapter 25

I don't turn my phone on at all the following morning. I can't face it. I help Greg load up the car with all his stuff before getting the bus to the gym. It's still relatively early considering it's the weekend, so the gym is quiet. Stuart isn't on duty; in fact, the only person I see who I know is Pete. At first he tries to avoid me, but I make a point of walking over to where he is.

"Hi," I say awkwardly, trying to judge his mood.

"Hi," he says, looking sheepish. His eyes dart about the room as if he's looking for an escape route.

"Look, I won't hold it against you if you want nothing to do with me," I plough on, determined to say my piece. "I just want to apologise for Greg's treatment of you at the pub. You did nothing wrong, Pete. I like having you as a friend, and I'm sorry my jealous husband can't see that's what it is, but I understand if you don't want the hassle. I'm just mortified that you got sucked in to the carnival of humiliation my life has apparently become," I say, looking at my feet. He's looking at me with more affection than I deserve now.

"It's okay, Lily, I understand. I'd probably be pissed if you were my wife and another bloke came sniffing round. I can't deny I like you, you know that, but I do understand you only want to be friends, and I respect your decision." He pauses, trying to decide what to say next. "He looked mighty pissed off with you, though. Were you okay after we all left?"

"Yeah, fine," I mutter, not wanting to get into that can of worms, but touched by his continued concern for my well-being.

"Just remember you have lots of people who care about you, Lily. If you need me, just call."

I nod before moving away to start my workout, hiding my eyes so he doesn't see the tears threatening to spill out of them, relieved he hasn't cut me off completely. *God, I am pathetic at the moment*, I berate myself. *Any kind words, and I fall to pieces.*

I channel my emotion into exercise for an hour and a half, and by the time I'm finished I feel amazingly better. *Endorphins are the best thing ever, it's official*, I decide. As I make my way home, stopping on the way to pick up some shopping, I wonder how Greg has got on with Annie. I've avoided talking about it with her because I'm so worried that if she hates his stuff it will impact on our friendship. When I walk the last bit home from the bus stop I can see the car is already back. I'm not sure if that's a good or a bad sign, but I've been out for a few hours so it could mean anything.

As I open the door a shout greets me, "Did you get my text?"

"No, my phone's off, and I forgot to turn it back on. Why?"

"She only loved them!" he says appearing out of the kitchen with a big grin on his face. It transforms his face, and I get a glimpse of the man from years ago. "She really liked my newer stuff and wants some pieces for the shop. If they sell, she'll keep featuring more. She's planning an evening event that she needs me to go to, you know to schmooze the punters, let them meet the artist, that sort of thing which she reckons will help if I turn on the charm," he says grinning, his voice full of excitement. "And then the icing on the cake is she's networked with a load of other galleries across the UK and even a couple abroad. She's going to share my details around, and if any of them bite I'll have to go and do the same for their galleries. It might mean a bit of travelling, but the costs should be low if I just stay in B&B's, and it could make all the difference. If the demand picks up then hopefully I'll start being commissioned regularly."

I think my mouth is hanging open at this point. I don't know how many years we dreamed about this happening, and I had honestly given up hope.

"I can't believe it – that's fantastic," I say, overwhelmed by the joy that is radiating off my husband. He grabs my hand and pulls me into a fierce hug, crushing me against his chest until I push away if only to breathe.

"It's going to get a bit busy for me, because I need to get some canvasses finished. She definitely prefers my newer abstracts, so I want to make sure I have a supply ready if she wants them. I left her a few today that she's planning to hang, so we'll see what happens." He's so excited, the change is phenomenal. It's like the small, pink, vulnerable male ego that had been withering inside of him has woken up, stretched and is now beating its proverbial chest. He's standing taller and straighter – he actually looks five years younger than he did when he left the house this morning.

"I'm proud of you," I say softly.

He grins before telling me, "This is the start, Lil, I know it is."

I can only nod as he launches into his plans for the rest of the day which basically involve him painting in the shed for the foreseeable future. When he leaves the house I have to sit down for a moment, unsure of what has just happened. I reach for my bag and retrieve my phone, finally turning it back on for the first time since last night. There is a short delay before the texts start to arrive. There are four altogether, two from James and one each from Annie and Greg. I read Greg's first:

She likes them Lil – I think this is it x

I smile at the joy he exudes, and a part of me is pleased he wanted to share his news with me first. I look at Annie's next:

His work is beautiful sweetie. Really. I know u well enough to know you'll be thinking I'm just doing you a favour. Believe me when I say as much as I love you I would never risk my business. He really is good A x

I feel a warm glow inside, both for Greg's sake that he has earned this chance on his own merit, and for Annie, because she already knows me well enough to want to reassure me. I send her a quick text back.

Thanks Annie, you have made him a very happy man x

Then I steel myself and open up the first of James' texts.

I knew you'd try and push me away again– it won't work

I don't even bother deleting it and just open up the second. It simply says:

Thinking of you, see you soon xx

I resolve to stay firm and not cave in to him, despite the fact that every communication he sends me increases my pulse. I manage not to reply to his text. *I really meant it when I told him we should stop*, I tell myself, and then wonder who I'm trying to persuade. The chance Greg and I have spent the last eighteen years waiting for has finally arrived, and I need to focus on supporting him to make the most of it, not spend all my time running around behind his back seeing another man. *So why can't I stop thinking about him?* I wonder in despair.

I am determined to distract myself by cooking a celebration dinner, texting Adam and Ethan to let them know the good news and asking Adam to call his father tonight so he can tell him about it himself, and for Ethan to be home to share the meal. They are both delighted. It's a small step and may never come to anything, but its significance to our family is huge – the boys know how much this means to their dad and promise to do as asked. I buy a bottle of prosecco so we can have something fizzy to celebrate with at the meal. When Greg finally comes in covered in paint and looking tired but happy, I swiftly pour us both a glass. Ethan arrives home five minutes later, and we sit down together to enjoy the first light-hearted meal since the night before Adam left. Thoughts of James flicker through my mind occasionally; I haven't checked my phone again today. I wonder if he has texted me again, and then I reprimand myself for even thinking about him.

I wash up while listening to Greg chatting happily on the phone to Adam. I wonder how different our lives might have been if this had happened sooner. *Would I have even looked at a man like James if Greg and I had been happier?* Who knew if we would even have been happier if Greg had had more success in his career, and life had not been so hard for us, who knew what it was that had made our marriage become so hard?

I can feel the desire to look at my phone building in me. I have suppressed it for a couple of hours now, but I can't resist any longer, rummaging in my bag until I find it. When there's no message my stomach drops, and I feel sick. *What if I have chased him off for good?* I worry inwardly and then berate myself for caving so soon. My fingers hover over the buttons, but I force myself to put it back in my bag and finish wiping the sides. Ethan has gone out with his girlfriend again – he seems surprisingly serious about her – so Greg and I are alone again as ever these days. When he comes into the kitchen I think at first it's to make his way down to the shed for more time painting, but he walks over to me instead and asks if I am nearly finished. He stands watching while I sweep the floor and then when I am done takes me by the hand and leads me up the stairs.

When we reach our room I walk to the window to close the curtains. There's a Mercedes parked in the road outside that makes me pause for a moment because we don't exactly live in an area where Mercedes are a common sight. I feel Greg step up behind me and put his arms around my waist, pulling me in to him, and I resist for a moment, closing the curtains before turning in his arms to face him. He kisses me gently and I close my eyes, willing my body to respond, but all I seem to see is James' face in my mind. Angry with myself, I kiss Greg more forcefully, and he takes it as a sign and moves me to the bed. I can see he's already aroused. We strip ourselves of our clothes and then move back together to resume our touching and kissing. I really want to feel something. I really want to be aroused and forget James and what he does to me, but my body remains resolutely unaffected. When Greg enters me my body seems cold and dry compared to my experience of the day before. Somehow knowing what it can be like makes this experience one hundred times worse. Greg is lost in the moment as ever, relentlessly pushing on towards his goal, while I lie there wondering what this means for me, for us. Can I do this for the rest of my life? Greg is grunting now, the precursor to his orgasm. The final thrusts are accompanied by a groan as he collapses over me, swiftly pulling out and leaving a trail of semen over my thigh. I shudder and hope he didn't notice. I feel like a whore must feel as I allow my body to be used as a receptacle for his sperm with no emotional involvement on my part – we barely even kissed. It's like night and day when I compare my experience with Greg to my experience with James. I know Greg cares for me in his own way, but I just don't know if it's enough anymore, and I'm not sure what it's all going to mean for Greg and me or for our marriage.

Chapter 26

The urge to text James is now so strong I don't know how I've managed to hold out for so long. I have become completely phone-obsessed, spending long minutes gazing at it, just willing him to text me. It's making me pretty miserable company; I am being horrible to patients and staff at work as well as Greg and Ethan. Greg is on such a high that he barely notices my moods, but Ethan has virtually moved in with his girlfriend – just to get away from me, I suspect, as I have been such a cow to live with. I know I'm doing it, but I just can't seem to help myself. The only thing that is keeping me going is I keep seeing Mercedes cars everywhere I go and have persuaded my deluded mind that James is watching me from afar, believing he still cares about me. I can't believe he has given up on me so easily; in my darkest moments I imagine him with another woman in his arms, and mostly they look like Sarah from the Peak District trip. I keep hoping I will bump into him at the gym – I have been keeping to my usual schedule after work in the hopes he will do what he said he did last time, but so far he has been noticeably absent. Even Annie and Emma noticed my flagging spirits, despite the news about Greg, when we met at the pub last night. Emma kept looking at me with a worried expression, while Annie looked at me more knowingly. I have a feeling Stuart is aware of some of what was going on between James and me and may have said something to Annie about us. I love her for not judging me. On a rare good note, things at the gallery are going well, with Annie reporting a positive buzz around Greg's work. He is building up to the evening event that will be featuring a selection of up and coming artists from the area, so I have hardly seen him the last couple of days.

As I walk towards the entrance to the gym I automatically scan the car park, looking for the Mercedes. I can't see it, and my spirits flag immediately. I slump my shoulders and throw my stuff down in the changing room, swiftly changing out of my work clothes, keen to get on with the workout.

I am in dire need of some shopping time – my clothes are now hanging off me because of my weight loss, which has only accelerated while I haven't seen James. I can't summon any sort of appetite at the moment, Greg is starting to give me a hard time about it at home and Annie and Emma have independently of each other asked if I'm eating enough. I step out of the changing room, totally miss the step and fall forwards, smacking my head on the pot plant to the side. Pete happens to be using the equipment close by, sees me and comes running over to see if I'm okay, but I'm too stunned for a moment and can't speak. He puts his arm around me and tries to help me to my feet, which proves to be more of a challenge than you might think. I have eventually managed to stand, leaning heavily on Pete, and am finally able to take in the extent of the witnesses to my most recent humiliation, only to look straight into a pair of very angry-looking bright blue eyes.

I think I actually gasp, and my legs give way again. James moves faster than Pete, sweeping in and lifting me into his arms, casting a throwaway comment over his shoulder to Pete, who is left just standing there gaping at us.

"Don't worry, mate, I've got her now," he says as he makes his way to the reception desk, where Stuart watches our approach with a bemused expression on his face.

"I swear to God, Lily, I've never restocked the first-aid kit so many times in the whole time I've worked here, as I have since you joined," Stuart says. "I've actually booked onto a refresher first aid course next week just because I'm terrified what you might do next. I think you're going to have a lump the size of an egg on your head from that wallop, I'll go and get the ice pack."

He disappears into the back office, leaving James and me sitting on the chairs by reception. I am gazing at him like I can't believe he's really here. I'm dying to touch him, and my hand actually moves towards his face before I realise where I am and what I'm doing. James is looking at me with a bemused expression on his face.

"I'm sorry," I eventually manage to say.

"So you should be," he says, his voice sounding gruff. "I'm very angry with you."

I'm taken aback by his directness and pull away from him, feeling mortified, but he grabs my arm and pulls me back into his chest, looking at me intently before continuing: "I don't know what to be more angry about, actually; the fact you just managed to fall over and injure yourself again – I swear to God, Lily, you are not safe to leave on your own; the fact you look like you haven't eaten since the last time I saw you or the fact that the first time I do see you in days, there is another man holding you in his arms."

I'm confused for a moment until I realise he means Pete, which makes me smile. "I promise you, Lily, if you hadn't collapsed and needed me to catch you, I was about to punch his lights out for putting his hands on you," he growls, and my heart soars to hear it. Stuart returns with the ice pack and effectively puts an end to our discussion, but I can't get rid of the happy smile that seems to be occupying my face for the first time since I last saw James. I can only imagine Stuart thinks I'm concussed. The pair of them sit there discussing my catalogue of my mishaps since they met me, while I hold the ice pack to my head, and for once I don't care; I'm just basking in the pleasure of being near him again.

"I don't think you should work out today, Lily," Stuart is saying. "This lump is huge. If you get any nausea or feel sleepy at all, you really need to go to the hospital and get it checked out."

James swiftly agrees, offering to see me home if I get my stuff from the changing room. I jump at the chance to be alone with him again. Pete rushes over when he sees me leaving to check I'm okay, and I giggle when I catch sight of James scowling at Pete as he waits for me by the door. I spend a couple of minute explaining I'm fine, just not in the mood to work out with the thumping headache I have now, and mentioning James has offered to drive me home. He takes a quick look at the glowering James at the door and swiftly excuses himself, wishing me well. *Poor Pete*, I think, *he's continually being scowled at by the men in my life.*

When we are finally in the car alone together, James turns to me. "Do you mind if we take a little detour before I take you home? Are you feeling well enough?"

"I feel fine. I, I'd like that," I say. He drives for about ten minutes and pulls into a gated driveway in one of the best roads in the area. I just know this has to be his house as I take in the enormous lump of property. Our different circumstances couldn't be more obvious, I realise as I gaze at my surroundings. He stops the car and immediately pulls me into his arms, pressing his lips gently to my own. He's so gentle, as if he's worried he might hurt me. My hands move into his hair, holding him to me as I breathe the essence of him in again like an alcoholic let into a pub for the first time since they got out of rehab.

"Come on," he says, "let me make you a coffee." He jumps out of the car, waiting for me to join him, and then leads me into the house. I can hardly look at the surroundings now; I can't seem to take my eyes off him, and I think he's the same with me. He puts the coffee machine on, and we sit beside each other, touching whenever possible, drinking each other in with our eyes as we wait for the coffee to brew.

"I'm sorry," I say again finally.

"Don't be. I understand," he says gently. "Tell me what happened."

"I don't know," I say honestly, "the day we had was so beautiful. The time I spent with you was such a contrast to my normal life," I try to explain. "I just couldn't see how it could continue when I got home and tried to get on with normality. I decided I couldn't think about leaving Greg because I knew he couldn't survive without me. I thought I could push my own needs away, that I was being selfish, but I didn't realise how deep my feelings are. I couldn't just push my thoughts of you away. Every time he touches me, I only know it's not you, and I want it to be you." I sob slightly, terrified he'll reject me.

"Oh, Lily," he says, pulling me to his chest, "I don't want him to touch you either. It kills me to think of him with you. We will find a way through this, I have to believe we can," he says fiercely. He kisses me then, and I am lost to him once more. My memories of him were not a patch on the reality. My body responds instantly, and I only know I want him. I start to pull at his clothes, desperate to feel the touch of his skin. He's doing the same, his hand reaching up under my gym top to grasp my breast through my sports bra. It's still not enough for me. I don't want to waste time, I just want to feel him inside me, and I reach for his fly to release him.

"Are you sure you're well enough?" he gasps while I bend to remove my leggings. I don't speak, just move to his chair and climb onto his lap. I raise myself up until I am high enough to enable him access. There is no preamble, and I don't need it. I've been wet and wanting him since I got in the car. In one slow move he pulls me down onto him, and I groan in satisfaction when I feel him filling me entirely.

"You are mine, Lily, you will only be mine," he tells me again and again as he moves within me, and in that moment I believe him. He kisses me then, and it feels as if we are joined, as if we are becoming one person. I think if I could crawl inside his body, I would probably try.

His thrusts become more urgent as he holds my hips and moves me above him – I can feel he is staking his claim, and I'm glad, I want him to. I don't want anyone else to touch me. The realisation thrills me, and I come whispering the words I have been holding back from him, "I love you", and I do. It seems to push him over the edge too, as he thrusts against me the last few times before spilling into me. We sit there for a few moments, me straddling his lap with him still inside me, trying to catch our breath, until he pulls back slightly looks at me directly in the eye and says:

"I love you too."

Chapter 27

We reassemble ourselves eventually, and he finally makes the coffee he promised. We sit looking at each other in silence for a while, both maybe realising that somehow we have tipped over into something new now, something more profound and meaningful than the sexual relationship I thought I was having at first. I know I have some tough decisions to make, but the last few days have shown me I can't just pretend I haven't changed at some fundamental level. It is impossible to go back to the way I was before, so now I have to move forward and make decisions about what that direction should be.

"How's your head?" he asks, looking intently at the bump on my forehead. A trip to the bathroom had shown me it was massive and I was going to be subjected to continual ridicule for the next week or so as a result. It actually doesn't hurt too badly now.

"It's fine," I smile. "Nice place," I say, finally taking in my surroundings. The kitchen breakfast room we are sitting in is nearly as large as the whole ground floor of our house and fitted with every kind of appliance you can imagine.

"Thanks," he says, and I see him grimace. "We need to talk," he says, and he seems uncomfortable.

"I know," I say, unable to shake the feeling that I don't think I'm going to like what he has to say. I look at my watch and realise I have already been gone for nearly three hours. I really need to get home. I also want to get my own head straight before we talk. "I want to talk too, but I don't think now's the right time. I need to get back, but I want to see you... if that's still okay with you?"

"More than okay. In fact, I insist," he smiles. "You need to know, I meant what I said Lily. This means something important to me. I'm not going anywhere; I need you in my life." He runs his fingers through his hair like he's anxious, and I immediately want to soothe him. I stand up and move to him, cupping his face gently in my hands as I kiss him, before pulling back.

"I know, and I feel the same. I'll text you some times, and we can talk then. It'll be okay, we'll be okay," I say with certainty.

He nods, and we kiss again before he takes me back to his car. I insist he drive me back to the gym so I can collect my own car; I feel fine to drive now, and it will just be easier than having to find my way back to pick it up some other time. James seems quieter since we spoke at the house. I understand; we have passed a significant point in our relationship in such a very short time, and yet somehow I feel like he's weaved himself into my DNA. It's both scary and exciting, but I know we have some difficult times ahead, whatever we decide to do.

We don't kiss when we get to the car park in case someone sees us, but he holds my hand, and everything I need is right there in his eyes.

"I'll text you," I promise again. He just nods and squeezes my hand tighter.

Alone in my car after I leave him, I realise how bad I have it. When I am away from him now, it feels as though there is a huge hole in my life; it's almost physically cold without him beside me. On the plus side I'm actually feeling stronger mentally now. I feel like I have finally made some decisions, that I am taking control of my own destiny, whatever the outcome. I know with complete certainty I love James, and whatever the outcome of our relationship, I can only rejoice in the love both physical and emotional he has shown me it is possible to have. I also know Greg and my marriage do not give me those things. I may have once loved him, but that changed to duty and responsibility a long time ago, and now that is no longer enough for me. As selfish as it may seem to many people, now the boys are independent, I want more from my life. I know I will need to end my marriage whatever happens with James and me. It is not fair to deceive Greg, and for the first time it feels as though Greg will have the strength to stand on his own feet in life, giving me permission to go. My sense of responsibility made me feel I needed to look after

Greg too, but now that his career is on the up he will need me less.

The last thing I know is that it is time for me to be independent. I need to be able to do this on my own and not rely on James for the strength. It is too soon to put that responsibility on him or our burgeoning relationship. The decision about my marriage has to be about me and Greg alone. Having made those decisions, I feel empowered and somehow excited. I know it can't happen overnight, I need to give Greg the chance to spread his wings, but I sense it will be soon.

When I get home Greg is in his shed as ever, so I sit down to write for the evening. The most difficult part of the decisions I have made is I know I don't want sex with Greg again. I don't want to be used in that way, so intimately. It is too precious to give that part of me to someone without the right emotional connection. I can't allow my body to be used that way. I know it will be hard, and Greg won't understand, but in the short term I determine to spend the nights writing. Greg is so distracted with his work at the moment we are barely having sex anyway, so it shouldn't be too big an issue before I tell him of my decision. I figure I probably have a couple of months in which to organise myself and think about how we will part, where I will go, how I will live. Greg will hate me, and I know I will probably deserve his hatred, but I hope we can move beyond it and find friendship again in the future, mostly for the sake of the boys. *Perhaps I'm being selfish wanting the best of both worlds.*

****

The next week passes quickly, and before I really know where I am, it is the evening of the gallery event. Greg is nervous, and Ethan and I are walking on eggshells around him, not wanting to make him worse. I have spoken to James every day since we last saw each other, and we text each other several times a day, but we haven't managed to sort out a date to meet. I told him I wanted to get the gallery evening over first, but I can tell he's getting impatient with me now. I dress carefully for the evening in a new black pencil skirt with an emerald green silk blouse that plunges lower than my usual and shows off my impressive cleavage. I still haven't bought myself any hair straighteners, but I manage to control my frizzy mop into some more orderly curls for once. The overall effect when I don my heels is pleasing, despite the purple bruise that's still in evidence on my forehead. The small amount of mascara and lip gloss I am wearing distract from it a little at least. I can finally admit to myself, as I take in my reflection in the mirror, that I look slim – I actually never thought I would see the day where I really believed that about myself. I look at my watch and realise the taxi is due any minute. Greg has already gone to the gallery to help set up and be there for the early guests, while Ethan and I are coming along a bit later for moral support. Emma has also promised to pop in, despite the fact she is getting close now to her due date. I make my way carefully down the stairs, endeavouring not to trip and add to my collection of bruises. Ethan hears me coming and gets up from the settee where he's been watching television while waiting for me. He looks shocked as he takes in my appearance.

"Do I look okay?" I ask anxiously, worried his expression means I look like mutton dressed as lamb.

"You look great, mum. I'm shocked to say you actually look hot." I blush, taken aback by this unexpected compliment. "I'm not sure I can cope with my mum being attractive," he adds. "I certainly don't think dad will be able to." His comment sours my mood slightly and makes me worry Greg won't like it, but it's too late to change now.

"Come on," I insist, dragging him behind me out the door to where the taxi is waiting. Because Greg took the car, Ethan and I can at least have a drink. "You look nice too, by the way," I add as we get in and give directions for where we're going.

"Feels like I'm going to work," he grumbles, and I can see why because he's dressed in his work trousers and a white shirt. "Sarah might pop in tonight," he mentions offhandedly.

"Your girlfriend Sarah?" I say surprised. He's been keeping her at arm's length from Greg and me, so she must be serious.

"The very one," he confirms.

"Well, it'll be nice to meet her at last."

"Please don't embarrass me, mum," he groans. "I really like her."

"Give me some credit; I wouldn't dream of it," I reply, trying not to show my amusement at how anxious he is at the prospect of his girlfriend meeting his mum. It also makes me feel incredibly old.

When we pull up outside the gallery we can see a good crowd has already arrived, and we are relatively late. I can see Greg chatting to a group of people, smiling and laughing. It's amazing to see the transformation in him. I'm glad he's happy. Ethan helps me out the car and pays the driver, and we make our way inside. I spot Annie instantly, as she's hard to miss, and she makes her way over as soon as she is able. Ethan's eyes nearly fall out of his head when he takes her in. I distract him by asking him to fetch us all something to drink; it's easier than having to avoid trying to maintain a conversation while he stands there gawping at Annie.

"How's it going?" I ask Annie.

"Really, really well," she assures me. "Everyone loves his work. I keep telling you it's really good – have you even looked at it recently?" she asks. In truth I haven't, and I tell her as much. It's different when you live with an artist somehow.

"He's already sold several pieces," she tells me, and I'm shocked.

"Well, that's good isn't it?" I ask.

"That's excellent; not all the others have," she says, pointing out some of the others who are stood in smaller clusters. When Ethan finally rejoins us with three drinks in hand, we make our way over to Greg. He is surrounded by people as we approach him. He looks up and frowns as he notices us. I sense he's reluctant to be disturbed by us, wanting to immerse himself in his role as artist, not be dragged back to the humdrum husband-and-father existence. In the past I might have found it hurtful, but now I understand. I'm actually happy for him. We wait patiently, chatting together and laughing at some of the more eccentric characters around while he finishes with the current group. Eventually he comes over.

"Lily, you're looking lovely," he says, taking in my appearance. But he accompanies the compliment with a frown before moving in to give me a chaste peck on the cheek, and I can't help but get the feeling he would have been happier if I had turned up dressed in my slacks and a cardigan. I take a moment to get a look at his work for the first time, and I have to say I am gobsmacked. It really is beautiful. There is a darkness in the abstract paintings, enhanced by flashes of colour, like emotions. They display so much feeling, so much of his pain in such a raw honesty, that I am speechless for a few moments, overwhelmed by both the beauty and the feeling of sadness they evoke in me. I had no idea.

"Greg, they're stunning, but when did your work become so dark?" I eventually manage to say, my voice choked with emotion.

"Thank you," he says quietly, but his face twists in an expression that resembles pain, and I don't know why. Ethan is oblivious to the undercurrent between us and is chattering on about the work, genuinely impressed by his dad's efforts. Greg is delighted by his interest and approval, I can tell, and seems to enjoy pointing out the various aspects and elements in his composition. I stand there watching them together, unable to shake the sadness that is overwhelming me.

"You okay?" Annie asks quietly.

"Yes," I whisper, swallowing down the lump that has formed in my throat. "They are so good. I had no idea," I say, ashamed to admit my lack of awareness at what stunning work the man I live with, and am married to, has been producing.

"They are good," she agrees. "If I were a betting person I'd say his future is bright; there's been a lot of interest from the press in his work, and several other galleries from my network want to show him. He's going to be a very busy man for the foreseeable future."

"I'm glad," I say honestly, looking over to where Greg is standing talking to someone, with Ethan watching on.

Annie has to move on and circulate, so I stand alone for a bit looking at some of the other pieces, none of which are a patch on Greg's. I hear Emma's little voice at my shoulder saying, "Hey sweetie," and I turn to smile at her. "You're looking pretty fine, lady," she says sweeping her gaze up and down my body. "I remember when I used to have a waist," she says sadly. I look at her bump (which now seems to almost engulf her) and laugh, trying to reassure her that she will again soon be able to wear trousers and skirts without elastic waists. "His work's lovely," she says, nodding in Greg's direction.

"It is, isn't it," I agree. "Do you know I had no idea, Em," I say sadly. "We live in the same house but we're virtual strangers now. How does that happen?"

"I don't know, Lil, but you've always done your best for them. I don't think you should beat yourself up," she says, hugging me as much as she is able given the large bump between us. I'm grateful to have a friend who always takes my side no matter what. We stand chatting about nothing in particular until I get a sense someone is watching me. I turn only to immediately see James over on the other side of the room. He's heading straight for us. I'm torn between being delighted he's here in front of me, having not seen him for a week, and horror that James and Greg are in the same room.

He looks strangely determined as he walks towards us, his eyes on me. I hear Emma whistle under her breath. As he gets to where we're standing he bends to kiss my cheek, like any acquaintance might within the art world, but I instantly blush. Emma doesn't miss a thing.

"Hello, Lily, it's lovely to see you," he says politely.

"James, I didn't know you were coming. Lovely to see you too. This is Emma, my best friend since college."

He holds a hand out to Emma and shakes hers warmly, saying, "It's a real pleasure to meet you, Emma. Lily speaks of you very highly." I see Emma blush under the intensity of his gaze and marvel again that this incredible man who can seemingly melt any woman is currently into me.

"I remember seeing you at the coach when I picked up Lil," I hear Emma saying – *Jeez, does this girl miss nothing?* I wonder – "What brings you to the gallery this evening?" For the life of me I have no idea what he's going to say. I'd kind of like to know myself.

"I'm a collector," he explains. "I come to a lot of Annie's new artist evenings. She's got a great eye, and I've picked up a number of pieces from artists who have since gone on to make names for themselves. It's been a great investment," he smiles. *Of course*, I think, deflated now, *he's not here for me, he's here for the art.* I vaguely recall the artwork on the walls of the rooms I saw in his house.

Emma's smiling at him, and I distantly hear them discussing various artists he's collected. I can tell by the occasional gasps she makes that Emma's impressed by what she's hearing, but I can only seem to gaze at him, until I hear Emma saying, "Isn't that right, Lily?"

"I'm sorry," I say apologetically, "what were you saying?" She gives me a smug grin that tells me she sees straight through me and my goo-goo eyes at James.

"Just that we all keep saying you need to eat a bit more now you've lost so much weight."

They were? Shit, when did the conversation move on? I wonder. James is looking at me fondly while they wait for me to say something.

"Well, I'm about the right weight for my height now," I mutter, hating being the centre of attention.

"I keep telling her she's getting scrawny," I hear Greg's voice behind me say, as I feel his arm slip around my waist in a rare display of public affection. Ethan joins the group behind him. My eyes flash to James, and I see his scorching glare focused on Greg's arm. I'm panicking to have them both standing here together, at a complete loss for words.

It's my beloved Emma that steps in to save the day. "Well she's certainly looking particularly lovely this evening. To Lily," she says, raising her glass to me. There are echoes of "Lily" from James and Greg and "mum" from Ethan.

"We haven't met before, have we?" Greg says, looking at James.

"No. James Lattimer," James says smoothly, putting out a hand for Greg to shake with the natural confidence of a man born to money.

"Greg Lambert," Greg says, shaking it. The two men seem to be sizing each other up, before Greg says, "How do you know my wife?" I don't miss the possessive choice of words he uses, and I'm not sure if anyone else does either.

"We met on a walking trip to the Peaks. Lily was sharing with Annie," he says, nodding his head towards the place where Annie is standing. She's looking over at us anxiously when we all lift our heads to look at her. I give her a small smile which she returns in kind, but James is speaking again which drags my attention back to the living nightmare I have found myself in. He's explaining what brought him here this evening, the same as he did with Emma. Before I know it James and Greg have moved away with Ethan hot on their tail to look at Greg's work. I watch them depart.

My expression must describe some of the horror I'm feeling because Emma puts a hand on my arm to steady me. "Hold it together, Lily," she says quietly. I look at her and she just raises an eyebrow. "It's written all over your face, sweetie, and if I can see it, then so can Greg. You have got to get a grip; this is neither the time nor the place for a scene." I nod to let her know I understand, and then take a long drink. Annie moves to join us, glancing anxiously over at Greg and James.

"Well, shit, Lily," she says. Emma snorts her orange juice out through her nose, and even I can't help breaking out a smile. It kind of sums up the situation, really.

"I think you and I need to have a talk," Emma says sternly.

"Ooo, can I come?" Annie says, jumping up and down on the spot, which makes us all smile again. I love these girls so much for helping me smile at a time of such stress.

The moment is broken by Ethan tapping me on the shoulder. "Mum, I'd like to introduce you to Sarah," he says. I turn quickly with a big welcoming smile on my face, only to feel it freeze as I find myself eyeball to eyeball with queen bitch Sarah from the Peaks trip. Queen bitch Sarah who was all over James, if I recall correctly. Ethan is looking at me waiting for a response as I try to reassemble my scattered wits once again into a response that doesn't sound like: 'get your slutty claws away from my son, oh and James, for that matter'.

"Sarah," I say, "what a surprise, it's so nice to see you again." To be fair she looks equally pained at the situation she's found herself in.

"Do you know each other?" Ethan asks, surprised by our exchange.

"Yes, we met on the Peaks walking trip, when you were doing your training," I manage to say. Sarah is scowling at me now, perhaps concerned I might start to describe her behaviour with some of the men on the trip once James made his lack of interest known. *How old is she, anyway*, I wonder, *to be going after James one minute and then Ethan, my beautiful eighteen-year-old son, the next?* I'm trying to wrack my brain for something else polite to say that isn't: *how old are you, anyway?* when once again Greg comes up behind me,

"That must have been one hell of a trip to the Peak district," he says to no one in particular. "Hello, Sarah, I'm Greg – Ethan's dad, it's nice to finally meet you." Sarah shakes his hand and starts to flatter him over the quality of his paintings while Ethan looks on like an adoring puppy dog. I turn to Annie, whose expression at this point looks as pained as mine must.

"Do you have a bathroom I can use?"

"Sure," she says, "through the door along the corridor, then it's the second on your right." I nod gratefully before making my way over. I sit in the bathroom with my head resting on my hands, wondering how it is I am participating in this comedy of errors. *It's karma*, I decide, before I wipe my face and steel myself to engage in act two of the unfolding farce.

When I exit the bathroom it's to find James leaning against the wall waiting for me. He pulls me towards him. "Not here,"

I despair, wishing my body weren't moving closer to him at the same time as I'm trying to tell him not to.

"You look so fucking beautiful tonight, Lily," he murmurs into my hair. "I wish you were coming home with me. I want you so much." He kisses me then, and I forget everything but him. When he finally lets me go, I feel bereft. "Will you be at the gym tomorrow?" he asks.

"Yes," I croak.

"Bring some dates," he instructs. I nod and watch him stride along the corridor and out the door. When I follow a couple of minutes after, the room is still abuzz. Greg is talking to some new people while James seems to have left. I sigh with relief as I look for Emma only to find Sarah staring at me with a smug expression on her face. *Shit, she knows*, I think. The question is what is she going to do about it?

Chapter 28

I wake late the next day. The rest of the evening had been relatively uneventful. Emma had left pretty much straightaway, claiming tiredness but promising to call me, which left me to stand around like a spare part on my own for another hour or so while Greg spoke to his admirers and Annie worked the crowd on behalf of her artists. Greg had already sold every piece on display, which was fantastic, and Annie had a list of people interested in seeing other pieces. They had all gone for a drink after the gallery closed, but I had made my excuses and got a cab home, unable to face more forced conversation. Ethan and Sarah had already left to go wherever the younger people were hanging out these days, but not before Sarah gave me yet another of her sly smiles. I know my choices are closing in on me, but I just need a little longer.

Greg is already painting when I stick my head around the shed door to let him know I'm going to the gym.

"Well done again for last night," I say, "it was wonderful."

"It was, wasn't it?" he agrees with a smile. "I've been invited to exhibit up in Harrogate next weekend," he informs me. "It's late notice, but I don't want to turn it down while my stock is high. Do you mind if I go? I'll go up Friday and come back Sunday morning."

"No," I say, surprised at the suddenness of his rise in fortune. It's all happening so fast. "I think it's great for you, and I couldn't be more pleased, so you must do whatever you need to in order to make the most of this opportunity."

"Thank you," he says, coming over to me and giving me a hug. "Maybe I'll be able to take you on a holiday for the first time ever," he says with a wry smile.

"Maybe," I smile sadly, knowing it's not going to happen. He looks at me with his head to one side for a moment, before he walks back to his easel and picks up his brush again. I know I've lost him again to his first love.

When I get to the gym I change and start my workout, my head shooting up every time I hear the door open. The minute James arrives, his eyes find mine and hold my gaze. He looks stunning in his tracksuit bottoms, which are hanging low on his hips, and t-shirt tight over his toned abdomen. I can't believe how strong the urge is to touch him. He starts his workout, but we can't stop looking at each other. He is fucking me with his eyes, and my body is responding. I want to get my own back so I deliberately make every move as erotic as I can, arching my back and spreading my thighs as if to stretch and pressing my chest out. The pec dec is particularly successful judging by the obvious response I see bulging in his trousers as I sit there with my legs open and my bust pushed out. I look at him and bite my lip, and I swear I hear him groan. When I finally finish I head for the changing room only to feel someone come up fast behind me, grab my waist and push me into the sunbed room, just to the side. I hear the sound of the door locking behind me and turn slowly to face him.

"Don't start what you can't finish," he warns as he stalks towards me.

"I don't know what you mean," I answer coyly, looking up at him as he reaches me.

"Don't get cute with me, Lily Lambert," he says as he pushes me up against the wall, his body hard in every way against me, grinding against me so I am under no misconceptions about what he wants. His hands are on me now, touching my breasts and teasing the nipples through the Lycra of my top, while his mouth claims mine and I respond with equal passion. We're pulling at each other's clothes, sweaty and panting. This is not going to take long, and I don't care. I just want him now. He pulls my leggings off and hoists me onto his hips, bracing my back against the wall. Next thing I know, he's released himself from his tracksuit bottoms and he's pushing into me. It's animalistic raw sex, and I love it, as I feel the same urgency in him as I'm feeling in me. When he bites my shoulder, the pain is exquisite and the combination of ecstasy and pain pushes me to orgasm, my muscles clenching around him until he loses control himself and collapses against me. My head rests on his shoulder as he turns so his back's against the wall and slides us gently to the floor.

"God, Lily," he says when he finally catches his breath, "what are you doing to me? I can't stop thinking about you and wanting you. Last night nearly drove me crazy, seeing him touch you. I was ready to do something crazy, like kiss you in front of everyone just to make sure they all knew you're mine, and that they should keep their hands and eyes to themselves. Did you have to dress so fucking sexily when I wasn't able to touch you?" he berates me.

"I haven't had sex with him since I last slept with you," I reassure him, resting my forehead against his. He looks at me, and I see a vulnerability he doesn't normally display.

"Really?"

"Really. I only want you too," I say simply. He kisses me then and hugs me tight for a long while.

"You do smell, though," he says eventually.

"You're fairly ripe yourself," I say, elbowing him in the ribs. We stand and pull our clothes back into position. "I hope no one was waiting to use this room."

"Well, you look flushed enough to have been on the sunbed," he observes. I blush, and he laughs. "Come on," he says and grabs my hand. "Wait for me outside," he instructs as he unlocks the door and pushes me towards the changing rooms. I glance around, only catching sight of some blonde hair before I'm immersed in the gloomy depths of the changing room. I stand in the shower, letting the water run over my body, touching myself and remembering his hands on me only moments ago. I wish he were here with me now. Then thoughts of him standing waiting for me outside make me hurry to wash myself, and I dress in record time. When I leave the changing room, I run straight into Sarah, who is leaning against the wall with her arms folded over her chest.

"Hi," I say, determined to be friendly, "did you have a nice time yesterday evening?"

"Yes, thanks," she says sarcastically, "did you?" and just the way she's looking at me with that smug tone convinces me she knows exactly what's going on with James.

"See you soon," I say as nonchalantly as I can before walking out to the reception. It feels like a big clock is ticking in my head, and I know time is running out. James is leaning against the wall in one of the archways as I exit, moving to join me as soon as he sees me.

"So when are you free?" he asks immediately as we walk towards our cars. I see he has parked next to me.

"Greg is going away Friday until Sunday morning, this weekend," I tell him, "if any of that is any good for you?" He looks delighted.

"All of it, please. I'll take you away for a weekend."

"You don't have to do that. I'd be happy just to come to your house."

"I know, but I want to. Please let me." He looks so earnest and excited at the prospect of a weekend together that I can't resist him and relent immediately.

"Okay, but let me contribute?" I ask.

"Don't be ridiculous," he says dismissively, "if I want to take you away, then I want to pay for it. I don't want to argue about money. Let me look after you; it gives me pleasure to do so," he insists.

I give in to him as ever, only insisting we can't leave until after my shift at work, which makes him pout because it limits how far we can travel; but eventually he accepts, and we separate to get into our own cars. I haven't even pulled out the parking space when my phone bleeps with a text. A quick look shows it to be from James. All it says is:

I can't wait

I smile at his obvious excitement, but inside my head the ticking clock is getting louder all the time.

Chapter 29

I don't see anything of Greg at all; he is like a man possessed with his painting now. In turn I am spending all my time writing whenever I am not at work or the gym. The book is nearly finished, which indicates just how many nights I have worked through in order to avoid sex with Greg. I know this burning the candle at both ends will lead to me crashing and burning soon, but I need to finish the book, and I want to do it before my world crashes down. It's going to happen soon... I can feel it.

The only break in my writing is for a trip to the pub to meet Annie and Emma. They are both already there when I walk in, and as I make my way over to them I'm reminded of how I felt when I went to my first job interview, desperate for approval and acceptance. After the usual drink-collecting courtesies from the typically unhelpful Brian, I am finally at the table opposite the pair of them.

"So what's happening with James, then, Lil?" Annie asks in her usual direct style.

"What makes you think anything is?" I ask, more because I'm intrigued to hear what they think they know than because I'm trying to be deliberately evasive.

"Lily, he practically grabbed Greg's hand off you at the gallery the other night in between the pair of you eye-fucking each other the rest of the time. How long has it been going on? Since the Peaks?" I nod, and Emma gasps.

"What are you going to do?" she asks, wide-eyed. "Does Greg know?" I decide honesty is as ever the best policy, something I seem to have forgotten over recent months.

"What I am going to do is leave Greg," I say with certainty.

Emma gasps again. "But you've hardly had a chance to get to know him! Are you sure he's worth walking out of an eighteen-year relationship for?"

I have to say I'm surprised Emma is defending my marriage to Greg, considering how down on him she's been over the years. Annie is just listening now and watching my face.

I sigh and lay my cards on the table. "I'm leaving Greg because my marriage to him is empty in every sense of the word. I have fulfilled my responsibilities as a parent, and now the kids are off, doing their own thing, I just want to have a chance to do my own thing too. I'm not planning to move in with James, although I do care about him, and I really want to see what happens with us. I'm going to find somewhere to rent and be on my own for a bit and just see what life brings." Emma's mouth is now fully open as I continue. "You may well think I'm mad, but I think madness would be living some sort of half-life until I die because I don't have the courage to do something different. The only thing that has held me there for so long has been the fact Greg needed me to look after him, but you've changed that," I say, looking at Annie.

"I've been waiting until I could leave knowing that he would be okay, and now he is – okay, I mean, better than okay. I've never seen him so happy. He may be upset about me for a while, but I know he will be alright in the longer term." I pause, waiting for their judgement.

"I'm proud of you, honey," Annie says, squeezing my arm. "I think you're doing the right thing, and I'm here if you need me." I lean over and hug her, my cheeks wet with tears.

Emma joins the hug, whispering: "I love you, Lil. I just want you to be happy."

"Me too," I say with a little sob, which just starts Emma off big time. "We need to stop this," I eventually say, "Brian must definitely have a hard-on over there behind the bar, watching this girl-on-girl action." I nod over to where he's standing, not taking his eyes off us. That makes them both laugh, in between making fake retching sounds at the thought of Brian with an erection.

"So, when are you going to tell him?" Annie asks, the mood sobering again.

"I'm not sure. After Christmas sometime, I think, I need to find a room to rent. Money's going to be tight for a bit because I'll still need to help with the mortgage, but hopefully now Greg's got some money coming in, things will be a bit easier."

"You're a good person, Lily," Emma says. "He's lucky to have had you."

"Is he?" I wonder. "I cheated on him, Em, and I'm not proud of it. Whatever his faults, he didn't deserve that. It's bad karma."

"So what about this James, then? What's he like, apart from the obvious?"

"The obvious?" I ask.

"Drop-dead gorgeous, of course," she laughs. I can't deny he is.

"He's wonderful," I say simply. "He's generous and kind and passionate, and he's shown me a whole new side to the world that I didn't believe existed. I still can't believe he wants me too," I whisper.

"Don't be ridiculous," they say in unison and laugh.

"Have you seen yourself recently? You're stunning. At the gallery there wasn't a man in the room that wasn't looking at you, Lil," Annie adds. "Greg didn't like it, though. Don't assume he's going to take this breakup well, sweetie." I know she's right. "To be fair, Lily, you didn't stand a chance with James. He wanted you bad, woman, all those panty-combusting looks he was giving you all the time. I did try to warn you."

"You did," I agree, "but I can't regret it. I feel alive again."

"But is he a good person?" Emma demands of Annie. "Is he good enough for Lil?"

I don't think I could love my friend more if I tried. She always looks out for me, and I thank God every day she is my friend. Annie's still thinking about the question, and I'm intrigued to hear what she has to say.

"I don't know him well enough to judge, Em. What I've seen of him round Lily makes me think he genuinely cares about her, and judging by what Stuart tells me he's picked her up off the gym floor enough times when she's damaged herself to make you think he must be a good person, but I can't say I really know him yet. I guess the jury's still out."

"I have a favour to ask," I say to Emma, and she narrows her eyes at me, but I plough on. "He wants to take me away for the weekend while Greg is in Harrogate. Can I tell Ethan I'm coming to you in case the baby comes early while Phil is on his course?" I hate dragging her into my world of lies, and I can tell she doesn't really want to do it, but she's my friend to the end and of course agrees. I thank her and apologise again for involving her.

We definitely need a change of subject, so I announce I have practically finished my book and intend to get it sent off by the end of the week to various publishers. Emma squeals with excitement, which has Brian running over convinced she has gone into early labour. It takes a few minutes to reassure him that is not the case and that he should return to the bar, but eventually we achieve it by telling him Annie and Emma both need new drinks, which has him scurrying.

"You have to give me a synopsis of the story," Emma declares, and I promise her that once I have sent it off she can have a copy to read and give me feedback on. I have low expectations, I assure her. She makes me promise to finish it by Friday and drop her a copy by for the weekend to read while Phil's away, since I won't be there and she's got to tell lies for me. It seems fair enough. With that in mind I tell them I have some writing to get back to do, so I say my goodbyes and leave them in the pub to talk about me. I know they will – I would if one of them had announced what I had this evening. As I drive home I feel as if the pressure has released a little by telling them. It matters to me that my friends understand why I've made the decisions I have and can still love me. It gives me hope I'll be okay if I can just get through the next few weeks.

Chapter 30

By Friday I am virtually dead on my feet, mostly because I have nearly killed myself to finish my book in order to fulfil my promise to Emma while still going to work and making sure Greg and Ethan are fed. But I've done it, and I'm thrilled. I've researched the publishers who might have any interest in my story and written the summary they request, but everything I read around the subject of getting published makes me feel it's probably hopeless to believe my book will be picked up – I'm more likely to win the lottery, I suspect, and I don't even buy a ticket. I have Emma's copy all printed off, thanks to the printers at work, and I'm going to drop it in to her on my way to work after I post my chapters.

First, though, I help Greg get the hire van he's got for the weekend loaded with all his stuff. He's worked similar hours to me all week, but I think it's paid off, and he seems pleased with his output. The canvasses I catch sight of when he's packing them for the journey look stunning – it's not only the stuff he's producing at the moment; there's some of his older stuff too that people now seem to be interested in.

The gallery event got a good write-up in both the local and national press, and Greg got the most mentions, all of it favourable, so it certainly seems like his time really is now. When the van is all packed, we stand and look at each other for a moment. It feels awkward, like there's a distance now that he senses and is less willing to cross. We've barely seen each other with his painting and my writing, but I'm unwilling to broach the subject yet, and so it seems is he. He gives me a stiff hug and a peck on the lips before climbing in, seemingly keen to be away. I can understand it; it's like we both need to move on from what we were stuck in during our life together.

With Greg gone, my chapters posted and my stuff packed for the weekend and in the boot of my car, it's like all the energy has seeped out of my body. I've been running on adrenaline for so long now I think it's all finally caught up with me. I sit at work in a daze, wondering how it is that my life could change so much in a few short months. I wonder briefly what would have happened if I had never joined the gym, never gone to the Peaks, never met James, what my life would be like now. Would Greg and I be happy now he is achieving success? But then I realise I would never have met Annie, she would never have asked to see his work, and Greg wouldn't have achieved the recognition he now has; so we would have been stuck in the same unhappy rut I was so desperate to break out of in the first place. It's a catch-22. James has texted me the address of the hotel we are staying at, the Buxted Park Hotel, about half an hour from Brighton. He's excited and keeps sending me texts telling me how much he's looking forward to seeing me. I'm excited too, but I can't shake the little worm of anxiety that keeps gnawing away in my stomach. I guess it's true the guilty never sleep; I remember reading something that said: "When you are guilty, it is not your sins you hate, but yourself." I think there is some truth in that. At least it explains how I'm feeling at the moment.

The workday crawls to a close, and I have been as much use as a chocolate teapot all day. I make my way slowly to the car. I'm not hurrying like I normally do when I'm going to see James, and I don't really know what the matter is. I think it's because I'm getting an increasing sense that I need to finish things with Greg before I can truly move forward happily with James. I have made some progress with my plans and circled some potential bedsits to see on Monday, so now I'm determined that as soon as I have one, I will sit Greg down and tell him. I think I will wait until after Christmas now, though, as Adam is coming home, and I selfishly want a last chance for us all to be together. I know it's not going to be easy to tell them, but it needs to be done.

I drive along the country roads, noticing the twinkling of Christmas lights in the houses I go past. I really haven't given it a thought, and yet it's only a couple of weeks away now. When I pull in to the hotel it's delightful. Set within beautiful parkland it's the quintessential British hotel, lit up with twinkling fairy lights. James is already waiting in the car park for me, talking on his phone. He looks stressed, but when he catches sight of me he smiles and all the stress vanishes. I like it I can do that for him. He ends his call and moves towards me, taking my bag from me with one hand and taking hold of my hand with his other before leaning in to brush my lips with his own. The hotel is just as lovely inside too, and not too ostentatious. I like that. Our room is not quite as immense as last time, but it is very comfortable. James pulls me into his arms and holds me there tightly for some time, and I relish the chance to just lean in against him and be held and comforted. When he finally pulls away he looks at me and frowns. "Lily, you look exhausted."

"I am a bit," I admit. He waits for me to explain. "I've been staying up late writing," I say by way of explanation. "It's finished," I add with a smile.

"My God, Lily, that's extraordinary, you've done it so fast."

"It just sort of flowed out of me once I started," I say, "and I didn't really have much else to do with myself. I loved doing it, though, whatever the outcome," I sigh.

"Well, that calls for some champagne," he announces, moving to the phone and calling down to reception. "You need to run yourself a bath and relax," he tells me. "I'll bring you a glass in when it gets here." So I do, and it's bliss. As I lie there soaking, feeling some of the anxiety seep away, I hear the knock at the door as the champagne is delivered, and he comes in with two glasses in his hands. He hands me one and then clinks his own glass against it.

"To you, Lily, and your future."

"My future," I agree with a smile. He puts his own glass down, as I slide down the bath sipping my champagne, and takes hold of one of my legs. He picks up the soap and the flannel, and then begins to wash me from my toes all the way up to the apex of my thighs before he repeats the whole exercise on my other leg. When he has finished there he begins on my arms, carefully taking my now empty glass from me and placing it on the side. It is blissful and oddly touching to have him taking care of me like this. When he reaches my chest the mood changes and my breathing becomes faster. He dwells on each breast, running his fingers around and over the ample flesh before lowering his head to take my nipple in his mouth, teasing it with his tongue and teeth until I am moaning, before moving to the other breast. Finally his hand moves to my clitoris, and he brushes it lightly with his fingertips before pressing first one finger and then another up inside me. We stay there like that, with him teasing my body to the brink and then calming, before doing the same again until I don't think I can cope with any more.

"Please, James," I say. When I open my eyes and look at him, his eyes are heavy with desire.

"Come, Lily," he says, holding out a hand for me and helping me to my feet. He wraps a large white bath towel around me and lifts me into his arms before carrying me through and placing me gently on the crisp white cotton sheets. His eyes never leave mine as he moves over me. I spread my legs wide for him, still damp from the bath, inviting him, needing him. I feel him at my entrance, and he presses into me so slowly, a centimetre at a time with his eyes still locked to my own. There is none of the lust-filled coupling of previous occasions. It's intimate, loving and exquisitely sensual. A connection of both our minds and our bodies, and I can see the emotions blazing in his eyes as he reaches the deepest part of me. I feel stripped bare, emotionally and physically as I offer everything I am to him. We are making love, I realise, and it reminds me of our first time together. As we slowly begin to move it feels so beautiful and gentle. He kisses me, and even his kiss conveys feeling. We move together until we both finally cry out our climax within moments of each other, and afterwards in post-coital drowsiness he holds me close until I fall asleep with my head on his chest, the sound of his heartbeat lulling me into the most restful sleep I have had in months.

I wake early entangled in James, with his arm still wrapped tight around me, and for a few moments I just lie there enjoying the closeness. He looks so beautiful in his sleep. I feel much better, more rested and content. The anxiety that has resided within me for so long now has lessened slightly. One blue eye opens sleepily, followed by the other, and he blinks at me.

"Morning, beautiful," he says with a smile. "Do you know how lucky I feel to get to wake up with you? How long I've wanted to do this?" He pulls me close to him.

"I wouldn't come too close to my breath," I warn him, "I don't think I cleaned my teeth last night." He smiles, rolling on top of me. "Even your breath can't force me away," he assures me, and then he shows me just what he means.

When we wake again for the second time, we order some breakfast to be sent up to the room and spend a happy hour feeding each other fresh fruit and croissants. It's a heavenly start to the day. The morning is bright and the grounds inviting, so we wrap up warm, put on our walking boots and follow the directions the receptionist has given us through the grounds to a local pub, about six miles away, where we have a drink and a light lunch before making our way back to the hotel. It is so nice to do such normal activities for couples, and I realise how much difference it makes to be able to spend this sort of time with him. James and I talk so easily about anything and everything; it all feels so comfortable and natural for us to be together. Even when we are quiet it is the comfortable silence of two people content just to be in the other's company.

We get back to the hotel and order coffee in the lounge. There's a wedding at the hotel, and we admire the happy couple through the windows as they pose for photos in the grounds while we sit by the fireplace sipping our coffee. They can't take their hands off each other, and it's sweet to watch. They look young and happy and in love. I feel old and jaded by comparison and tell James so.

"Rubbish, Lily," he snorts. "You really don't see yourself as other people do, do you?" he says, bemused. "Let me tell you what I see." He begins, effectively silencing me with a finger over my lips when I start to protest. "I see a petite, perfectly proportioned woman who is in danger of losing her beautiful curves if she loses any more weight; with the most enticing big brown eyes that make me want to lose myself in their sweet depths when I look at them, and lips which are full and make me think of kissing all the time. When you walk into a room I see all the men check you out, but what's amazing is you never even notice, and that just makes you even more attractive in my eyes. Add to that you're intelligent, funny, insightful, caring and…"

"Stop," I say, embarrassed, pushing his chest with both hands.

"I was going to say bossy and a bit of a bully."

I laugh, and I see his gaze fall to my lips again. I can tell he doesn't want to talk any more. I take his hand, and we make our way back to our room where we lie down together on the bed.

"The thing is, Lily," he says, "a man is very transactional when it comes to what is attractive. You only have to look at the type of porn a man goes for. Crappy videos with no real story featuring women with big tits doing sexy stuff to men. It's all very superficial. With women it's different; they like books where they can visualise the sex themselves, not pictures. It's more cerebral. A woman needs to feel beautiful to allow herself to behave erotically; I think that's why so many women don't have orgasms with men, because the men are too transactional; they don't help the woman to feel beautiful," he says, stroking my thigh all the while.

He reaches for the sash from my robe and wraps it around my eyes so that I can't see anything, only feel the sensations as he touches me. "You have to give yourself to the moment, Lily, to the sensation," he says, caressing me. The lack of sight means every new touch startles and thrills me, and I respond with little gasps because each touch is amplified.

"Do you trust me, Lily?" he asks. I don't have to think to answer:

"Yes."

As soon as I say it I feel him securing one of my wrists with some sort of tie, and then the other one, before moving to my ankles. The fastenings are soft on my skin, but when he finishes I can't move and am spread-eagled on the bed. I feel vulnerable but aroused at the same time. He resumes his touching, all the while whispering to me how beautiful I am and how much he wants me. I feel him move between my legs, and my heart rate accelerates. When his tongue touches me, my body jerks but the ties hold me in place. My natural instinct is to want to close my legs or reach down to touch him, but I can do neither. I am entirely in his control, with my body at his command. His tongue is teasing my swollen bud, and the sensation is intense; when he pushes his tongue up inside me, I groan. His tongue resumes its work on my most sensitive place while his fingers take over probing inside, seeking more response from me. I am writhing now, wanting to pull him to me, to satisfy the ache inside me. I would do anything to have him enter me now; my body is aroused, arching to thrust my breasts towards him, trying to tempt him higher so I can ensnare him within me.

"No, Lily," he says, "this is just about you first of all," and he continues to tease until I am moaning in a place between despair and desire. I feel beautiful and desired as he worships my body with his hands, lips and tongue, until my body can take no more and I spiral into a climax made all the more intense because I cannot close my legs. For a few seconds I cannot think; I don't even know my own name until I feel James, as he releases the ties on my hands and feet before he enters me. I am still sensitive at first, and he moves gently as if knowing what I am feeling. Eventually the pace builds and I feel myself rising again with him this time, my body craving the feel of him moving inside me, until we both cry out, his name on my lips. It is the most intense orgasm I have ever experienced, almost exquisitely painful.

I don't know how much time passes until he finally takes my blindfold off, my eyes blinking in the light of the room. I look up at him shyly, feeling embarrassed at the abandon I exhibit to him, and "thank you" is all I can think to say.

"No, thank you," he replies with a sweet kiss before pulling me back against his chest and wrapping his arm around me as we drift off to sleep.

By the time we wake up, have a shower and dress for dinner, the wedding meal is well underway. James has booked us into the hotel restaurant for dinner, figuring we would want to spend most of the time we have left alone together in the room. I feel so close to him now, a deep connection I don't ever remember feeling with Greg, as we walk together down the stairs and head for the restaurant. When James halts me, I am not sure why until he points to the mistletoe hung directly over my head and pulls me into his arms for a kiss.

We are disturbed by a strangled voice crying: "Mum?" followed by the sound of a tray filled with glasses hitting the stone floor and smashing into a million smithereens. I pull away from James and turn to look straight into Ethan's horrified face.

Chapter 31

"Ethan," I say, my voice sounding appalled. I am so ashamed he has seen us like this.

"Mum, does Dad know you're here?" he asks, sounding much younger than his eighteen years for a moment, his voice almost pleading with me to give him some reason to make sense of all this.

"No, Ethan," I say gently as I put a hand out to try to reassure him, console him, but he steps away hissing:

"Don't touch me." He's getting angry now, and James takes a protective step in front of me, which only makes matters worse. "Sarah tried to warn me what you were like," he says, looking at me, his eyes narrow and hard, his voice louder now. "We had a huge row, and I told her she didn't know what she was talking about, but she was right, wasn't she? She saw right through you," he says, looking at the pair of us with hatred in his eyes. "You're fucking him, aren't you?"

"That's enough," James growls.

"Please," I beg the pair of them, "let's not do this in public."

"Why not, Mum, are you afraid people will find out what a slag you are?" Ethan is shouting now. The entire wedding party in the room behind us has gone silent now, and they have all turned to watch the spectacle unfolding at the door. I am mortified.

"I said that's enough," James says flintily, taking a step towards Ethan to try and calm him. Unfortunately it seems to be the final straw for Ethan as he pulls his arm back and slams his fist hard into James' cheek. To his credit James doesn't retaliate, stepping away instead with his hands up in an effort to try and diffuse the situation that is rapidly spiralling out of control.

"Ethan Lambert!" a stern voice to the side of us shouts. When I turn, a middle-aged woman who can only be his work supervisor is standing and looking on horrified. I watch her take in the smashed glasses on the floor and the guest who has obviously just been assaulted. Ethan is looking unrepentant, though, more like the teenager he is than the responsible worker he has shown her up to this point.

"Fuck you, Mum," he says, "Dad doesn't deserve this. Don't think I'm going to protect your dirty little secret. I'll be calling him in the morning to tell him what I've seen, you can count on that. The only reason I won't call him tonight is because I don't want to spoil his show. I hope he was worth it," he says, squaring up to James again.

"Ethan!" the supervisor intercedes yet again, desperate to end the horror show that is fast becoming a fiasco.

"Fuck you," he says to me and James, "and fuck your job," he says, turning to the supervisor before shoulder barging James as he pushes past along the corridor and out the front door of the hotel.

I stand there watching him go, devastated at the hurt I have caused him through the selfish pursuit of my own happiness. I have no idea how to begin to put it all right. I become aware of the whispering within the wedding group and James at my arm urging me to move. "Come on, Lily," he says, gently trying to steer me back towards the stairs. "Please put the cost of the glasses on my bill," he instructs the supervisor, who is still standing and staring at us as we walk past her.

I think she's unsure, judging by her expression, whether to treat us like guests or some sort of troublesome riff-raff that she needs to kick out. The superior tone James adopts ensures she assumes the former and defers to him with a submissive "yes, sir."

I manage to hold it together until we make it into the room and James pulls me against his chest, and then finally the tears begin to fall.

"I'm so sorry, Lily," he says, stroking my hair, as he continues to just hold me. I don't know what to say, *and what is there to say, really?* We stay like that for some time until my sobs subside, and he gently asks me: "What do you want to do?"

"I don't know," I mumble, just wishing the whole horrible nightmare would go away. "I never wanted to hurt him like that, and now he hates me, and I don't blame him, really," I say.

"Don't be so hard on yourself, Lily."

"Why not? I've been unfaithful to his father; he was just standing up for him in his absence." I pause, remembering the altercation. "I'm sorry you got hurt," I say, reaching out gently to touch the bruise forming on his cheek.

"It's nothing," he says dismissively.

"Thank you for not retaliating," I say.

"He was defending your honour in his own way, and I can't blame him for that." His voice is gruff as he continues; "I'm so sorry I have caused this to happen in your life, Lily."

"I had a choice, James. I could always have said no."

He looks at me anxiously for a moment before he asks: "Do you wish you had?"

I think about it for about a second before I say: "No, I wouldn't change anything except for how Ethan found out." He looks relieved and yet still filled with guilt at the same time.

"James, I'll be honest. I'm not proud of how I've gone behind Greg's back and been unfaithful to him, but I can't regret what you and I have had, what we have now." I pause, thinking about what I'm trying to say. "You've brought me back to life, shown me how life can be in a loving sexual relationship. I've been half-dead for too many years now. I was going to tell you anyway that I've been looking at bedsits and planning to sort something out for myself. I intended to tell Greg after Christmas I was moving out and wanted a divorce, and I guess this just sped the process up a bit." I try to smile, but it comes over as a twisted sort of grimace.

"Are you sure?" He pauses like he wants to say something, and for a moment I wonder if he's going to ask me to come and stay with him, but he doesn't. "Do you know what you're doing? It's a big thing to leave a marriage after such a long time," he says, looking at me intently.

His comment surprises me. I'd hoped he'd be pleased I was leaving Greg, even if he didn't want us to live together yet. I take a deep breath before I speak again. "All I know for sure is that I can't live the next eighteen years in a relationship like the one I have at the moment with Greg, and I can't have a meaningful relationship with anyone else, including you, that is based on deceit or dishonesty, which is what it would be if I stayed married to him and carried on creeping around behind his back. It's not a good foundation for something you want to last," I say with certainty.

He nods as I continue, "This weekend has been wonderful, having all this time with you. I want to be able to do that all the time, not be sneaking around worrying who might have seen us. My relationship has been over for more than twelve years, and it's well past time for me to move on now; I just hadn't counted on Ethan getting caught up so directly as collateral damage. I always knew the boys would be shocked about me leaving Greg, but I guess I selfishly hoped I could tell them about you after I had left him, and not have them think of you as a cause of the breakup. You have to believe the marriage was dead well before I met you; you just gave me the strength to do something about it."

I take his hand as I say it and give it a squeeze. He smiles bleakly at me. To be honest, he's taking this harder than I expected; he seems really unsettled.

"Do you think it's worth trying to get hold of Ethan? Trying to persuade him not to tell Greg?" he asks.

"Why would I want to do that?" I ask, surprised by the suggestion. "Why would I want to tell my son to lie for me?" The very idea of it is abhorrent to me.

"I don't know," he says, running his hand through his hair anxiously, "I just have a bad feeling. I like this bubble we've been living in."

I don't know what to say, and I think my heart splinters a little just to hear him say it. I've been so focused on the future, our future, I had assumed he felt the same way. A tear slips down my cheek. "Don't cry, Lily, I didn't mean to make you cry."

"I know, it's fine," I say, but I feel just a bit more alone than I did before.

James orders room service for us, as neither of us can face the restaurant for fear of bumping into the wedding guests again, but I can't eat. My stomach is churning too much to cope with food. I have a bath and try to think about how best to approach tomorrow with Greg. I know he'll be angry and want me gone, *I suppose I'll have to find a B&B to stay in until I sort a bedsit out. It's going to be a miserable Christmas*, I realise. *How on earth am I going to tell Adam?* All these thoughts are flying round and round my mind. *Ethan will probably have already told him.* The boys might not be close all the time, and they bicker like any brothers do, but when one of them needs help or support, they always have each other's backs. I know in my heart that Ethan will already have called Adam and discussed with him how best to tell Greg, and I'm glad to know they are looking out for each other. I hug my arms across my chest, holding on to my shoulders, feeling hollow from all the emotional exertion, trying to give myself some sort, any sort, of comfort I can.

Once I'm finally out the bath and ready for bed, James hugs me close again, stroking my hair and trying to reassure me that it will all be okay, but I'm not quite sure if he's trying to persuade himself or me more. I know it's ridiculous to think for one minute you can make this sort of change in your life and not hurt some of the people around you, but I wish I didn't have to. I never wanted to hurt anyone, and it makes it all so much harder; *but that doesn't mean it's not the right thing to do*, I tell myself. Now I just have to believe it.

It's a very long and lonely night – I spend most of it listening to James sleep. I watch him for a long time as he lies there in all his beautiful, breathtaking splendour, marvelling that this handsome man seems to care for me in his own way. It might not be quite how I would want him to just yet, but I know he cares. In the morning we pack our stuff, and James goes down to settle the bill. I'm glad to be away from the scrutiny of the other guests, who clearly remember us from the debacle the night before.

"Will you be okay? With him, I mean?" James worries as we both walk to the cars. I know he's been thinking about it for a while, but this is the first time he's said it out loud.

"I'll be fine," I say, because I know that's what he wants to hear. In truth I'm not quite sure how Greg is likely to react to the news. I certainly would not have wanted him to hear it from one of the kids like this if I had had a choice.

When we reach the cars James cups my face in his hands and looks intently into my eyes. "Call me and let me know what happens, when you're away from him, I mean. I'm going to be worrying about you." He looks like he means it, so I promise I will when it's done and I'm settled. He pauses like he wants to say something more but then thinks the better of it and just kisses me goodbye instead. There are no worries about anyone seeing us now, but it seems it's hard to shake the habit as I see James look over his shoulder to see if anyone's watching us. I tease him about it as we climb into our respective cars, and he just gives me his funny twisted sort of smile.

The drive back is frighteningly swift, which is so typical when you don't want it to be. I know given the length of the drive he has to make that Greg won't be back from Harrogate until this afternoon at the earliest, so I decide to stop at Emma's on my way back. I want to let her know what's happened, in case she gets any grief for me having used her as an excuse when I lied about my whereabouts. She comes to open the door and when she sees it's me she bounces up and down on her toes – well, as much as a 38ish-weeks' pregnant woman is able to.

"Oh my God, Lil, it's brilliant," she enthuses, and for a moment I can't for the life of me think what she's talking about. "You have a gift," she continues. "I just couldn't put it down. I swear all I've done since you dropped it off is read. I literally finished it twenty minutes ago, and now I don't know what to do with myself. There has to be another book! I have to know what happens next," she beseeches me.

I smile, finally realising she has read my book. I'm genuinely glad she liked it, but it is so far from my list of things to think about at the moment that the smile doesn't really meet my eyes. "What's the matter?" Emma asks, looking at me more closely now, her excitement fading. "What's happened? You look funny."

"Can I come in for a bit?"

"Of course," she says, moving aside to let me pass and following me into the kitchen, where we both sit at the table.

"What's happened?" she asks again, more serious now, the book forgotten. So I tell her. I tell her about the beautiful time at the hotel with James, about going down for dinner, about kissing James and about Ethan seeing us. When she looks confused I explain he was working there, that the agency must have sent him because of the wedding. I watch her eyes widen in shock as she works through the implications.

When I describe our exchange, what he said about telling Greg, what he called me, she just says: "Oh my God, Lil," and then she moves to hug me. "I'm so sorry, darling. I know you must hate it happening that way." I nod, glad she understands me so well, that she isn't judging me, always my friend to the last.

"I wanted to warn you," I explain, "I don't know how Greg will be, but I told him I was with you. I don't want you to get sucked in to any nastiness. I just wanted you to be prepared. You know how he is." She just nods at that, her face sad.

"Don't worry about me," she says confidently, "I've got Phil. More to the point, what are you going to do? You can't go back there."

"I have to."

"You have to be joking, Lil, he's going to go mental."

"I have to explain it to him. I have to let him know I'm leaving him, but not for another man. He needs to know; I owe him that much."

She doesn't agree and tells me so. "I'm scared for you, Lily. I don't think he's just going to sit there and listen to you tell him you're leaving and then watch you walk out the door. He's too possessive about you already; it's only got worse over the years. There's no way he's going to hear anything you say except that you've been seeing another man behind his back, and he's going to be batshit angry. What does James say about it?"

"What can he say? It's my marriage, not his. He's worried about me, of course, but I told him I'd call him when I was settled."

"And he's okay with that? You going off, I mean, to stay somewhere after walking out on your marriage? He hasn't asked you to stay with him?"

"No," I say defensively, "that was never the deal. It's too soon for us to live together."

"Okay, I'd get that if you were just leaving Greg in a controlled way like you planned and had already sorted out the place you were renting, but this is all so sudden. Surely he should be supporting you a bit more?"

"I can't think about that now," I say, on the defensive again, although something about what she's saying does touch upon some of my internal anxieties. I squash the thoughts down. "I just have to get through the next few hours with Greg, and then we can all move on. I know it's going to be shit for everyone, and I so wish I could have held off doing it until after Christmas, but the situation's the same as it was when I spoke about it in the pub the other night. I was already planning to leave Greg because our relationship died a long time ago. Hopefully he'll see the truth in that, and we can both move forward with our lives."

Emma nods, but her face looks doubtful. "Well, don't worry about me," she says, "I won't take any shit from him, and you just make sure you look after yourself. Look, Lil," she says, thinking out loud, "why don't you stay in my spare room tonight? Until you get yourself sorted with somewhere, I mean. I can't stand to think of you in some dingy B&B somewhere over Christmas."

"Are you sure you don't need to speak to Phil first? I don't want to bring all my shit into your home when you're so close to having the baby and all."

"Phil will be fine, Lil, I want you here so I know you're alright." I blink and realise I have yet more tears spilling down my face due to her unexpected kindness. I hadn't been looking forward to being on my own over Christmas.

"I thank God for the day I met you, Emma. I don't know what I did to deserve a friend like you. I certainly don't know what I'd do without you," I tell her with feeling. We hug again, and she wipes my tears away with a tissue before telling me to bring my bag in from the car and leave it here for later.

About an hour and a half later, after a cup of tea and much circular conversation which ends with Emma still worrying that I should stay away for today and see Greg on another day, when she figures he's likely to be calmer, I climb into my car, promising I won't be long and that I'll text her to let her know I'm on my way back. I haven't heard anything from James since we left the hotel, but then I didn't really expect to, despite checking my phone constantly. I drive the short distance to the house and am surprised to see the hire van is already parked on the driveway. He's already back. It must mean he's driven like a bat out of hell to get home. My stomach sinks. I leave the car parked on the road, grab my bag and walk to the door, rummaging for my keys as I go. When I let myself in, the house is completely silent. At first I think Greg must be in the shed because the house is so quiet, but when I walk into the kitchen

I am confronted with Greg sitting at the table, slumped over with his head in his hands. He looks up as I walk in, and his eyes are bloodshot. I can tell he's been crying.

"You're back," he says, looking up at me, his lip curling as he says it. "Ethan called," he says, and then he waits for me to say something. I am momentarily at a loss for words. All the planning I have done in my head to prepare for this moment flies out the window when I am confronted with the broken man in front of me.

"Greg, I'm so sorry," I start to say, moving towards him to touch him, my way of offering comfort.

"Don't fucking touch me," he says with a snarl, jerking away. It reminds me so much of Ethan last night.

"I'm sorry," I say again. I seem to have forgotten the speech I had prepared.

"So you keep saying," he says in the cruel tone he sometimes uses that I hate. "Ethan tells me you were fucking that bloke from the gallery, James. How long's it been going on?" he demands.

"Not long," I mumble, unwilling to let the discussion focus on my relationship with James. "We've been broken for a long time you and I," I try to tell him.

"So that means it's okay for you to go off and fuck someone else, does it?"

"Our marriage is over, Greg."

"You're leaving me for him?" He sounds genuinely shocked, like he hadn't considered I might actually leave him.

"I'm not leaving you for him, I'm just leaving you, leaving this marriage. I can't do this anymore. I think it'll be better for both of us to part and lead our own lives."

"Is it because he's rich?" he says derisively.

"I am not leaving you to set up with James." I say, getting angry at the repetitious nature of his questions. "I'm sorry I was unfaithful to you, and I'm even sorrier Ethan got caught up in this, but the truth is that, with or without James, this marriage was still over. I'm going to find a place to rent for a bit while we get things sorted," I say moving to walk out of the kitchen.

"Don't you fucking walk out on me," he bellows, and I freeze in the doorway, unsure what to do next. I start to move again, I want to go upstairs and pack a bag to take with me to Emma's, but he's up and grabbing my arm, pulling me back into the room. "I said don't fucking walk away from me." His voice is low and sinister now.

"Greg, don't do this," I plead.

"Don't do what, Lily? Don't let you walk out of our marriage after eighteen years, don't let you fuck up our family, don't let you fuck another man? What is it you don't want me to do?" he yells in my face. "Did you really expect me to sit here like some pussy while you told me you were leaving to go and fuck some rich prick who'll no doubt cast you out once his dick's had its fill of you? Did you think I'd just wish you well? You've treated me like a complete fool. Tell me how long it's been going on!" His skin is bright red now, and he's shouting in my face; little specks of his spittle keep landing on me. I can feel yet more tears falling down my face now.

"We met in the Peaks," I tell him finally.

"The fucking Peaks, I might have known," he says, rolling his eyes. "And how many others have there been? How many other men have you fucked while we've been together?" That shocks an angry response from me.

"None, there's been no one else, only you. I've looked after the kids, and the house, and you, and nothing else for the last eighteen years. There has never been anyone else, only you – until James. Now the kids are older, you've got your art, and I want my life back."

"I don't believe you," he says, and I realise he's losing it. There is no reasoning with him now. He's demented, convinced I've been sleeping around with numerous men behind his back. I need to get out; we both need space to cool down. I pull my arm free and move to leave the room.

"I said don't fucking walk away from me," he bellows, grabbing me with one hand, while his other arm swings and gives me a backhander across the side of my face.

I am stunned for a second as pain explodes in my head. He's still shouting at me, "I think you're a fucking slag who has been fucking anything and everything she can. Ethan's girlfriend told him how you were putting it out with all the men on the trip. You don't give a fuck who you're with, do you?" he says. "You're just a cheap tart."

I'm still holding my face and trying to pull away from him when I feel him push me hard so that I careen into the doorframe. I feel something crack in my chest, and more pain hits me like a wave.

"Please, Greg," I plead, the pain in my chest making my voice come out as a whisper.

"Oh you want it from me now, do you?"

"No," I say, horrified. But he's not listening to me, not hearing what I say as I plead with him to stop. He pushes me to the ground onto my back, making me bang my head again, but somehow I have enough awareness to try and move away from him, my feet kicking out at his body, trying to drag my body away from him with the backs of my elbows. But he's stronger than me. He lashes out again to stop me kicking him and catches my eye with his fist this time. I think I lose consciousness for a few moments. When I regain my awareness he has my jeans and panties off, and his body is over mine. His arm is pressed over my throat, making it hard to breathe.

"No!" I say weakly, "stop, please stop," but he doesn't. He forces himself inside me, his body thrusting into me hard, and he's grunting with his eyes shut tight. My body is screaming with the pain of his relentless assault, but my mind has switched off now. I've stopped fighting him, knowing I can't win this fight. I have to just wait until it's over now. And eventually it is. Eventually he comes, and then pulls out of me, standing there looking at me sobbing in a heap on the floor, in front of him, while he covers himself up again, before stepping over me and walking down the hall and out the front door. I try to move myself now he's gone, but the pain is just too much, and I lay my head down again and allow myself to fall into blissful unconsciousness.

Chapter 32

When I wake up I have no idea where I am. The room is white and bright, and it hurts my eyes. I try to move, but my body hurts too much, and I just groan with the effort.

"Lily, you're awake," I hear Emma cry beside me. She leans over me, her face looking so worried. I want to reassure her I'm fine, tell her not to worry, that it's not good for the baby, but I can't seem to speak and my throat hurts. "Don't speak, baby, you're fine," she croons, "it's all fine now," and I close my eyes and allow myself to drift back to blissful oblivion.

The second time I wake I am alone. I feel more with it this time, but that means memories of Greg and the fight come flooding back, and I start to cry. A nurse comes into the room and sees I'm awake, rushing over to check if I'm in pain. She gives me some pain relief and tells me she'll fetch the doctor, but all the while she's there and after she leaves I can't stop the tears that are flowing down my face. I wonder absently if I will ever stop crying.

Eventually an older female doctor with blonde hair streaked with silver enters the room and moves to the chair beside the bed.

"Welcome back to us, Mrs Lambert. I'm Dr Brown, and I've been taking care of you since you came in yesterday. We're very happy to see you awake again. Did the nurse give you some pain relief?"

"Yes," I whisper, unable to get more from my throat. "Where am I?"

"You're at the hospital," she informs me. "You've been hurt quite badly, I'm afraid." I nod to show I understand while she continues. "You have two cracked ribs, a fractured cheekbone and a serious concussion, along with a fair bit of other bruising, including some crushing to your windpipe. That's why you'll find it difficult to speak for a while. Fortunately we don't think there is any other internal damage. You've been unconscious for nearly a day; your friends have been quite worried about you." *Emma*, I think.

"Mrs Lambert," she continues, looking serious, "I'm sorry to say that, as part of the examination when you were brought in, we also found significant evidence of a serious sexual assault. We have had to inform the police, and they will want to speak to you when you are feeling a bit better. Do you have any idea who did this to you?" I just blink at her for a moment. I wish my head were clearer so I could think what to say. Greg is the father of my boys. Whatever he has done to me, however wrong it is, I cannot put them through the horror of watching their father defend himself against criminal proceedings. Not when it's my fault we're in this position in the first place. If I hadn't slept with James, made him so angry when I told him I was leaving, then none of this would have happened.

"I fell," I whisper, and I move my head to look away from her and at the window instead, unwilling to look her in the face and see the disappointment I know will be clear in her expression.

"Very well, Mrs Lambert," she says eventually, "we can talk about this again later when you're feeling a bit better." I can tell she disapproves of my decision to protect him. *She doesn't understand – no one can who hasn't walked in my shoes for the last few days.*

I hear her pause when she reaches the door, her hand on the handle. "I'll tell your friends they can come in and see you now," and she smiles gently at me, more forgiving of me than I feel I deserve, to be honest, before she closes the door quietly behind her with a soft click.

I am alone for a few moments until the door opens again, and this time Emma puts her head in.

"Lily, thank God," she says, moving quickly to my side. "You had us so worried," she says.

"Don't worry. It's not good for the baby," I say, trying to sit up, but it hurts to move, so in the end Emma uses the remote to raise the bed electronically until I am more upright. I look at her then and ask: "How did I get here?" I've been wondering what happened after the fight.

"When you didn't text me I got worried. I called Annie and got her to contact James to see if he had heard from you, and no one had. I called and called your phone, but there was never a reply, so I came round to yours. When I saw the car there I got really worried, so I called the police and they knocked your front door down. The neighbours told them they'd heard some shouting and screaming, so we were terrified what we might find." She pauses for a second, her eyes full of tears. "I thought you were dead, Lil. You were just lying there on the floor, and you looked so small and broken." She sobs a little, and I take her hand.

"I'm sorry," I say, "for worrying you."

"You have nothing to be sorry for; it's Greg who should be sorry. He should be locked away for this," she says angrily. "James wanted to kill him, and I only just managed to stop him going out to find him when he saw the state you were in by telling him you needed him here more. He's just popped home for five minutes to shower and get some fresh clothes, but he's been here by your side for the last day."

James has been here, and a small part of me, not devastated by the turn of events, is happy he cared enough to come and see me. "No one's seen Greg," Emma continues. "The police have been looking for him, but he isn't anywhere he usually hangs out. Ethan came by, but he didn't want to see you. I think he feels bad about what's happened, and he wanted to know you were going to be okay."

"He has nothing to feel bad for. Please tell him so from me if he comes back."

"I will, Lil. You just need to get better. They said you'll be in for a couple of days or so, but then you can come home."

Home. I wonder where that is? I think. *I need to find somewhere.*

"James seems to think you'll be going back to his, but I keep telling him you're staying with me." *James thinks I'm staying with him?! I can't believe it.*

"Emma, you've got to get ready for the baby. You don't need an invalid to take care of," I whisper, my throat at the limit of its ability for now.

"Lily, we'll talk about this when you're a bit better," she fobs me off. "You look tired. Get some sleep now; we'll look after you," she assures me. I nod and squeeze her hand. I am tired again, so I close my eyes and drift off back to sleep.

When I wake the next time, the first thing I see is a pair of beautiful blue eyes gazing intently at my face. He looks so worried, and I immediately want to reassure him I'm okay, so I reach out and squeeze his hand, and he smiles and raises my hand to his lips.

"Hi," he says.

"Hi," I whisper back, my throat still husky. He frowns when he hears it.

"I thought I'd lost you, Lil. When Emma rang to tell me what he'd done, I thought you were dead. It was the worst moment of my life. I want to kill him," he says angrily.

"No," I say, "it's over now. He knows it, and so do I. I don't want the boys dragged through anything more. I won't press charges," I say, knowing he needs to know the truth sooner rather than later.

"He deserves to be punished, though," he says, the shock clear on his face. "I know what he did to you. I heard the doctors talking. He raped you," he whispers, and his agony at the knowledge is there for all to see. A tear runs down my face, I seem unable to stop crying. "What if he does it to someone else? Could you live with that?" It's a horrible thought, but I don't think he will. He was just so angry with me and what I'd done and the fact I was leaving him.

"I can't hurt the boys any more than I already have." That's my only concern now, I decide. I'm not important in the scheme of things. Greg knows what he did, and he will have to live with that every day from now on for the rest of his life, and in a fucked up way he's done me a favour. I can leave him now and feel no remorse whatsoever. He has finally given me my freedom.

"You're tired," James tells me. "You just need to rest and focus on getting better. We can discuss all this when you're feeling more yourself." I decide to nod, as I don't have the strength to argue any more. "The doctor said you'd probably be in for another couple of days, but then you can go home. Lily, I want to look after you, will you let me do that?" he asks intently. I nod again, not trusting myself to speak, a warm feeling building around my heart at his words. He smiles at me then and strokes my hair until I fall asleep again.

The next couple of days I am put under relentless pressure to press charges against Greg. The police make it clear they believe they have enough evidence to press charges against him with or without my support, but I can tell they would prefer not to have to do it without. Greg has no previous record, and the chances are he would be given the benefit of the doubt without my testimony. For a while I'm concerned when Emma and James gang up and threaten to give evidence against him; they certainly know enough about us to make more of a case, but in the end I plead to them not to hurt my boys and me any more, and they relent.

The first time I am allowed to see myself in the mirror, I am appalled. Greg has destroyed my face – these bruises will take quite some time to heal. The emotional damage is harder to understand – I find myself crying continually. On one level I can rationalise what happened as a purely physical act, one I had performed with him countless times over the years, often when I wasn't particularly into the idea, just letting him get on with it. On another level I feel I have been invaded. I had always consoled myself that if I had said no it would have been enough for him; I trusted he would stop. I feel vulnerable in a way I have not felt since I was a child. It's hard to explain; I feel alone and afraid.

The boys have still not visited me, although I did get a 'get well soon' card that gave me hope we could rebuild bridges eventually. I have to believe it's going to be possible, as I can't imagine not having them in my life. Finally, I haven't heard anything from Greg, and for that I am grateful. I am terrified of being alone with him again. James has become my own personal guard dog, taking my safety as his cause and rarely leaving my side. He insists on working in my hospital room beside me, much to the nurses' annoyance. I have finally agreed with him and Emma I would stay with James during my recuperation before looking for a bedsit to move to. He grumbles when I say it, but I'm determined not to force myself into his house permanently under these circumstances. If we were ever going to live together it would be because he wanted me to and had invited me and I had accepted, not because I was an invalid and he felt guilty.

When the day finally comes for me to be discharged, James arrives bright and early. Emma had taken it upon herself to borrow my keys, go to my house and collect some clothes for me. Fortunately Greg was not there when she did, or if he was he was sensible enough to stay in the shed and did not come out to see her. He must have known he would be skating on thin ice if he made any more trouble. My clothes, apart from one set she brought in for me to wear home today, are already at James' house waiting for me in my case where Emma had dropped them off. She was beside herself after she saw James' house.

"Bloody hell, Lil," she had said, "I want to play at your house, please." I had smiled and reminded her it wasn't my house, and I was only staying there until I was well enough to live on my own again. "Whatever," she'd replied.

Christmas is now just over a week away, and as I'm wheeled out the hospital to the waiting Range Rover, there is a real nip in the air. It's nice to be out in the seasonal cold. James is treating me like I'm wrapped in cotton wool, as he insists on lifting me from the wheelchair into the car. I still hurt a lot, especially my ribs, but I've had enough injuries over the years to know all I need is time to heal the injuries on the outside. I think it might take longer to heal the ones inside. When we get to the house James insists on carrying me in and up to the bedroom where he settles me into the bed and then proceeds to offer me every type of food he can think of. It's sweet, and I enjoy being looked after for once.

"Thank you," I say when he brings me yet another cup of tea in bed. "I'll be able to be up and about a bit more soon, and I can start helping a little around the house," I reassure him.

"Don't be ridiculous," he says, "you are not to lift a finger. I have a housekeeper, Mrs Reynolds, who sees to all that. I'll introduce you to her tomorrow." And with that he kisses me sweetly on the lips and curls up beside me. I feel safe for the first time in days, and it feels like heaven.

Chapter 33

I've been here a week now, and the time with James has been wonderful. He has taken remarkable care of me. The only fly in the ointment has been the housekeeper, Mrs Reynolds. I can tell she hates me, and I don't know why. I can't think what I have possibly done to upset her. I'm now up and about; my bruises are still awful and unsightly, but I am healing well. Every time we are in the same room I can feel her eyes on me, watching everything I do, everything I touch. I try to discuss it with James, but he brushes it off and tells me not to be so silly. So now I just feel awkward. I try to clear up after myself constantly, but that just gets James irritated with me, and he insists I sit back down and let Mrs Reynolds help me. James has to work quite a bit, so I spend long hours in the house with just Mrs Reynolds, and frankly it's a nightmare. Fortunately the house is big enough so I can avoid her a fair bit, but it could never be big enough for me unless she wasn't in it in the first place. This morning I have miraculously managed to avoid her entirely, which has been heavenly. I am just sitting in the corner of the brilliantly stocked library, curled up in one of the large armchairs, when she sticks her head around the door. I know she hasn't seen me because she would have scowled if she had. I'm about to say something to alert her to my presence when something stops me. I hear her go out into the hall and pick up the landline phone to make a call. I can't hear everything she says, but what I do hear makes me curious:

"I'm sorry to bother you at work .... yes, very well, thank you................... so are you planning a trip here soon?............................ we have one of Mr Lattimer's guests..................seems very settled here...............no, I don't think she does.....................yes, I think that would be best, I hope you didn't mind me calling..................no, quite, that's what I thought.................yes, whatever you think best. Goodbye, goodbye."

I wonder who on earth the person on the other end of the phone could possibly be, because I know from what I heard Mrs Reynolds say on this end they can only be discussing me. It bothers me a lot for some reason to think she's talking about me, and I resolve to call Emma and get her to drive me round some of the bedsits I have found so I can move out straight after Christmas. James keeps telling me he wants me to stay, but I don't think I can, given the current climate in the house.

Emma is delighted to help when I call, and we agree to go to a couple of shops while we're at it so I can pick up gifts for James and the boys. I've already got Emma's present; a beautiful handbag I saw online that is big enough to hold stuff for the baby but means she won't have to sacrifice style entirely. I can't really afford much else, given my current predicament, but I decide it would be best to save money after Christmas; I want to enjoy the here and now. Fortunately work have been very kind and insist I should take as long as I need, giving me extended paid sick leave – I guess being a reliable employee for so long has finally paid off. They even sent me some beautiful flowers and a 'get well soon' card that everyone had signed. The benefit of being as accident-prone as I am is that I have had very little challenge to my story about falling down the stairs at home.

Emma and I have a wonderful day; we are a right pair with her enormous bump and my ribs, so we can't walk far. We see three different bedsits, which are all fairly grim but will do at a push, and then head to the shops. We pretty much only make it to one department store and stay there, given our combined invalid status. But we find everything we want, and the rest of the day we have coffee and lunch and chat like we always used to. I get the boys a shirt each from the designer I know they like, and I buy James two gifts: a first-aid kit that I figure he'll need if he's going to spend any time with me, and a book of walks in the Peak District. I hope he'll take me back there one day and we can do some more walking together. Emma laughs a lot at the first-aid kit. The shop agree to wrap all my parcels for me which is a bonus.

By the time we get home my mood is much lighter. James comes to the door when he hears Emma's car in the driveway, and my heart does a little flip when I see him again. He's pleased to see the smile on my face and tells me so as we stand there holding hands while we watch Emma drive off. She's offered to drop the presents for the boys off at the house on her way home as it's Christmas Eve tomorrow; I want the boys to have them before Christmas Day, but there's no way I want to go near the house yet. I know I'll have to soon, but just not yet. I realise I'm going to need to find a lawyer after the New Year and start to sort my life out properly, but I decide I'll worry about it 'tomorrow'.

"Is Mrs Reynolds here?" I ask as we turn to walk into the house.

"No, she's already gone home. Just you and me," he says with a smile. We haven't made love since Buxted Park – I've not been well enough – but when I look at him and he smiles at me, I feel the heating of my body that only he provokes in me. He senses it and laughs. "You seem to be feeling better, Lily."

"I am," I say, giving him a coy look as I walk up the stairs.

We have to be careful; he can't lie on me at all, but we find a way. And when he's inside me at last, having touched and kissed and licked me to the point of climax, it feels so good that neither of us can last long. I have missed this closeness with him.

"God, Lily, I've missed being inside you," he says as if reading my mind.

"I love you James," I say, looking into his beautiful blue eyes.

"I love you too," he says simply.

We spend the rest of the evening making dinner and planning what food we want to buy for our Christmas dinner – he promises to go out and buy it all in the morning – and he gets excited when I show him the two parcels I have bought for him. He looks like a little boy again when he gets excited, rather than the 42-year-old man he actually is. When we finally fall into bed again, close to midnight, my heart is much lighter. I'm up for a replay of earlier, but James insists we need to take it carefully so that I don't end up hurting my ribs again. I grumpily agree, only cheering up when he proceeds to kiss and cuddle me until I proclaim I'm finally happy with him again. I fall asleep in his arms, and it's heaven.

I'm disturbed in the morning by the sound of a door slamming. James is still wrapped around me, in the same position we fell asleep; I don't think we have moved all night. I assume it's Mrs Reynolds arriving for the day until the bedroom door is slammed open, causing James and me to sit up quickly. I wince as my ribs protest about the sudden movement.

A vaguely familiar blonde woman is standing in the doorway staring at us. She is stunning, and I become acutely aware of what a wreck I must look. I realise I am naked beside James and pull the sheet up to protect my modesty. James is staring at her, his mouth open.

"Close your mouth, James," she says in clipped tones. Her accent is American. I realise she is familiar because I recognise her from the photo in the Peak District; it's the woman James was with who he mentioned was his ex-partner. "Can I suggest you get your clothes on and pack your bag," she says to me coldly, "you're not welcome in my house." *Her house?* I think. "I'll see you downstairs," she says to James before sweeping out.

"Amanda," I hear James saying as he gets out of bed, grabbing his robe and trying to follow her while putting it on at the same time.

I sit there for a moment after they leave, and then I slowly get out of bed and begin to dress as quickly as I am able in my clothes from yesterday, which are the first things I can find. I need to know what's going on. I throw my things into my case but struggle to carry it, as my ribs are just too sore. When I see the little wrapped parcels for James I pause for a moment, wondering what to do. In the end I leave the little gifts on James' pillow. Eventually after the pain of trying to move my case becomes too much, I decide to leave it at the top of the stairs and make my way down towards where I can hear raised voices in the kitchen. Mrs Reynolds is standing in the entrance hall, a smug expression on her face, just watching me as I descend the stairs. I hold my head up and walk past her, determined to uncover what is happening. When I walk into the kitchen I see James by the table. He has his hands on it, and he is leaning heavily on them; he looks like a broken man, and my defensive hackles immediately rise.

"Ah, here she is," Amanda says as she sees me walk in. James lifts his head briefly, and the look in his eyes nearly breaks me; I have to stop myself from running to his side. "I must say, James, you've lowered your standards somewhat," Amanda continues, giving me a scathing look.

"Can somebody please tell me what's going on?" I say quietly.

"Why yes, dear, I'd be delighted," Amanda says.

"Amanda, don't do this," James beseeches her.

"Why, James? The poor girl deserves to know the truth, don't you think?" I look at her expectantly, knowing she's delighting in her little performance. I try to hold my head a little higher in order to retain some shred of dignity. "In case you don't know who I am, my name is Amanda Lattimer. I'm James' wife," Amanda announces grandly. My head swivels round to James, whose head has dropped even further.

"You're married?" I say, shocked, my mind trying to process what I've just heard.

"Yes, he's married," she answers for him. "Has been for nearly fifteen years. I live in America. I'm an actress – you probably recognise me?" I shake my head absently.

"I don't watch a lot of films," I murmur. She seems annoyed by this.

"Well, anyway, while I'm over there, James seems to prefer to spend all his time in this godforsaken little country; for the love of God, I have no idea why. We have an arrangement. It suits me to have a handsome English husband to roll out when I need him – they're quite the fashionable accessory these days, you know – and it suits him to have access to my money," she says, gesturing to the room around us.

"All this is mine, you see. James has burned his way through his own money, it seems, what little he had to begin with." I look at him, hoping to hear his side of things, but he won't even look me in the eye. I realise Amanda is still speaking, "So you see, while I am quite modern enough to tolerate the odd dalliance with some local slut, something James has always seemed so fond of, I will not tolerate one of his sluts moving into my house," she says, looking at me. She looks at James now when she hisses.

"I will not be made a laughing stock of, James. The maid had to call me to let me know what was happening." *I knew Mrs Reynolds was a snake.* "You're only lucky the paps didn't get wind of this; you know how they lap up sordid stories like these. So anyway," she says imperiously, turning back to me, "please say your 'goodbyes' and crawl back under whichever stone you crawled out from in the first place. There's nothing more for you here."

"James," I whisper, unable to believe he's just going to stand there and let her talk to us like this. No matter what has happened, I have to believe he loves me enough to defend me. I wait, but he still doesn't even look at me.

"Oh, how sweet, she thinks you're going to choose her over me! Oh, that's delightful." She actually laughs like I made a funny joke and claps her hands, before she leans forward again. "Now listen to me, darling, because I'm getting tired of having you in my house and I want you gone: James will never leave me. He's too fond of the money, you see, and he knows if he leaves me he gets nothing. Now I know you've had your fun, but it's over now, and James knows he needs to be a good boy again, so get your bag and get out."

I'm mortified, mostly because I realise James' silence means I was merely a meaningless dalliance to him; he can never really have cared for me if this is how he treats me. I rush out of the room and up the stairs. I grab my case, dragging it down the stairs and ignoring the protests my ribs are making.

I have no idea where I'm going; I just know I need to get out of this house and away from this shit. I open the front door and, only then, as I am leaving, I finally hear an agonised voice say: "Lily."

I turn to look at him. He is standing there in the hallway watching me leave, his face twisted in despair. "Where will you go?" he asks.

"I don't think that's really your concern," I say as I lug my case out the door, tripping along the gravel until I am beyond the gates. I must look a complete sight with my face covered in bruises, my hair ratty and un-brushed, my clothes creased from yesterday. I stand on the pavement for a few minutes until I collect myself enough to find my phone and call a cab. When it arrives I give him Emma's address.

I sit in the back, dry-eyed. I really thought he loved me. I thought he was different, but it seems it was all a lie. So much makes sense now I think about it; his caution about being seen even after Ethan saw us, his reluctance to invite me to his home. He was so clever telling me she was his partner but that they were separated. It was all technically true, but the more salient points, like the fact he was still married, he omitted to mention. I never questioned him, more concerned with righting my own wrongs first. Well it sure all came back to bite me. I feel such a fool.

As if a man like him would ever choose someone like me when he had a beautiful, rich actress like her at home, I think. *I was exactly what she described; a stupid little slut, and now I have nothing.* The cab pulls up outside Emma's, and I climb out, pulling my case with me. I throw a ten-pound note at the driver, not waiting for any change, and then stumble up the path to the front door. I don't know what I will do if she says I can't stay. I ring the bell, and when the door opens she is standing there, all pregnant and beautiful. She takes one look at me and my case before opening the door wider and pulling me into her arms, where finally my tears begin to fall.

Epilogue – 8 weeks later

The last eight weeks have been something of a fog, a time of pain and darkness from which I am only now trying to emerge. I am sitting in my bedsit with three letters still in their envelopes laid out in front of me. Emma popped them round earlier after Greg had dropped them in to her. I still haven't told Greg where I live. I can't face seeing him yet.

Emma had her new baby with her – a little girl called Rose. She finally had her on New Year's Day when I was still staying with them. Emma insisted she wanted me with her for the labour when it started. She was in so much pain, and Phil was panicking, unable to cope with seeing his beloved Emma in pain. I was the only one who could calm her and help her focus through the contractions. So I went with the pair of them to the hospital, and it was a truly beautiful moment – at a time of darkness – that I will always treasure, to see their daughter born and hold her just minutes after her birth. Emma asked me to be her godmother, and of course I accepted, although what hope I have of guiding another soul through life when I've made such a mess of my own, I have no idea. Emma told me she named her Rose because she is planning to build her own special bouquet of precious people around her in her life – she now has a Lily and a Rose, she says. I worry for the baby who gets called Daffodil. Rose is, as expected, an angelic baby who already sleeps for six-hour stretches at night, which is completely unlike my own experience of early motherhood. Emma is, also as expected, a complete natural at motherhood. As I watch the love she and Phil have for their daughter as they care for her, I realise how parenthood should always be between two people who love each other and choose to have a child. It is beautiful to behold, and Rose is very blessed.

The downside was that once Rose arrived I knew I had to leave. They needed their special time together as a new family without the black cloud of despair I have become spoiling it. Before Emma was sent home from the hospital with the baby, I had found myself a bedsit not far from them and moved out.

It's small and lonely, but it kind of matches where I feel in my life at the moment.

I have been sitting here for an hour, trying to build the courage to read the letters. I know I must. The first one is from Greg himself; I recognise his handwriting. It is past time we talked, so I finally tear open the letter, unfold the page and begin to read.

Lily,

I have given this to Emma with another couple of letters that came for you, as I don't know where you live. I heard you are no longer with the other man – Ethan told me after he saw you last week.

Thank you for not pressing charges. You could have, I know. I hurt you, Lily, but you have to know you hurt me too.

I loved you. I always have in my own way. I know our life was hard, but I was always trying, whatever you may think. The irony is that you have left me at the very time when my work is on the up, my art is in so much demand I can barely keep up with it.

You asked me once, when we were at Annie's gallery, when it was that my art had started to become so dark. I was surprised you had noticed. The truth is, Lily, that it got dark when you started to leave me. I could feel you pulling away from me, and I just didn't know how to talk about it with you. I always knew you would leave me in the end, which is why I just tried to hold on tighter.

The pain I felt when you began to change I poured into my paintings, and the irony is people liked them far more than my other stuff.

On the plus side I have so much fucking pain now, the art is pouring out of me and people are lapping it up – ironic, huh?

So the other guy was married? You know what they say, Lily – what goes around comes around. I hope you're hurting too.

Greg

I might have known Ethan would tell Greg about James. The letter was spiteful; I suppose I should have expected no less. I have an appointment with a solicitor next week, and I intend to start divorce proceedings; it's time to move on, I have decided, and this letter only confirms things. I knew his art was going well – I see him featured everywhere at the moment. Whatever he may believe, I am actually glad for him, as I never wished to hurt him. I need to close the wave of feelings his words have opened up in me again, so I move to open the second letter.

Lily,

Please let me know where you are. Emma and Annie won't tell me anything. I just need to know you're okay. I am so ashamed I lied to you, but by the time I knew how important you were to me it was too late to correct. Please give me the chance to explain about my relationship with Amanda.

I love you, Lily. I always will, whatever you may think of me now.

Please forgive me

James

After I got to Emma's, when I was at my lowest point, I couldn't speak about James. Emma was brilliant and never asked; she just waited until I was ready to talk. Eventually I had some time to think, and I Googled James and Amanda's names to see what came up. There were a few pictures of them together at some of Amanda's premieres, but not too many. Mostly there were pictures of Amanda alone. I could see where they were together that James was always in the background – he didn't seem to enjoy being in the limelight in the same way she did. I had no idea she was such a big deal, though; she was what they call an 'A' lister over there. I was so caught up in my own little world, and Greg had always been so dismissive of the whole celebrity culture thing, that it seemed completely alien to me.

Several times I had nearly caved and contacted James. He had called and texted relentlessly in the first few weeks, but lately it has begun to reduce. I know I should be glad, but it just hurts all the more. I stopped going to the gym too, for fear I would bump into him. I have taken up running instead, and now I run for miles and love it – *who would have thought a few months ago?* It helps me to clear my head when everything feels too much – that's quite a lot of the time at the moment. His letter hurts, and I can't deal with emotion anymore. I've decided to block it all off, so I screw the letter up and throw it in the bin.

I reach for the third and final letter. It looks official, and for a moment I wonder if Greg has beaten me to it and already started divorce proceedings. I open it and begin to read:

Dear Mrs Lambert:

We were very excited to receive your chapters and would be delighted if you could contact us at your earliest convenience. We are keen to see the rest of the manuscript and would like to discuss options for publishing.

We look forward to hearing from you,

Dan Simmonds

Elite Publishers

So much has happened I had completely forgotten about my book. The letter is dated from two weeks ago. I sit and stare at the letter, reading it again and again, trying to make sense of it. Eventually I pick my mobile up, fearing I may have missed my chance, and call the number on the letter.

"Hello, Dan Simmonds speaking."

"Oh hello, my name is Lily Lambert, I just received your letter today about my story – The Flight."

"Oh, Mrs Lambert! Thank goodness; we were worried you might have been thinking about going with someone else when you took so long to get back to us."

"No, no, I moved recently, I only got the letter today."

"Good, good, well, when can you come and see us?"

I make arrangements to send him the rest of my book, and then go in to meet him. He seems genuinely excited about it. After I end the call I sit there for a few moments, wondering what the unfamiliar sensation is that is running through my body. And then I smile as I realise what it is – hope.

The End

NOW AVAILABLE

Full Circle by O.C Shaw

Part 2/2 of Lily's Story

Author's Note

I wrote 'What goes around comes around', my first novel, because I wanted to, just to see if I could. Unfortunately, as with many authors, writing has to slot in around paid work, and the needs of my very patient husband and children. But I got there in the end, and have loved doing it. I was keen to write about a slightly older heroine, because I think a lot of us more mature women are romantics at heart too. I hope you liked Lily.

I owe the fact it is published to a few people who gave me the confidence to put it out there when I didn't know if anyone would want to read it. Particularly I want to thank Paula, Lynne, Penny, Kathryn and Sonya.

I hope you might have enjoyed it too. You can keep in touch with my progress, or get in contact via any of the following:

Twitter: **@shawhopeful**

Facebook page: **O.C. Shaw Books**

Blog: **myblogformybooks.blogspot.com**

My email is: **Olivia.c.shaw@me.com**

Be happy

O.C Shaw

Made in the USA
Charleston, SC
15 February 2014